Totally Bound Publishing books by Mina Jane Madeley

Ground Rules
On Common Ground

Ground Rules

ON COMMON GROUND

MINA JANE MADELEY

On Common Ground
ISBN # 978-1-80250-974-8
©Copyright Mina Jane Madeley 2022
Cover Art by Erin Dameron-Hill ©Copyright August 2022
Interior text design by Claire Siemaszkiewicz
Totally Bound Publishing

ON COMMON
GROUND

Chapter One

Homecoming

Slouched in the back seat of a cab, I rub a hand over my two-day stubble as the driver parks, the streetlamps almost blinding my sleepy eyes. I step out into the chilly wind and retrieve from the trunk the three bags containing everything that's left of my life in Paris. It's all I'll need for a fresh start. The rest would only be a reminder of Pauline's betrayal.

A surge of anger engulfs me again, not as strongly as it has the past five weeks, but despite putting physical distance between us, the disgust, resentment and sense of failure still weigh heavily on my shoulders.

I stretch my aching muscles, stiff as if I've ridden planes and taxis for an entire month. Even in the foggy darkness, my building hasn't changed much since I last lived in San Francisco—four stories high on a steep hill, with typical bay windows.

Inside the lobby and up the stairs, my surroundings still feel familiar, and so does the cold metal of my key in my hand. I've always clung to it, even after moving across the world. Deep down, part of me knew I'd come back. I'd planned to. Yet, not once did I imagine my return in these circumstances — alone.

I reach for the lock but hesitate. Madison lives here now, and I shouldn't barge in. I knock on the door once, impatient to surprise my little sister — twice, the anxiety creeping its way back into my gut. *How will Madison react after all this time?* I hope she'll be happy to see me. The impromptu visit seemed a good idea when I planned a one-week stay for my job interview. The intended short trip has turned into a permanent move back, and Madison might just be upset with me landing on her doorstep when I haven't even called in months.

Another apartment door unlocks behind me, and a young man comes out, dressed in black jeans and a hoodie, his long blond hair poking out of a beanie. With the shadow of a beard on his jaw and his six-foot height, I almost don't recognize him.

"River?" I ask.

His eyes widen. "Adrian? Great to see you, dude."

I drop my bags to shake his hand. "You, too. It's been a while." My gaze sweeps over him from head to toe.

The last time we crossed paths in this hallway, he was still a teen who looked up at me as if I were a rock star, tried to sneak in when I hosted parties and spied on every woman who left in the early mornings. A lifetime ago, it seems. The past few years have turned him into a man, and me into a boring adult.

River nods toward my front door. "Are you visiting?"

"Moving back, actually." My voice sounds serene, as if uttering the words aloud marks the start of my new life. "I knocked, but Madison's not here. Do you know when she'll be home?"

River pauses, one eyebrow cocked. "Dude… Madison won't be here anytime soon." He blows out a small laugh, cut off by his phone buzzing in his hand. "Gotta run, but let's catch up, all right?" He walks down the stairs and out of the building before I can ask him to clarify his cryptic words.

Showing up unannounced wasn't the brightest idea, but after months exchanging only rare and impersonal texts with Madison, the fallout from my failed engagement isn't a topic I wanted to discuss over the phone.

I knock a third time, just in case. The key prickles my palm. I'd hoped Madison would be home this late on a Thursday. Wherever she is, I can't wait in front of the door for however long it'll take her to come back.

I call out with the door half-opened. "Madison?" The fatigue in my voice echoes in the silence. No answer.

The living room has changed. A flowery fragrance floats in the air. Apart from the furniture, each trinket and piece of decor is different from what I left behind. In the dim glow of the standing lamp, wherever my eyes linger, the light touches of gold and soft blue turn my apartment into a stranger's place.

The shimmering night view of the bay through the windows, still as staggering, comforts me. I take in a deep breath and bask in that sentiment. I'm home.

My limbs are numb from hours of travel, and my eyes drift closed. The urge to lie down is hard to resist, but if I cave, sleep will overtake me in seconds. A shower seems essential at this point.

Dropping my bags by the guest room door — unpacking postponed until tomorrow — I rehash the carefully chosen words to explain my return without mentioning the humiliating reason.

Pauline and I are over. So is my life in France.

Simple enough. No reason to share the sordid details that led to our breakup.

Madison will need to move out of my apartment. I can't keep lending it to her. I won't stand sharing it, not even with my sister. Finding some peace, alone, is the first step to getting my life back on track.

Just like the rest of my apartment, the bathroom is different. Dozens of girl products cover the countertop, all arranged by size. I place my toiletry bag next to the sink and dig for my shower gel.

My fingers brush the pack of condoms. A bitter chuckle escapes me. A one-night stand wasn't enough to erase the damage Pauline's cheating inflicted on my ego. Switching back to being single and playing the field after a decade in a relationship isn't easy or fulfilling. Instead, the meaningless night had left me hollower and more lost.

I swallow the frustration in my throat, bury the pack deep inside my bag and undress, avoiding even the smallest glance at myself in the mirror. I can't stand that beaten look in my eyes, lately.

The shower's scalding water pours down my back, washing away some of the exhaustion and misery.

A clank in the hallway startles me. I step out of the shower and slip my sweatpants on. With a long calming breath to regain some composure, I exit the bathroom to face Madison. But the brunette standing in the living room in a tight dress and stern ponytail is not my sister.

Chapter Two

The Stranger

Shifting from one foot to the other, I attempt to ease the searing pain in my toes. I'd take off my heels if there was the slightest chance it would go unnoticed by all the people gathered in the conference room for our law firm's quarterly town hall meeting. The reason why this always requires a three-hour presentation with a buffet and a thirty-minute speech from the managing partner is beyond me. If only it wasn't mandatory for secretaries, I'd be chilling on the couch, or even better, relaxing under the hot shower spray. A longing sigh threatens to escape me, and I clear my throat to cover it.

Several faces around the room look as bored as mine. My fake rapt expression fades with each passing minute.

As the speech drags on about teamwork and motivation, Colin's massive frame leans toward me, his light-gray suit bringing out the dark color of his skin.

"Cheer up, Eva," he whispers, his gaze following our talkative boss. "You look like you're slowly dying of boredom."

"Aren't you? Don't get me wrong, it's great that the managing partner takes the time to share his vision for a more 'socially open workplace', but—"

"But can't he just shut the fuck up already so we can go home?"

We exchange a glance and try to repress our laughs, doing our best to keep our friendship discreet at the office. Enough rumors are spread about our supposed affair.

As if on cue, the monologue ends, and the entire room claps.

"Thank fuck. Finally," Colin mutters. "I'll go shake some hands, pretend to be a devoted senior partner, and I'm out of here. You, go home." Colin winks at me.

He ambles to the front of the crowd while I exit in the opposite direction, ignoring the judgmental side-glances several colleagues throw my way.

After the short commute home, the pain in my feet is too unbearable to wait until I'm inside my apartment, so I kick off my stilettos in the building's hallway. Shoes and jacket dangling in one hand, I rummage through my purse to find my keys, then slide the right one in the lock.

I pause. The door is already unlocked.

My stomach flips as I step forward, eyes riveted to the light coming from inside, ears buzzing at the sound of water running in the bathroom. Madison kept a spare after moving out, but there's no reason for her to be here. Not at this hour, and not in the shower. None of the men I've dated ever had a key. My current state of tiredness hinders my efforts to analyze the situation. There has to be a simple explanation that I'm failing to see.

I place my bag, shoes and jacket on the floor, wedge the keys between two fingers to use as a defense weapon, silencing the voice inside my head snickering at me for such a ridiculous move, before I sneak down the hallway to take by surprise whoever this intruder is.

The beating of my heart resonates in my ears. I push the bathroom door ajar and peek inside.

A stranger. In my shower. Naked.

Part of me expected to recognize my uninvited guest, and that it would all make sense. It doesn't. I don't know this man.

In my head, I yell and demand an explanation, but no sound comes out of my mouth. The words are trapped somewhere between my brain and my lips. All I'm capable of is staring at him.

The man faces the opposite wall, his back turned to me through the glass shower door. My focus travels with the stream of water pouring on his light brown hair, cascading down his strong back, undulating over his muscles and the curves of his perfect ass. They linger on the massive tattoo, dark and intricate, that runs from the left side of his back, over his shoulder and around his ribs, and the other thin one around his right forearm. Neither of them is decipherable through the steamed-up glass.

Is he some kind of pervert with a weird shower fetish? How dangerous could he be? I should be worried, I should panic, but the sight is too enticing, the situation too absurd.

The stranger shifts to his side, and my eyes catch sight of the light stubble on his masculine jaw, of his muscular torso and defined abs. The keys slipping from my fingers startle me out of my daze, and they fall on the floor in a loud clank. I pick them up and sprint back to the living room, embarrassed that this man may have caught me staring.

The water stops. Rumbling sounds echo in the other room. I steel myself for the confrontation, yet this reminds me of the scenario from some mediocre porno. If my nerves weren't on edge, I might find it funny.

"Maddie?" the stranger calls.

In the midst of the thrill, it takes me a second to process. *Why is he calling for Madison?*

He walks into the living room, a big smile on his mouth and a pair of sweatpants hanging low on his hips, drops of water trickling down his torso. The image of his well-rounded ass under the shower is fresh in my mind, and the adrenaline rush still dominates my brain.

After a few quiet seconds, the puzzle pieces come together. This man has a key. He didn't break in. He isn't a stranger at all, and I even know his name. It indeed all makes sense — *he's Madison's older brother, Adrian.*

The adrenaline subsides, nerves and worry taking over. My mind is assailed by the dozen questions that he will ask me and that I need to find answers to. Adrian has no idea who I am. Madison never told him she moved out of his apartment, and it's not my job to tell him where she lives.

Adrian's face is etched with a baffled expression as he looks at me, silent. His inquisitive gaze stirs my self-consciousness, and I blurt out the first question that pops into my head.

"What are you doing here?"

"This is my place. What the fuck are *you* doing here? Who are you?"

His rudeness brings my full focus back, and I mimic his cold tone. "I live here."

"No, my sister lives here. Where's Madison?" He runs a hand through his damp hair, his eyes searching mine. "And you still haven't told me who the fuck you are. I assume you have a name?"

"I'm Eva. Madison is my best friend. She lives elsewhere, so I'm subletting the place."

"What? Since when?" His voice rises.

Surprise is understandable, worrying about Madison, as well, but not this anger. "More than a year and a half ago... Look, the situation can be easily explained if you'd just tone it down a notch." My voice sounds a little snappier than I intended, and his eyes narrow.

"Well, I walk out of the shower and find a woman I don't know in the living room. You'll admit I have some fucking reason to be upset."

"*Well*, I walk inside my apartment and find a man showering in my bathroom." My voice rises, too, as annoyance overcomes me. "It's not just upsetting. You scared the shit out of me. And you still haven't told me who you are, either, but I assume you're Adrian."

"At least you've heard of me." He shakes his head, and his gaze fixes on me. "I'm calling Madison right now. This is my home. You shouldn't even be living here." Adrian turns around to enter the corridor before disappearing.

His words sound too familiar. They uncover the remnants of past wounds, like a crack in my chest that never healed. My knees are weak, my heart accelerates and blood rushes to my cheeks. I can't smother the unwanted feeling.

Adrian's hard voice blasts from the guest room.

"Maddie, what the fuck is going on here?" he yells. Either the man has a bad temper, or I don't know what his problem is. "Who's this woman living at my place? Yes, she told me that, but... I am moving back to town… No, I don't want to talk about it now, Maddie. And where the fuck do *you* live, by the way?"

A pause, then Adrian walks back into the living room, his phone wedged between his shoulder and ear as he pulls down on the hem of a T-shirt.

"Fine, but I'll need some explanation." He hangs up with a defeated sigh and shoves the phone in his pocket. "Madison will come by tomorrow, and we'll sort this out."

"Okay." My heart is pounding, nails digging into my palms. "But, what do you mean by 'I'm moving back'?"

"What don't you understand? That's a pretty simple sentence."

I want to slap his handsome face so hard my hand twitches. "You're kicking me out."

"Not right this second, but I own this place. It seems obvious to me that I'd want to live in it." Adrian's tone borders on condescending. He runs his hand through his hair, pulls at a loose strand then briskly rubs over his face. He seems on the verge of a nervous breakdown. "I can't… I can't do this. This is my place. You have to move out."

"What? When? And how? Do you realize how hard it is to find a place in this city, especially on a secretary's salary?"

"Look, I don't know…" He sighs and drops his voice, almost as if he were sorry. "I don't care."

"Me neither. Couldn't you give Madison a tiny heads-up, before storming in?"

"No, it wasn't…" He pauses, and never finishes his sentence.

"Couldn't you crash at your parents', or even a hotel, until we figure it out?"

"No!" He pulls at his hair again, and I'm not sure whether he's answering my question, or only shouting at the situation.

There's no point replying if I'm not going to insult him or hurl the first object within reach at his head. No matter his issues, he's rude, infuriating, and unfair.

I storm past Adrian to my bedroom, but he follows me.

"Wait…"

He's close behind when I turn around. "Why? So you can yell at me some more?"

He rubs both hands over his face and drops them to his sides. He breathes deep, holding it for a moment before releasing it in a slow, controlled blow.

My head held high, I wait for him to speak with my hand on the door, ready to close it. His blue stare, sharp as a knife, pins me to the spot.

"Look, Eva," he says in a calm voice, and it's obvious it's an effort for him. "I don't… I can't…" He pauses, jaw flexing.

I raise an eyebrow, waiting for the rest of his sentence, this time.

"Going to my parents or to a hotel is not an option. Or to my sister, for that matter, since she lives fuck knows where." He snickers. "I'm staying. This is my home."

Behind his cutting gaze and bridled tone, his message is clear. It's not my home anymore, and I have to leave as soon as possible.

Having never signed a lease, I have no choice, no right, no control over any of this. I can't force him to leave, but he can evict me. My throat tight, I remain silent. Our dispute morphs into a staring contest. Neither of us is willing to stand down.

When he takes a step back, I slam the door shut, almost in his face, before we start arguing again.

His footsteps resound as he walks away, and the guest bedroom door shuts with a loud thump.

Chapter Three

Arrangement

Eva slammed the fucking door in my face.

The surprise and irritation, added to my already exhausted nerves, are too much to handle. My heart is beating too fast, my body restless, I'm losing my mind. This situation is unreal.

After an hour of pacing the guest room, I stomp to the kitchen to find some decent alcohol to numb my brain. I need some sleep.

A soft ray of light flows from the bathroom door left ajar just enough to catch my eye as I pass by.

I freeze in the hallway as a shudder runs down my back. I heard a noise while I was in the shower, and the door was open when I got out. Eva was there. She must have seen me. Was she peeking?

My stomach flips. In other circumstances, I'd find it arousing, but Eva caught me in a vulnerable moment, the culmination of five weeks of anxiety, of self-doubt. The safe space I thought I'd come back to is anything but.

Boundaries be damned, I rummage through the fridge and cupboards but find nothing. Eva isn't making a good first impression at all.

I lean on the counter and concentrate on my breathing. Slow, measured breaths until the frustration subsides, until the adrenaline abates enough for me to walk back to bed and let the exhaustion knock me unconscious.

The sound of water from the bathroom startles me awake at six thirty in the morning, and irritation rushes back into my body like a reflex I can't control. Eva exasperates me so much that I fight the urge to storm out and scream at her. Yelling is my primary reaction to everything these days. Her presence seems to worsen my temper outbursts, no matter whether it's justified. Blaming her for getting ready for work is insane. *I need to get a fucking grip.*

So I lie in bed, listening to the sounds of her morning routine until the front door clicks shut and it's finally quiet.

One hot mug of coffee isn't enough to straighten my mind. I rehearse what to tell Madison while steering clear of the sore subjects, prepare my questions, search for my words, but fatigue obscures my reasoning.

On second thought, Madison has more to explain than I do. The situation needs to be sorted out so I can settle down. And I need Eva to leave.

The morning drags on as I wait for Madison to arrive. Unpacking my bags in the guest room doesn't sound too appealing, but it'll have to do. The reckless idea of putting my clothes in the large bedroom and throwing Eva's in the hallway crosses my mind as payback for pushing my buttons so hard, but I'm not that much of a jerk.

My suits are put away in the closet and the rest of my clothes folded in the drawers. I leave my toiletry bag on top of the dresser for now. My three bags are empty — no souvenirs from Paris, nothing to remind me of the life I had there. Most of it was a lie, anyway.

I drop by the store to buy some beer and a few groceries to fill the nearly empty fridge, so I don't wipe out Eva's stock of food, and pace the living room again. The wait is unbearable. I need to occupy myself to appease the whirlwind in my head.

Without going through Eva's property, the need to reclaim my apartment in any way becomes vital. All the furniture is still mine, so I push the couch a little to the left, move the TV further into the corner and reposition the bookcase — as they were when I lived here.

My gaze lingers along the book spines, and I pause. Some of the books seem like mine, yet I don't recall leaving any behind when I left.

The Principles of Project Finance... Secured Transactions: Teaching Materials...

I studied them years ago when I was at Berkeley, but these are new editions. They're Eva's.

Between a shelf of crime thrillers and a few satirical graphic novels, at least two dozen practice guides with topics ranging from mergers and acquisitions and debt finance to market regulations compose an impressive textbook collection. Almost all of it is introduction to either finance or banking law. As an investment banker, even *I* don't own that many books on the subject. *Who the fuck is this woman?*

By the time I'm done rearranging the furniture, Madison knocks on the door. As soon as I open it, she jumps into my arms. We hold each other close for a long moment, neither of us talking, until she pulls back and looks at me.

"I'm mad at you," she says.

"I'm mad at you, too. What's going on here? I know I haven't visited in a while, but — "

"In a while? It's been almost two years!"

"It didn't give you the right to lend my apartment out without telling me."

Madison follows me to the living room, and we both sit at either end of my old chesterfield couch. I plop down on the soft morning-blue cushions covering the worn-out brown leather, and she faces me with a concerned frown.

"Adrian, why are you here?"

"Because..." The words catch in my throat. I wish Madison didn't have to see her big brother so broken. "I don't want to talk about it, Maddie. Not yet, please."

"Why didn't you call me? To tell me you were coming back, at least..."

"It was supposed to be a one-week trip. I wanted to surprise you. And...I thought it'd be easier to explain face-to-face. It isn't."

"You left Paris for good?" The hopefulness in her voice is obvious.

"Yes, I'm never going back there."

"Okay, but you'll have to tell me what happened eventually." She raises an eyebrow, her tone worried but her gaze resolute. My baby sister has turned into a strong woman without me being here to witness it.

"I know, but I need to breathe, for now."

She just smiles and nods.

"Why don't you live here, Maddie? Where do you live?"

"Somewhere else. I don't want to talk about it now, please." She throws my words back at me, her head cocked to the side, with a playful glint in her eyes to lighten the mood.

"Seriously, you're going to play it that way?"

"Yes. What we need to talk about today is you sharing this apartment with Eva."

"Me doing *what*?" I jump from the couch.

"Are you willing to stay with Mom and Dad until she leaves? Did you even tell them you were back?"

"Not yet." My heart pinches. "I'm not ready to face them."

"So, it means you'll have to live with Eva for a while. Because you can't ask her to leave tonight. It's not right. You realize that, don't you?"

"I never said *tonight*. I never even said this week. I'm not a complete asshole, thank you. But there's a gap between tonight and living together." The exasperation grows in me, along with the debilitating feeling of having no control over my life. It smothers me. "I can't do this. This is too much for me, Maddie. I can't come home to some woman yelling at me and slamming doors in my face. Not again."

"Adrian, I get that you're going through a rough phase, but you can't reappear without warning, throw her out and expect her to be happy about it. You already moved the furniture, for fuck's sake!" Madison stares at me, daring me to contradict her, and I can't. "Eva is a smart woman, she understands, and she *will* look for another place, but you have to give her a few weeks, at least."

My mouth opens but no sound comes out—no valid counter-argument—and I close it in a tight line. Eva shouldn't have to pay for the wretchedness of my life, even though she did nothing to temper our first exchange and overreacted as much as I did. I battle with myself to rein in the anguish, hold on to the faith showing in my sister's stare, and after a few deep breaths, I cave.

"A few weeks. Okay, fine."

"During which you'll be nice?"

"I can't promise anything," I deadpan. Deep down, I question my ability to stay calm.

I slump back on the couch as Madison walks to the kitchen. She returns a few minutes later with two cups of coffee and hands me one before sitting down.

We both avoid the personal or painful subjects. Her eyes light up when she mentions her job at the veterinary clinic, but she remains cryptic about where she lives and, I realize, with whom.

"You met someone, didn't you? I mean, you live with someone."

"Yes." Her expression hardens, her fingers fiddling with her empty mug.

"You never mentioned him. Every time we called or texted... I didn't even realize you were dating someone."

"Adrian..." She pauses, her eyes warm but determined. "This is a conversation for some other time, when you're ready to hear what I have to say. Not today."

"When the fuck did you become wiser than me?"

"I always have been!"

We laugh, and some of the tension I carried with me from France evaporates. Madison and I have always been close, and I've missed her the last few years.

Chapter Four

A Bad Day

Adrian sparks anger in me that I haven't felt in a long time. My mind can't calm down, invaded by his words playing on a loop since last night.

Madison sends me several texts to apologize, both for never telling him she'd rented me his place, thus putting me in this predicament, and on behalf of her brother as well, as if his rudeness was her fault. I don't blame her, neither of us could've anticipated him turning up without warning. She plans to come by the apartment to talk to him right after the last dog neutering on her morning schedule. Even though I trust her to defend my interests, I can't keep the worry from settling in my gut.

Itching to relay the crazy story, complain and vent my frustration to Colin, I barge into his office. Madison won't insult her own brother, but Colin will have no qualms. I slump down on one of the big leather chairs facing his desk and sigh.

A peaceful, majestic view of the San Francisco Bay stretches out behind him through the floor-to-ceiling windows, in complete contrast to my restlessness.

Focused on the papers in front of him, Colin doesn't look up. "Good morning to you, too," he jokes and lifts his gaze to me. His face falls. "You look like shit! What's wrong?"

"You're not going to believe this," I vent. "When I got home last night, I found Madison's big brother naked in my shower."

"No shit?" A smile forms on his lips, eyes dancing with amusement. "You got a good look at him? Is the big brother really *big*?"

"I didn't look!"

"Yeah, I've known you since we were six. I can tell when you're lying." He winks and reclines in his chair. "Did you join him in the shower? Is that why you're so tired?"

"Are you finished?" I ask, feigning annoyance.

"I don't know. Did *you* finish?"

I'm making this too easy for him. He bursts out laughing, and I can't help but join him.

Most people are as intimidated by Colin's tall frame, strong features and deep, masculine voice as by his blunt honesty and inappropriate humor, but I never have been.

"You need to get laid, Colin. Your brain is suffering from the lack of sex."

"Look who's talking. When was the last time you went on a date?"

"Not that long ago," I say, and he raises an eyebrow.

Dating hasn't been a priority lately. Or ever. I'm thirty-four, and I've been through enough in my life to always put my wellbeing first. I like my independence, and it scares most men away. Between meaningless dates with uninteresting guys I end up rejecting, few ever see beyond the wall I put up to protect myself.

I hold Colin's dubious stare. "Maybe it never turns into anything serious, but I have more sex than you do."

"Well, I work too much to get laid. You know that."

Colin is handsome enough that he could seduce any woman he might desire, with his dark caramel skin and even darker brown eyes. Over the years we've known each other, I have witnessed more than a few women swoon over him. Now he works long hours, spends his time either at home or in his office and never meets anyone.

Colin leans forward on his desk, resting on his forearms, serious. "OK, tell me the whole story, Ev."

"There's not much to tell. Adrian just turned up last night and wants me out of *his* apartment."

My exasperation rises when I relay the details about our short exchange and Adrian's behavior.

"Funny," Colin says. "I always thought Madison's, or even more so Luke's, opinion of the guy was to be taken with some caution. I mean, they had been friends forever until Adrian left. But it sounds like he really *is* an entitled prick."

"And Adrian doesn't know yet that Madison and Luke are engaged. It wasn't easy answering questions without telling him that's where his sister was."

"It's Madison's problem, not yours. What is Adrian even doing here? Wasn't he supposed to be getting married in France or something?"

"I don't know, but he was alone. Madison will talk to him today. We'll see."

Colin lounges in his chair, careful eyes on me. "How do you feel about all of this?"

"There's not much I can do about it, so—"

"That's not what I mean." He studies my face, my reaction. No matter how hard I want to pretend, he knows which feeling I'm trying to hide.

"I..." I pause, search for my words, just how I learned years ago in therapy, and take a deep breath. "I know, *rationally*, that the situation is different. He's not my stepfather, and I'm not fourteen anymore..."

"Rationally. But in your gut?"

Colin is pushing me. He's the only one who's allowed to, who saw how hurt I was years ago and understands how it still affects me.

"I never thought I'd feel this way again in my life. I was so careful not to put myself in that position, to be reliant on any man I dated, or anyone. I didn't see this one coming. But I'll be fine."

"Okay." Colin nods. "On a legal note, he better allow you time to find another place to rent," he says in a poised and professional voice. "And you know you can always stay with me, if you have nowhere else to go."

"That's nice of you to offer, but I don't want to reignite the rumors of an affair between us. Enough of our colleagues still believe you gave me this job because we were sleeping together. If they heard I was staying with you, that reputation would never leave me. But thank you." I give an earnest smile, and he nods again.

"Do you need the day off to take care of it?"

"No, that's fine. I'll wait for Madison to call me back."

"Okay, then get your ass to work," he orders in a bossy tone but winks at me as I exit.

Focusing on work is nearly impossible, and I'm not very efficient. My phone lies on my desk, within close reach, the screen turned so I can see any incoming calls or texts from Madison. I can't refrain from checking every few minutes nonetheless, just in case I missed one.

Whenever the office phone rings, my heart skips a beat, but it's never Madison. The absent-mindedness forces me to read every email twice, my mind constantly drifting back to Adrian and his cold words.

"You shouldn't even be living here. This is my place. You have to move out."

My brain creates a dozen different versions of the conversation Madison will have with Adrian, each of them more unrealistic and ludicrous, but all of them resulting in me sleeping in a hotel tonight. The wait is maddening.

No matter how hard I stare at my phone screen, Madison doesn't call. Hours pass without anything productive getting done.

A case holds Colin up at the courthouse, so I eat lunch alone in the bistro across the street. On my way back to our office floor, I press the elevator up button, and a petite redhead rushes inside. Her slim body slides between the closing doors, her grace and pale skin giving her the allure of a porcelain doll. If I had tried that maneuver, I would have either knocked myself out on the doors or fallen on my face inside the elevator. She offers a flat "hi" without bothering to look at me, and I answer in the same tone.

The doors open, and I follow behind her confident stride when I overhear our receptionist's voice.

"You should see her, that *Daphne*, all cold and arrogant." Patricia leans over her desk, engrossed in her usual gossiping with the mail delivery guy. Her black dress rises too high for a woman her age, her blond over-teased hair doubling the size of her head. She speaks with one hand next to her mouth as if pretending to be discreet, but she's loud enough for anyone to hear in the entire reception area. "I'm telling you, she was sleeping with her boss, that's why she had to leave her previous firm in Los Angeles. Probably going to do the same here. What a slut!"

The redhead stops and turns to Patricia, catching her attention with a loud and pointed throat clearing. I slow down a few feet away, rather amused at Patricia's shocked expression and the mail carrier's sneaky escape.

"Excuse me, I didn't mean to interrupt." The redhead's voice is strong, unyielding, in complete contrast with her frail physique. "I just heard my name. I thought maybe you had something you wanted to say to me."

She was mentioned during our last staff meeting, but I didn't get a chance to meet her. She's Daphne Harwell, our new paralegal in the Banking & Finance department.

Patricia's mouth hangs open, but no clever answer comes out. None ever does.

"No? All right, then," Daphne concludes with a sickly sweet smile etched on her lips. The porcelain doll is not as fragile as she looks, and she has some nerves of steel underneath her fair skin.

Daphne turns on her heels, and her stare crosses mine. I expect a snarky comment about my eavesdropping, but she walks away with a hint of a smile.

An hour later, she struts to my desk, her face expressionless. She *does* come across as arrogant.

"Hi, I'm Daphne Harwell."

"Eva Duncan. How may I help you?" I smile too widely for the dullness of our exchange when I recall how amazing she'd been in front of Patricia. Daphne doesn't return the gesture.

"Here are the case files you requested for Mr. Wilder."

"Thank you. And, Daphne?" I hold her attention as she was already turning around. "I'm sorry I was eavesdropping earlier. I didn't mean to —"

"Don't apologize." She waves a dismissive hand. "You seemed to enjoy watching her being put in her place."

"Patricia loves spreading rumors. She had it coming."

"Sounds personal." She cocks her head to the side. "I overheard some shit about you. So I guess it means you're not fucking Colin Wilder?" Her bluntness and hard tone of voice were conflicting with her delicate appearance, and her crude language accentuates the contrast.

"Wow, you're straight-forward!" I chuckle. "No, I'm not. We're friends."

"I never had an affair with my previous boss, either. Nor will I ever be that stupid and naive. It's not why I left L.A." She smiles and strides back to her desk with the poise of a ballet dancer. Once again, she leaves me speechless with her unexpected behavior.

Before I can focus back on work, my phone buzzes on my desk, and I snatch it with a hammering heart. *Madison, finally.*

"Did you talk to your brother?"

"I did." The yelps and barks of her furry patients seep through the phone. "I have an emergency at work. I can't replay the entire conversation right now. But I'm sorry, he *is* moving back to San Francisco permanently, so he'll need his apartment back..." A loud bang and distressed meowing cries interrupt her. "Shit! I have to go, Eva, sorry. I'll call you back but in the meantime, talk to Adrian. It's going to be fine, I promise."

She hangs up before I have time to ask for more details. Her few words haven't reassured me much.

.

Chapter Five

Harder Than Expected

The concession I promised Madison spins in my head — endure Eva's presence in hopes she'll find a new place to live, sooner rather than later. With luck, when she comes home from work, my conversation with her won't be as disastrous as last night.

A run along the Marina helps me clear my mind and avoid spending the afternoon mulling over the situation. The magnificent views of the Golden Gate Bridge spur me on, my breathing even, my strides in rhythm with the soothing sound of The Chemical Brothers blasting in my earbuds. I walk the four miles back to my place drained but relaxed.

The serenity lingers in me as I step under the shower. Even though the situation isn't as peaceful as I expected, this turn in my life brings a lightness inside my chest that I haven't felt in a long time.

The run-induced endorphins get my body buzzing, and my mind drifts as I undress. The condoms taunt me from my toiletry bag. I crave the touch of a woman, just for one night. Just sex. No feelings, no trust given or betrayed. Meaningless sex isn't the most satisfying, but I haven't had a woman's body writhing under me in weeks, and I miss it. At only thirty-six and healthy, I shouldn't need to jerk off like a teenager.

I relax under the hot water, close my eyes and conjure up the image of a random porn star. My left hand rests on the wall tiles while the other reaches for my cock. I breathe in deep and move my fingers, picturing the woman's hand stroking me. My dick grows in my palm as I graze all the sensitive spots, in all the ways I love it, but it doesn't rival the delicate feel of a woman's touch. In my imagination, she moves on all fours, or kneels with my dick in her mouth, but alone in the shower, the sensation is not nearly as pleasurable as what a true connection feels like.

Not entranced by my own movements, I open my eyes. Through the steamed-up glass, my gaze lands on the closed bathroom door. The same door that was open last night, with Eva behind, peeking while I was showering. I can almost see her in my head. I can't shake off the idea of her standing there, watching me naked.

I exhale loudly as my heart skips a beat. Behind my closed eyelids, Eva is wearing the same tight dress she had on last night, her gaze locked on me, and my body ignites. After months of tepid desire, one simple vision of Eva makes my cock grow harder without even trying.

My hand moves on my length as if I can't control it. My mind shouldn't drift in that direction. *Stop!* We have to share my apartment, I shouldn't let myself fantasize about her, but the vision is too exciting to restrain it. My instincts are stronger than my will, and the image of Eva watching me through the barely open door is carved in my mind.

My heart speeds up, my breathing labored, the movements of my hand more eager. I'm more aroused by Eva than any other woman my imagination could create, or any real woman I met in a bar this past month. In my head, Eva walks to me and gets in the shower, her eyes filled with lust, her breasts showing through the wet fabric of her dress. My fingers slip inside her cleavage, between her round tits, pulling her closer. Her hand, trapped between our bodies, closes around my throbbing cock, moving up and down in slow strokes.

It takes all my strength to stop and not lose myself in the sensation. I open my eyes and take a deep breath, torn between desire and guilt. I need to force my body to settle down because I couldn't look Eva in the eye if I jerked off thinking about her. Our situation is complicated enough as it is. I move the faucet and gasp when the water turns freezing cold.

For the first time in weeks, I'm aroused beyond the urge to satisfy a primal need, and I can't act on it. *This is a fucking nightmare.*

I fight with my own brain to discard the memory of my little fantasy before Eva gets home, and cook dinner with a frustrated frown etched on my face. Pasta with diced chicken breast and vegetables is simmering on the stove. I hope it'll get me on Eva's good side for the conversation we need to have. Madison made it clear that Eva is important to her, so I'll make the effort of a peace offering in the form of a home cooked dinner. If, in addition to my sister's gratitude, I get some tranquility at home, even better, for both Eva and me.

Uneasiness creeps in my stomach now that I have to face her after fantasizing about her. My memory of her might be more alluring than the reality, yet I wonder how my body will react to being near her.

The front door opens, and Eva's footsteps resonate in the living room.

"Eva? I'm in the kitchen, I'm cooking —"

She appears in the doorway, livid, hands planted on her hips. In that tight black skirt and purple blouse, with her high heels and hair in a bun, she'd be the living cliché of the sexy secretary if it weren't for the scowl on her face.

"Are you fucking kidding me? You couldn't even wait until I got back to move *your* furniture? I assume you also threw my clothes out of *your* room? You're a jerk!"

There's the answer to my doubt. Despite the fantasy in the shower, Eva is still the annoying woman I want out of my apartment as soon as possible. My promise to Madison to give her friend a few weeks and make cohabitation easy will be more difficult to keep than anticipated. I could've explained and even apologized for the furniture, had Eva let me pronounce a word before shrieking like a shrew.

Her stare moves from me to the food on the stove behind. I inhale a lungful of air, struggling not to appear too irritated.

"Eva, I'm trying *really* hard not to be a jerk. I'd appreciate it if you helped me a little bit."

"What's that supposed to mean? How is any of this my fault?"

I can't tell if her harsh tone is a defense mechanism or natural bitchiness, but I'd bet the nicest words coming from me would still be offensive to her. Her prejudice is tiresome.

Behind the anger, a hint of worry shows in her fierce green eyes. Perhaps she still doesn't know that she has some time ahead of her to find a new place.

"I talked to Madison."

"And? What do we do?"

"I want to be in my apartment. Like I said, I won't crash on my parents' couch," I say in the calmest voice I can muster. "And you can stay for a few weeks, at least, until you find something else."

Eva shakes her head, eyes shut, and a loud sigh escapes her lips. "Can't you go —?"

"I told you, no. And for how long would that even be? Can you give me an estimated time? How many hotel nights would I be paying for so you can enjoy my apartment alone?"

"Great, then, a few weeks of living with you." An exaggerated eye roll accompanies her sarcastic tone.

"I'm not thrilled about the idea, either!" I snap.

My eyes never leave hers, neither of us willing to surrender first.

"Looks like there's no other choice." Her voice sounds resigned, but her eyes throw daggers at me. "So am I supposed to say thank you?"

Once more, her reaction to me is unfair, and I can't bite my tongue hard enough not to answer. "No, you're not. But since you mentioned it, you could give me back the large bedroom."

This is the opposite of what I promised Madison, but I couldn't refrain myself. Eva's aggressiveness annoys the shit out of me.

She rolls her eyes again and walks back to the bedroom, slamming the door. I follow her, even more pissed than last night. Her behavior is exasperating. She has to stop acting like a persecuted girl and treating me like the worst prick in the world.

I bang on her door until she opens.

"What?"

"Are you going to do that every time?"

"Yes!" She grabs the door and tries to slam it in my face, but I stop it midway with my hand.

"Don't! I'm not the only one being a jerk here."

Eyes narrowing, she reaches for the door one more time, and I block it again.

"Goddamn it! I never said you actually had to do it, but if you want to have it this way, fine. Move your stuff out of my room. *Now.*"

"Asshole!"

I walk back to the kitchen without answering, grab a beer and sit down for a while, unable to calm down.

Eva rummages through her things, groaning and mumbling.

"Are you going to get your shit out of the guest room, or do I have to do that, too?"

I grit my teeth so hard I might break one.

At the end of the hallway, she goes back and forth between the two bedrooms, still perched on high heels, arms filled with clothes. A twinge of guilt pinches my chest; this is unfair, but it's too late to stop it, or I'm too proud, maybe, so I let her continue.

I move my three bags' worth of clothes to the large bedroom and sneak back to the kitchen, getting out of Eva's way to avoid another fight. I take the pan off the stove before the food burns and chug my beer too fast. My heart still hammers from anger, my head now spinning.

An hour later, no sound is coming from her room. Just as I get up from the couch to check on her, Eva yells from her open door in a mock-cheerful voice. "I'm done!"

This woman has the skill to upset me with only one sentence when I am calm.

"I also made room for your stuff in the bathroom," she continues with a shade of sadness in her voice, and these are her nicest words to me since we met.

"Thank you, Eva."

She doesn't come out of her bedroom. Spending several weeks together won't work if we can't speak in the same room, and since she has to move out, I'll make the first step. Or second one, if we consider the now-overcooked pasta, but who's counting?

I lean on her doorframe. All her clothes are put away, personal things aligned on the nightstand. The room is tidy, except for the sheets I slept in last night rolled up on the floor. The pinch in my chest redoubles.

Eva lies on the unmade bed, gazing at the ceiling. She has changed out of her clothes into loose-fitting jeans and a T-shirt, her long brown hair sprawled around her. In this outfit, she doesn't look so uptight, but the severe expression returns as soon as she sees me.

"What?"

"Are you hungry?" My tone is gentle in hope she'll stop being aggressive, but my efforts remain unnoticed.

"No."

"Fuck! Can't you at least try?" I lose my temper, and she bolts upright on the bed.

"Okay, fine. Yes, I'm hungry."

"Then come and grab a plate. I made enough for two."

"You did?"

"Yes. I'm not a complete asshole."

I expect a snappy comment as she follows me to the kitchen, but she doesn't say a word.

Eva sits at the table while I fill our plates with the pasta. An uncomfortable silence stretches between us. Her entire body seems tense, and so is mine.

"I'll leave as soon as I can," she says between two bites, eyes on the food.

"All right. Until then, can we try not to fight every day?"

Her head snaps up, and she glares. "Sure."

Every word I utter offends her. Every comment she makes irritates me. The next few weeks are going to be fucking torture.

Chapter Six

Make Her Scream

I sneak out before Eva wakes up. My Saturday morning run eases some of the remaining tension from our fight and the night of blurry turmoil, tossing and turning in bed.

The next two days promise to be more nerve-racking than I hoped. I don't know how Eva usually spends her weekends, but the less we see of each other the better, considering we barely managed to remain civil until dinner was over. I don't see us chilling on the couch together all Sunday afternoon.

Before the week starts, my head needs to be clear and focused on my job interview. Even for a transfer from the Paris office to San Francisco, I'll be evaluated, and I need a positive outcome for both mental and financial reasons. With the alternatives being either going back to Paris or being unemployed, this is crucial.

After a vitalizing six-mile jog, I enter the building as River calls out from the corner of the street, and I hold the door open. He saunters toward me wearing what seems like yesterday's clothes.

"Walk of shame?" I joke.

"No shame here, dude. Only post-coital happiness."
He winks.

The proud look in his eyes fishes for my approval,
and I realize I may have set a bad example for that kid,
a few years back.

We make our way up the stairs, and he slows down
as we approach our front doors. "So, you met your *new
tenant*?" His voice lowers, a mischievous glint in his
eyes.

"Why didn't you say something the other night?"
My tone sounds more curious than reproachful. Not
that I blame him for my catastrophic first conversation
with Eva, but had I known the situation, it could've
gone better. For one, she wouldn't have seen me naked.

River laughs. "You expected your sister, and you
end up with a smart and sexy stranger... I thought it'd
be a nice surprise."

"It wasn't."

"How is that possible? Eva's the sweetest person in
the entire building."

I raise an eyebrow. "Are you sure we're talking
about the same woman?"

He chuckles, pauses for a beat and shakes his head.
"Dude, you remember that time before my father
bailed on us, you got into an argument with him? That
time he was pissed because you'd fucked a woman all
night, and we could hear her moan and scream your
name in the whole building?"

I cringe at this reminder of the man I was before I
met Pauline, my face contorting in an apologetic
grimace. River must be in his early twenties now, but
part of me still sees the boy he was before I left. "Fuck.
How old were you when that happened?"

He shrugs. "Fourteen, maybe... Old enough not to be shocked. Anyway, the answer you gave him that day stuck with me. I apply it in the way I treat any girl I meet."

"I wonder what valuable advice could possibly be taken away from that situation."

"You told my father that, unlike him, you'd rather make a woman scream in pleasure than in anger or sadness." He cocks his head to the side with a defiant stare.

His clear message hits me like a gut punch. "You could hear us fight?" I gesture toward my front door, toward Eva.

"Walls are still as thin. Look, she can be feisty and stubborn, I'll give you that. And I may or may not be mad at her for brushing me off 'cause I'm too young for her or whatever," he jokes, making me chuckle. "But, seriously, she's the best."

River's maturity and insightfulness stun me, and no wise words come out of my tired brain as we each enter our apartment. Even though it crossed my thoughts in a brief moment of mind drifting, making her scream my name in pleasure isn't the plan. Yet I'm also not happy about how upset she's been because of me.

At the end of the hallway, Eva's bedroom door is still closed, so I keep as quiet as possible so as not to wake her, swinging by the kitchen to drink some water before walking to the bathroom.

After peeling off my sweaty T-shirt, shorts and briefs, I lean inside the shower to turn on the hot water. Behind me, the bathroom door creaks open. I spin around to find Eva in her gray pajamas, hair ruffled and eyes barely opened as she yawns.

"What the — ?" I mumble in bewilderment, one hand covering my junk just as hers covers her eyes.

"Shit!" She steps back, but then forward again with her other hand hovering in front of her, groping in the air for the door handle. She's not even close, and the scene is rather comical.

I snatch my towel and wrap it around my waist, inhaling deep to keep from laughing. Coming from me, no doubt she'd take it as an insult. "It's okay, Eva. You can open your eyes."

She peeks between two fingers before removing her hand. "Old habit," she mumbles. "I'm not used to living with someone."

The bathroom fogs up with the steam of the hot water pouring. River's words still echo in my mind, and I fight with my instincts to remain silent and not make a tactless joke or shitty comeback. *Breathe in. Breathe out.*

A few seconds pass, the air heavy and awkward, and I become very aware that I'm almost naked in front of her. Again. At least she has the decency to keep her gaze on the floor.

"I'm not used to having to lock the door, either. I should have." I don't mention it's the second time she's opened it while I shower. I also refrain from asking if she's doing it on purpose, to tease her. That conversation might not end well, we're far from that level of familiarity, so I say nothing.

Eva fidgets, her gaze still avoiding me. "Are you going to be long?"

At this point, I'm starting to wonder if she's testing my resilience deliberately. I chuckle. "Why?"

She clears her throat. "I need to pee."

I stare at her, dumbstruck. In the course of three days, she has managed to render me furious, guilty, horny, furious again. And now... I don't know how to react.

My nerves are on edge. My head is a mess, torn between the persistent impulse to yell, and the flickering desire for her eyes on me, filled with lust like in my fantasy.

Astray in the whirlwind of my emotions, I blurt out, "Are you fucking serious?" My tone is cutting, much more than I intended, but she speaks before I can rectify it.

"I just woke up. I need to pee. I won't be able to hold it very long. So..." Her eyes glance all around the room, but never land on me. She waves a dismissive hand. "Never mind. I'll ask across the hall to Mrs. Matthews or River."

Once again, a random situation with us becomes uncomfortable in a second. I run a frustrated hand through my hair, the other clutching the towel knotted on my hips so it doesn't fall. "This is fucking stupid."

Her eyes snap up to mine. "So what am I supposed to do? Pee in the kitchen sink?"

This is *not* what I fucking meant. The frustration inside my chest grows. My inability to align a simple sentence to her without it turning into an argument is exasperating. Perhaps I *am* being a jerk. Perhaps Eva's too susceptible.

The air suffocates me, the unease between us smothering me. The little patience and resilience I had left is wearing too thin.

River might be right about making her scream, but fucking her senseless to extract some amiability from both of us isn't an option. A sour chuckle escapes me before I realize.

"What's funny?" She glares. "You know what, don't bother..." She turns around with an appalled eye roll.

"Hold on..." I might not have my manners in check, but I also won't let her rebuff me every time we talk.

I lean into the shower to turn off the faucet, water scorching my arm and shoulder before it stops. Turning back to Eva, I take a slow step toward her, breathing even and voice low. "Let's try this again." I clear my throat as she watches me with furrowed brows. "Good morning, Eva. No need to apologize for entering while I was naked. It happens." I shrug with a smile, hand still clasping my towel. "Is there anything I can do for you, now?"

Eyes narrowed, she plasters a fake smile on her face. "Adrian," she says in a syrupy tone. "Would you mind letting me use the bathroom for a minute?"

I cock an eyebrow, head tilting to the side as you do with a child who forgets the magic word.

"Please," she adds in the same forced tone.

"Sure." I fake a sweet voice, too, and walk past her with a smirk.

Sweetest person in the building, my ass.

Chapter Seven

Ugly Truce

The fifth real estate agency website I search doesn't have much better to offer than the previous four. All the rental ads within my price range look similar — too small and too shitty. Even with lowering my expectations, finding a decent place to live is going to take forever.

And I don't have forever. Sharing the apartment with Adrian has been tense and awkward. The only moments we manage not to bicker are when we avoid each other. I won't bear that situation for several weeks.

Neither will he. My mere presence bothers him, his aloof behavior and tired gaze betraying his annoyance every time he looks at me. After only a few days since Adrian's return, the comfort the apartment used to bring me has plummeted. It's not my home anymore. I never thought I'd feel so unwelcome again. My stomach cramps as a reflex every time we cross paths, dreading a possible clash, so I avoid the common areas. Every day, instead of relaxing in front of the TV, I retreat to my room to watch a movie on my laptop.

Instead of enjoying a quiet meal in the kitchen, I wolf down the quickest dish I can prepare and again, flee to my room before Adrian exits his. Just like I plan to do tonight.

Still wearing the pencil skirt and high heels I had on for work, I swallow the last bite of my mixed salad, clean the table and pour myself some coffee. I've already drunk too many cups at work, and it might keep me from sleeping, but it's not like I'd have a restful night anyway.

I sink down on my chair, scroll through the depressing rental ads one more time, and sigh. Holding back from banging my head on my laptop keyboard, I shove it aside and rest my forehead on the cold tabletop, my arms sprawled around my head.

"Hi," Adrian says in a meek voice.

I jolt up in the chair and push my hair out of my face, clearing my throat as if it'll help me regain some composure.

He pauses at the door with a mug in hand, hesitant, in worn-out jeans and a black hoodie. His gaze lands on my screen displaying the rental ads, and I shut it in an abrupt move, too embarrassed by my meager budget. He'd probably find my options pathetic compared to his real estate property and the ease with which he flies to and from Paris whenever he feels like it. I'd rather spare myself the condescending comments he might make about my finances.

"Hi," I answer, and take a sip of my coffee.

The air around us fills with an uncomfortable electric charge. We haven't spoken since I walked in on him in the bathroom. We haven't spent any time in the same room since that dinner he cooked. Why bother pretending?

Adrian strides toward the sink to rinse his empty mug, silent. I consider making small talk but stop myself. No doubt we'd end up arguing again. The awkwardness stifling me, I stand up and grab my laptop with the intention to go isolate in my room.

Adrian turns around, leaning on the sink with his hands in his pockets and a distant look on his face. "You can stay. I'm not chasing you out."

A bitter chuckle escapes my lips at his word choice before I can hold it back. I steel myself for the harshness of his response, but nothing comes.

He opens his mouth and closes it in a tight line without speaking. His prying stare doesn't leave me, sweeping over me from head to heels before settling on my face again. The hairs on the back of my neck prickle. I expect him to demand an update on my move, but he says nothing, his body oozing nervousness for some reason that evades me. *Is bumping into me in the kitchen so insufferable?*

Overcome by the urge to justify myself like when I was a teenager, I snap at him. "I'm looking for another place, don't worry."

His hands raking his hair, he whispers, "I didn't say anything."

It's true, he didn't, and my comment could start the fight I wanted to avoid. I should've kept quiet, but the intensity of his eyes on me puts my nerves on edge, like tiny pins pricking my skin, forcing me to react. Seizing the last shred of opportunity to dodge an argument, I clutch my laptop and flee to my room. However, as he has every time I've tried to retreat to avoid confrontation, he follows me and persists.

"Eva, wait. Please." He sighs. "I haven't blamed you for not finding something fast enough."

From the doorway, I toss my laptop on the bed then stand in front of him. "You don't need to say it aloud."

"Wh...?" His brows furrow. "What's that supposed to mean?"

I stare at him, stunned. He's too self-absorbed to realize that he's treating me like a nuisance. I'm not sure whether it makes it better or worse. I shake my head, dejected. "Nothing."

"No, tell me."

"You really want to know what I think?"

He chuckles, his palms together in front of him in a begging gesture. "Yes, please," he says in a collected tone, almost as if he were teasing, and I wonder if he's mocking me. "That mind of yours works in mysterious ways, all of them leading to hating my guts for no reason."

Another chuckle bursts from my throat, and this time I don't try to contain it. "For no reason? The effort you make to avoid taking any responsibility is awe-inspiring." The sarcasm in my voice is obvious. *Too* obvious.

For a second, our exchange could almost pass for some light banter, but the flash of disappointment in his eyes betrays him. We're not friends who have the luxury of teasing each other without any offense taken.

He snickers and pauses, running a hand through his hair again. "This is not going to work." He turns on his heels and walks back to the kitchen.

My heart drops. Is he backtracking on his decision to give me a few weeks to move? I stride after him, my throat tight. "What do you mean?"

"Talking to you, I mean." He stops and turns around to face me with a stern expression. "I swear I'm really trying, but no matter what I say..." He shakes his head.

"Talking to you doesn't work, Eva... For either of us."
His blue stare pierces me like a blade, a hint of sorrow
veiling his eyes for only a second, and he drops his
voice low. "So maybe we should just... *not* talk."

A shudder runs through me, leaving me cold. For a
fleeting moment, I'm fourteen again, in front of my
mother and stepfather, being told to shut up and
disappear. The scar inside my chest cracks.

I won't explain to Adrian how his behavior affects
me, how hurtful his words are to me. How his
withering stare knocks me back to my teenage years.
Adrian probably wouldn't care, and I shouldn't have to
lay bare my deepest trauma in order to be treated with
kindness.

I swallow hard. My nails dig into my palm, my eyes
prickling with tears from resentment, and from
sadness, too. Once again, I'm nothing but an annoyance
in someone's life.

Chapter Eight

Night Out

Another email that can wait until Monday.

My main preoccupation at work is to prioritize what has to be done and skip the rest so I can leave early.

Tonight can't come soon enough. Madison and I haven't talked much or seen each other at all since Adrian's return last week, and I've missed her. Going out for drinks with her is the breath of fresh air I need to escape her brother's suffocating presence. Being home early is my best chance of avoiding him. However he spends the day, he comes back quite late every afternoon.

Allowing myself a thirty-minute break to pick up my lunch, I run into Daphne looking lost on the corner of the street.

"Are you okay, Daphne?"

"Yes, kind of." She turns her icy blue eyes to me. "Is there a good restaurant around here? I've been eating a sandwich alone at my desk every day. I just can't take it anymore."

The small crack in her confident façade takes me by surprise, and I feel for her. I've been in her position. "There's a nice place right behind you. I wasn't planning on taking a long break, but if you like, I'd love to join you."

Her eyes widen. Her relations with most colleagues in our department haven't improved much, from what I've heard.

"Sure. Thank you for offering. I appreciate it."

We sit at a table, and the waiter takes our order soon after.

"Things are still rough at the office, huh?"

"I don't consider work as a place where you make real friends, but people here aren't even civil. It's insane." Daphne shakes her head.

It's difficult to contradict her. "The rumors at Rees & Lovett are indeed persistent, but there are a few people who are nice, once they get to know you."

"Like who?"

"Apart from Colin, who's a childhood friend… there's Hannah, from Real Estate. She's a sweet girl. She's on maternity leave, though."

The waiter brings our plates. Our initial easiness fades. Daphne and I stay in an awkward silence until I fill the void with a forced cheerful voice.

"How do you like San Francisco so far?"

She lets out a long sigh. "Let's cut the crap, okay? I'm too tired for this shit."

I put my fork down and wait for her to speak her mind. Rays of sun are glowing on her pale skin, shiny red hair cascading down her shoulders. She looks flawless, immaculate, innocent. Until she opens her mouth again.

"Every single woman at the office is a bitch. Except you, maybe, but I don't know for sure. I mean, I just met you. People are way less friendly than in L.A., and I didn't think that was possible. I don't know anyone or anything here, so I spend every evening alone in my hotel room. It's fucking depressing."

"Okay." I ponder for a moment.

She almost insulted me without being apologetic about it, but I appreciate her forwardness. Honest and blunt people are refreshing amidst an ocean of hypocrites forcing themselves to say the right thing. *I like this woman.*

"I've had a shitty week, too," I say. "I'm being thrown out of my place, and I don't know where to live. Tonight, I'm going out with my best friend with the firm intention of getting shitfaced. Do you want to join?"

A smile creeps across her lips. "I like you. And it doesn't happen to me very often, so you should feel honored," she says in feigned arrogance.

We both laugh, and the conversation returns to a natural ease.

"Tell me. What's this shit about you getting kicked out?"

"I'm subletting from my best friend Madison — with whom we're getting drunk tonight. The owner's her brother. He just got back from Paris and wants his place back."

Daphne looks at me with a frown. "Without warning?"

"Yes. He just appeared out of nowhere."

"What about your friend Madison in all of this? I mean, it's her brother. Can't she intervene?"

"She did. And she has issues of her own with him, so there's not much else she can do."

"I would've *at least* kicked the guy in the balls." She manages to drag a smile out of me.

"Not slapping him is a daily challenge, to be honest, so apart from the basic 'hi' when we pass by each other, I stay in my room, and I think he does the same." I sound miserable and defeated.

"Shitty week, indeed. Do you have somewhere to go?"

"I'm looking, but when I eliminate any apartment that's over budget or too far away, there's nothing left. I'm not sure how long I can stay in *his* apartment, and I don't want to have to crash on a friend's couch for weeks."

She stays silent for a moment, eyes unfocused, lost in her thoughts. "My aunt's a realtor. Maybe I could ask her if she can find something."

"Wait, your aunt's a realtor? You just said you lived in a hotel."

"I'm staying at the Hyatt Regency until I have the keys to an apartment in Dolores Heights in two weeks. She found this little gem for me. She managed to get me in touch with the owner before it was even listed. I can't promise anything, but maybe she has another miracle up her sleeve."

"That would be awesome. Thank you so much."

"I might be extra kind right now because of your invite to tonight's drunken debauchery. If you find something on your own, perfect. And if I can help, I'll be happy to."

Coming out of Daphne's mouth, it sounds like my problem is solved. I struggle to wrap my head around her offer. She'd be my savior if only I could extricate myself from Adrian's oppressive presence without having to settle for a shitty place. I try not to put too much hope in her proposal, but it still brings a smile to my face.

Daphne's grin widens. She is far from being the arrogant bitch people think she is.

* * * *

As planned, I leave work early, and Adrian is nowhere in sight when I arrive home.

My ultra-tight pencil skirt is discarded for black skinny jeans and a comfortable, loose-fitting white top. I release my hair from the bun I've worn all day, let the curls fall around my shoulders and adjust my makeup.

Madison is waiting for me when I arrive at our favorite restaurant, and Daphne comes soon after.

After a meal peppered with random questions to get to know each other, Madison dives into the fundamental matter.

"So, Daphne, did you run to San Francisco for a guy, or away from Los Angeles because of one?"

"That's the most sexist question I've heard in a while," I say. "Why does it have to be about a man?"

"True." Daphne nods in my direction. "Although, I *did* run away because of a guy."

"What happened?" Madison asks.

"I was dating this man for over a year. It was great, and we were happy together, or so I thought. For some reason, it wasn't relevant to him to mention that he was married," she deadpans.

"Shit! How did you find out?" I ask.

"His thirteen-year-old daughter DM'ed me on Twitter."

Madison shakes her head. "That's fucked up on so many levels."

"Yeah… So I'm happy to be single now. I think I will be for a while."

For the first time since we met, her fragile soul and the remnants of broken pieces appear from behind her strong façade. That side of her, somehow more consistent with her physical appearance, makes her look even more delicate.

The waitress clears our table, and we make our way down the block toward one of the most praised bars in town.

"What about you, Madison?" Daphne asks. "That huge rock on your finger has blinded me all evening."

Madison's face lights up, eyes bright, and a big smile graces her lips. "Luke is the most amazing man."

"When's the wedding?"

Madison slows down on the sidewalk as we approach the bar. Her face falls, and I answer for her.

"That's the issue I mentioned, with her brother."

"I don't get it." Daphne frowns.

We enter, then sit at a high table with beers in hand. The dim light from the lamp offers some privacy, but the volume of the music forces us to speak louder.

"Okay, long story short, Luke used to be my brother's best friend. They were in school together, grew up together. When Luke came out as bi at fifteen, Adrian became his truest ally. They were inseparable."

"And they're not friends anymore?"

"Luke's the kind of man who speaks his mind, sometimes too bluntly, and my brother's a stubborn wiseass. They got into several fights about Adrian's girlfriend, and when Adrian decided to follow her back to France, it blew up. Bad words were said, punches were thrown, and now they haven't spoken in, like, six years. Adrian doesn't know we've even been dating."

"How do you feel about that?"

"He's my brother. I don't want to get married without him." She swallows a big gulp of her beer. "Luke understands, and I know he feels the same way. That's why we haven't set a date yet."

"Now that your brother's back, you have to tell him," I say.

"I know, I know. Shit, we were supposed to have fun tonight. Enough depressing stuff." Madison gets up and drags us to the dance floor.

We spend the next two hours drinking or dancing. As we sit back at the table with our fourth beer in hand, Daphne throws her arm around my shoulders.

"Oh, by the way, I texted her earlier. She's on it." She winks.

"Who? On what?" Madison sits up straight on the stool, eyes wide open in anticipation as if we're about to reveal a big secret.

"My aunt's a realtor. She's going to help Eva find an awesome new place." She claps.

If someone had told me a week ago that Daphne could be this cheerful, I never would've believed them.

"That's great!" Madison raises her beer.

"Yes, let's hope your aunt *does* have miracles up her sleeve so I can move out soon."

"How is it going with Adrian, anyway?" Madison asks. "I haven't heard from either of you for days. I thought you had killed each other."

"It's fine. We manage not to fight every day. Not talking helps."

"You don't talk at all?"

"No, but it's fine." The annoyance builds up again. The awful memories from my youth crawl back to the surface, and I drown them in a mouthful of beer. "Feeling like an intruder in my own home is shitty, apartment hunting isn't easy, and Adrian being a jerk to me doesn't help. I'm getting claustrophobic. But I'll be fine."

Daphne snorts. "You said 'fine' too many times for it to be true."

Madison places her hand on mine with an affectionate smile. "You can't see it because you need someone to blame, and I'm mad at him, too, for leaving and coming back the way he did, but deep down, Adrian is a decent guy."

"He doesn't act like one."

"I don't know what happened in Paris, but I'm glad he's here because that woman was not good for him. I've never seen him so hurt."

"Whatever happened to him, I'm paying the price, and I don't appreciate it. He acts like my mere presence sickens him, and it's not fair."

I'm not willing to let myself be the bad person. I expect Madison to respond, but before she can open her mouth, Daphne snaps out of her observation mode and speaks.

"Listen, Eva, I have to play the devil's advocate here." Her firm voice comes out a little slurred. "From what I gather, Adrian must have gone through some shitty stuff with a woman he thought he'd spend the rest of his life with—and my money's on she fucked around. He comes back home to discover that some woman lives in his apartment, and his sister has a life that he knows nothing about. Put yourself in his shoes for a second, and maybe cut the guy some slack."

"He's mad at me, you know," Madison adds before I answer, "for renting out his place and not telling him where I live. But he needs someone to be on his side, so he won't fight with me. However, he can fight with you."

"We're not saying any of this is fair to you," Daphne says. "But I don't think it is to him, either."

"Okay, maybe you're right." I drop my head into my hands and sigh. "It's just so hard to feel unwelcome. It's hard having to go through that again." I lift my eyes and Madison offers me an understanding smile. I don't explain further at Daphne's questioning look. I don't want to dwell on that tonight, and she doesn't pry. "Ugh, you were supposed to bitch about Adrian, not defend him. I should've gone out with Colin!"

Madison laughs, and Daphne sips her beer, deep in thought, before speaking again.

"You know, you and Adrian should just fuck. That'll calm you down a bit."

"Gross!" Madison grimaces.

"I take my last comment back," I say. "You sound just like Colin."

"What does Adrian even look like?"

"I don't know, he's…" I search for the most suitable adjective to describe Adrian.

"Really hot, obviously." Madison whips her long golden hair over her shoulder in mock arrogance. "I mean, it runs in the family."

She doesn't realize how right she is. She's pretty enough to be overconfident, yet most of the time she's self-conscious and shy. It only adds to her beauty.

"I know he's my brother and all, but if we're being objective, he's a handsome man." She pulls out her phone, scrolls through her camera roll, and turns the screen toward Daphne. "It's an old picture but see for yourself."

Daphne gives an appreciative nod, and stares at me with a raised eyebrow, waiting to see if I agree with Madison. For the first time since that night, a memory of him naked under the water spray flashes in my mind. My brain fogs up, my cheeks blushing, and they notice it.

Daphne slaps her beer bottle on the table. "So, you think he's hot, too."

"He's still a jerk. To me, at least, so I won't fuck him."

"This is uncomfortable," Madison says, but Daphne and I ignore her.

"Why not?"

"*You're* the one who should get laid, Daphne."

"Damn right!" She laughs.

We speak loud enough for the man walking past our table to stop in his tracks. The lewd smile on his face is as disgusting as his libidinous stare.

"Not with you. Keep walking, dude," Daphne says, and the combination of disappointment and surprise on his face to see this perfect porcelain doll speaking in such an unrefined voice is priceless. Madison and I can't contain our laughter.

We spend another few hours swinging between deep and meaningful conversations — or so they seem in our drunkenness — and carefree dancing. We order a few more drinks, and by the end of the night, none of us is sober enough to walk home.

Madison calls Luke, and we wait for him on the sidewalk, welcoming the fresh air. He arrives with Colin driving his car, both of them getting out at the same time. Madison throws herself at her fiancé, her entire body crashing into his tall, slender frame. Her arms reach loosely around his neck, almost hitting him in the face when her hands circle back to the top of his buzzed, dark-haired head. The amused look Luke and Colin exchange at our state of inebriation isn't very subtle.

"Okay, let's put everyone to bed," Luke says.

Colin opens his car door for us. "Daphne, you look…"

"Shitfaced? Yeah, big time!" She slurs with a wide smile and slaps him on the shoulder.

His eyes widen. "Okay… So here's the plan, Luke walks home with Madison, because you are literally right around the corner" — he stresses each word with a raised eyebrow — "and I'll take the two of you in my car."

"You wish!" Daphne walks past him to get in, and Luke laughs before he lets Madison hop on his back and waves us goodbye.

As I'm sitting in the rear seat of Colin's BMW with Daphne, the movement of the car makes me nauseous. Even with the window open, the effect of all the alcohol I ingested is overwhelming. My head spins, and the ride home is a long struggle not to vomit.

Colin drops me off first on the way to Daphne's hotel. He parks in front of my building and opens the car door for me. Once I'm on the sidewalk, he pulls Daphne by the elbow, ignoring her unattractive groans, and forces her to follow us to avoid her either passing out or throwing up on his leather seats.

Before I can comprehend, we're at my front door. I consider searching for keys in my purse, but Colin doesn't wait for me to move and knocks. I'd never find them, anyway.

Adrian swings the door open, eyes wide. He speaks to Colin who answers with a few words I can't grasp.

The floor wobbles beneath my feet as I struggle to stay upright. All I can focus on is the dark tattoo on Adrian's bare chest.

Chapter Nine

Drunken Disclosures

An incessant banging on the front door startles me awake. The clock shows two-thirty in the morning. Eva must have forgotten her keys and has no qualms about waking me up in the middle of the night. So much for the quiet and solitary life I longed for. *Fucking perfect.*

After slipping into the closest pair of jeans I can find, I stomp to the door and swing it open with an exhausted sigh. The sight in front of me leaves me dumbstruck. Eva is barely able to stand up by herself, and nor is the redhead behind her, leaning on a huge black man who seems to be the only sober one.

"Hi, I'm Colin. You must be Adrian," he says. "The ladies were drunk, so I'm the chauffeur."

I must have been the topic of some discussion, so I skip the unnecessary introductions. "Where's Madison?"

"Already home safe." He gives no more information on where this *home* might be. "And now I'll drive Daphne."

The redhead who I assume is Daphne is a mess, eyes unfocused, head resting on his shoulder. My gaze then falls on Eva, who stares at my bare chest without reserve. This is new, and my exasperation morphs into unease.

"Can you take it from here?" Colin asks in a very protective tone, although I doubt he's her boyfriend. Even without being the jealous type, he wouldn't leave her with me.

"Um… Yeah, sure."

Colin pushes Eva through the door and walks away with the redhead holding on to his arm.

Eva totters to the living room and trips over her feet. Her hand reaches out, grabs mine to steady herself, and the last trace of exasperation in me vanishes. Eva's vulnerability is troubling. I'm not sure how to act with her in this context. I dealt with my fair share of tipsy girls back in the day, but our situation is different, complicated enough, and I'm not quite the same man, either.

Her hand clutches mine, very tight for such a petite woman, until we're sitting on the couch.

"Maybe you should take off your heels."

Eva turns to me, her eyes studying me, scrutinizing every inch of me for long seconds. Her slightly see-through top, ruffled hair and smeared makeup make her look a little dirty. The mischievous glint in her eyes and the small smile lifting the corner of her lips don't help. She's ogling me.

"You're hot!" she blurts out.

I'm stunned. *More than a week insulting me, and now she's hitting on me? She's unbelievable.*

Appealing to women is always nice, but the satisfaction inside me now is more than pride. I like *Eva* finding me attractive when she usually makes such big efforts to hate me.

A little — or perhaps a lot — of alcohol was all it took to loosen her up. If she's in a better disposition when she's drunk, I should enjoy it while it lasts. "Hot is better than a jerk. I'll take it. Thanks."

"Don't be so humble now." Her words are slurred, her voice loud and cheerful. "You know you're hot. I just realized it, though."

"Did you?"

"Yeah." She nods with wide eyes, a huge smile on her lips, making me laugh. Who knew she had that kind of spunky cuteness in her, even drunk?

Eva talks to me with no restraint or resentment for the first time since we met. With her eyes shining and her face relaxed, she's pretty.

"You seem to have enjoyed yourself tonight."

"I did. It was so much fun. Daphne's amazing. I don't know why everybody thinks she's a bitch. Well, they think I'm a bitch, too. But all the women in the office are bitches." Her lips turn into a little pout. She takes off one shoe and throws it over her shoulder, knocking a few books off a shelf as it lands on the bookcase. I struggle to stifle the laugh.

"Daphne's your colleague, then?"

"Yes. She just moved here. Hey, kinda like you!"

I bite my tongue not to retort that I didn't really *'just'* move here. I'd rather not see her irritation amplified by the effect of too many margaritas or whatever shit she's been drinking.

Instead, I circle back to the original topic because those words in her mouth are very satisfying, perhaps more than they should be. "Does Daphne think I'm hot, too?"

"Of course, she does. Madison also thinks you're handsome, but not in a creepy gross way, you know? And I think you're hot, but you're an asshole." She speaks fast, but her tone is casual. Joyful, even.

Eva has insulted me enough for me to know her opinion, yet hearing her say it aloud is still upsetting. I never meant to be an asshole to her. The situation just seems to get out of hand, my self-control thrown out the window, each and every time we talk.

"Is that what you think of me? Really?"

"Maybe you're a nice guy, but you were an asshole with me." Her cheery tone never falters. She doesn't even realize that she's insulting me.

Eva remains silent for a few moments. She leans forward, her hands fiddling with the strap of her remaining shoe, but her eyes are locked on my tattoo. Brows furrowed, lower lip trapped between her teeth, she must be trying to decipher it.

Her gaze on me is disarming. My heart speeds up, my skin warming.

"You're staring, Eva."

All week, I have avoided closing my eyes in the shower, afraid I'd see Eva pressed against me in a wet see-through dress. That my cock would grow hard at the vision of her, and I'd have to deny myself the pleasure again in my foolish determination to act like a respectful person. In my head, it was only a fantasy—I never wanted it to become true. Now, with that naughty twinkle in her eyes, Eva is too close to my mental picture.

"I like your tattoo. Can I touch it?"

"What? No!"

"Oh come on, don't be a baby." She launches herself at me.

I fall back on the couch with her on top of me, her face inches from my torso, arms on either side of my waist.

What the fuck is happening?

Eva doesn't grasp how wrong this is, how uncomfortable it could make me. I don't know how to handle her staring at my chest with such hungry eyes. Her thighs press between my knees, her long hair falls on my waist. Her belly pushes against my cock with every breath she takes, and she offers me a plunging view inside her loose top, her round breasts almost spilling from a black lace bra as they rest on my stomach.

Eva might be the most infuriating woman I've ever met, but right now she's fucking sexy, and I like her on top of me. My whole body is pulsing, aching to grab her and pull her closer. My cock hardens against her, and I struggle to think with my brain.

Hands closing into fists on the couch, I take a deep breath. Eva is swaying, too drunk to be aware of how inappropriate this is. I straighten up and push her back with careful hands on her arms so she's sitting on her side of the couch.

She resumes her fiddling with her left shoe and takes it off as if nothing happened.

"I'm hungry," she says, "and I miss feeling home."

"I'm pretty sure those two things are completely unrelated, though."

"I don't know... I need to sleep..."

"Clearly," I mutter, unable to make sense of the weirdness of our exchange.

Eva lounges against the armrest, a sad smile on her lips. Guilt tightens my chest. My coming back has affected her more than I'd let myself notice, but the last thing I want is for her to start crying. I couldn't deal with her tears any better than her advances.

"Eva, this is your place for as long as you live here. Until you go, consider yourself at home."

"Not true." The smile on her lips doesn't fade. "You don't want me here. You act like a jerk, like this situation isn't such a big deal for me." Her voice remains cheerful as she speaks almost without taking a breath, slurring half the words. "But I have to leave, and I could never afford a place like this. I'll move into a shitty small apartment, in a shitty neighborhood, with three weird-ass roommates. Well, maybe not anymore, thanks to Daphne's aunt who's got miracle places inside her sleeves. Daphne's awesome. I'm going to miss living here, though. I miss living here with Madison, too, sometimes, but she could never live without Luke, and it'd be so weird once they're married, so I'm going to find a great apartment just for m—"

"Wait, wait, hold on a sec! What did you say about Maddie and Luke?" I sit up straight, and her eyes grow wide.

"Nothing."

"Madison and Luke are fucking *engaged*?"

"Noooo..." She shakes her head. "I never said that. Please tell me I never said that."

"Fuck! I can't believe this!" I slouch back on the couch, staring at the ceiling, my hands tangled in my hair.

"I'm sorry."

"She's engaged to Luke. Goddamned Luke! And she didn't tell me..."

After several minutes of struggling to overcome the shock, I lower my gaze back to Eva who's falling asleep in a sitting position.

"You should go to bed, Eva."

"I'm still hungry, though."

"There are leftovers in the fridge." This conversation was entertaining — to a certain point — but not enough that I'll cook for her once more. No doubt she'll be resentful again tomorrow.

"Awesome!" She claps her hands and jumps from the couch but loses her balance. She tilts to the side and leans against me for support as I stand. Before I can react, her hands are on my bare torso, her body against mine, and she looks at me from under her lashes, biting her lip, green eyes filled with lust. She's doing a fucking good job of tempting me, whether it's on purpose or not.

The issue hasn't changed in the last ten minutes. This is still a bad idea. Chances are she'll still hate me in the morning when she's sobered up, and regardless, Eva's drunk, I'd never touch her in that state.

When I step back to walk away, she pushes her body harder against me, lifting on her toes to bring her mouth close to my ear. Her warm breath tickles my neck, sending a shiver down my back. My cock grows hard, and I can't fucking believe I have to ignore it…again!

"Can I tell you a secret, Adrian?" she whispers in a sultry voice.

"Yes," I blurt out too quickly.

"I saw you."

"Where?" My heart gallops. I know what she's referring to, and I want to hear her say it.

"In the shower, I watched you. I saw everything." Her hand slides down my chest until it reaches the waistband of my jeans, leaving an electric tingle on my skin. My breath catches, I can't move, I can't think. All my blood runs straight to my cock.

Eva brushes her index finger over her plump red lips. "Shhh…it's a secret."

My fists tighten at my sides, so stiff that my knuckles hurt. I move away from her before my primitive instincts take over, before I slam her against the closest wall and fuck the shit out of her.

I leave her on the spot and flee to my bedroom. Basic manners require staying by her side, making sure she's fine and goes to bed safely, but I'm too aroused to be a fucking gentleman.

She watched me on purpose. Eva made my fantasy real, but tomorrow morning, she won't remember admitting it.

After weeks of lukewarm desire, barely aroused by dull women in dull situations, real or imagined, now my dick is rock hard because of Eva, and I can't take advantage of it for the second time. Life fucking sucks. This woman is killing me.

I pace my room, jaw clenched and breaths ragged, torn between two choices. Too bad walking back to Eva and fucking her on the couch isn't one of them. Either calm down and go to bed like a good boy, or sneak into the shower to jerk off thinking about her eyes on me, hands sliding down my chest, lips close to my skin… *Fuck!*

The hunger is too wild to tame, sleeping won't be possible, and I don't want to cockblock myself again, anyway.

Lights switched out, I jump into bed, jeans and boxers off and my hand grabbing my cock, my movements irrepressible. Behind my closed eyes, Eva is flirting, pressed against me. My hand moves on my length in slow strokes, teasing. I'm out of breath, drowning in the thrill I haven't felt for so long, and I quicken the pace.

The muffled noises Eva makes permeate through my closed door. I imagine her in the next room, undressing, revealing her tight ass covered only in black lace, reaching behind her back to unhook her bra and let it drop to the floor. The idea of her naked body slipping under her covers spurs me on.

This is wrong. A part of me is fighting my instincts, trying to make me stop. I force my brain to erase the face of Eva from my fantasy, to settle on another woman, but I can't. I only see Eva. Some other part of me wonders how she'd react if she came in and saw me touching myself. That intoxicated, she could forget that we switched rooms.

An electric jolt courses through my body, firing up. What if she caught me? Would it turn her on? Would she join me?

The moon casts a dim light through the window, enough to peek at the door. I imagine her entering and whispering my name. My hand moves faster on my cock, as uncontrollable as my mind picturing Eva crawling on the bed, her warm hands on my chest, her slender, soft legs on either side of mine, heat radiating from her, burning my skin.

The sound of a door opening seeps through the confines of my bliss, but my eyes shooting open obliterate the illusion that she could've entered for real. The pounding of my heart resonates in my ears. I slow the rhythm of my rubs and focus on Eva on the other side of the corridor. She's in the bathroom, and whatever she's doing, she left the door open. My mind goes wild at the possibilities. All I want is to join her, crash my body against hers, thrust into her.

"She's drunk, she's drunk, she's so fucking drunk," are the only words I can mutter, the only thought I can form and repeat to myself as a shield saving me from a very bad decision. I must stay on my side of the door.

Eyes falling closed again, I dive back into my first fantasy, and I'm in the shower with her. Only this time, I won't stop.

I grab my cock a little tighter and accelerate, shifting my hand up, palm brushing the head, then down, my muscles tensing as I pull Eva in the shower with me, tear her dress apart and slam her against the tile wall. I stroke faster, breathing labored, heart racing from the whirlwind of sensations gushing over me as her leg locks around my waist, eyes begging, tongue darting out to taste mine, and one hand reaches my ass to pull me closer. I slide inside her pussy, and the most blissful orgasm overtakes me, my heart exploding, hips bucking and legs trembling, until my mind goes numb.

I catch my breath, come back from heaven, and open my eyes to clean up with a tissue. My breathing slows down, muscles relaxing.

The place is quiet, Eva's not making a sound. I can't discern what room she's in. I lend an ear, but there's only silence and peace as I drift into sleep.

* * * *

I wake up in the morning with a heavy weight sprawled over my abdomen, and I know it's Eva even before I open my eyes.

What the fuck is she doing here?

She lies on her stomach across the bed in only her white top and silky black panties, her lean body over the covers, one leg bent at the knee, the other foot dangling off the side. Her right arm over my chest, her head rests on my belly with her nose facing my crotch, hot breath blowing on my cock through the thin fabric of the sheet barely covering me. Her left arm is draped over my thigh, with her hand an inch from my growing erection.

None of my dreams could compare to waking up to such an arousing sight.

How she ended up in my bed and in that position is a mystery, but her mouth is too close to where I want it. My brain is useless, stuck on the vision of my fist clutching those long brown locks to guide her as she sucks me.

I rub a hand over my face and fight to reason. Eva might not even realize she slept in my bed. How ironic that part of my fantasy came true while I was unconscious. In any case, she shouldn't wake in that position, facing the tent I'm pitching. I shift, hoping to remove myself from under her, but she follows the motion and ends up even closer to my throbbing cock, almost touching it.

This is too much. She has to wake up, no matter what happens next.

"Eva." My hand squeezes her shoulder. She budges a little then freezes. I can't see her face, but she's awake. I remain immobile and silent as I brace myself for her reaction.

Eva gasps, pushes herself away from me and almost jumps from the bed. In her haste, she falls backward, flips over the edge and lands on the floor in a loud thud with her feet flailing in the air.

Chapter Ten

Hanging Over

My head is heavy, hurting as if crushed in a vice. Opening my eyes is too difficult. Never again will I drink as much as I did last night. I danced and laughed with Madison and Daphne, but the rest of the night is a blur. All the memories have been washed out of my brain by the alcohol in my system.

"Eva?" a deep, raspy voice whispers as a hand squeezes my shoulder.

I emerge from the confines of my semi-consciousness with a body under my head and a slow rhythmic breathing motion under my ear. I'm not alone in bed, and there's no other choice but to come back from my blissful coma to meet this stranger and face the hard, shameful reality.

Lifting one eyelid, I chance a peek. My head rests on his stomach facing a happy trail of hair leading to an impressive peak lifting the sheets. I freeze. My mind arises from its haziness and recognizes whose voice woke me, whose fragrance lingers. Even without paying attention to it, I'm positive it's Adrian's.

Fuck! I'm in bed with him.

I jump up and, in my haste, fall backward from the bed, knocking my ass on the wooden floor, with the horrific confirmation from the corner of my eye that the man is indeed Adrian.

"Fuck! Eva, are you okay?" He kneels on the bed, both hands clutching the sheet to cover his crotch.

"What are you doing here?" My voice comes out more high-pitched than intended as I pick myself up in a clumsy maneuver.

"This is my room —"

"Are you kidding me? You want to use that argument *again*?"

"Yes! I slept in my own fucking bed. You're the one who didn't. How can you turn this into being my fault?" His voice rises to mimic mine. He grabs at his hair and lets out a long breath.

Adrian turns around to put on his jeans and a T-shirt, offering me an unimpeded view of his ass in the process. I divert my gaze and snatch my pants from the floor to get dressed. My head throbs. I'm confused.

"Look, Eva, calm down. You came home drunk, you probably just got in the wrong bed, no big deal. It's not the end of the world."

"Waking up with your boner in my face is pretty close to it. What happened last night? Are you telling me you didn't notice I was here?" My voice still sounds hysterical, and his rises again.

"If I did, I would've asked you to leave."

"Yeah, you're good at kicking me out."

"I can't believe this," he says under his breath. "I can't believe how unreasonable you are. You want to know what happened? Fine." Adrian takes a step toward me, running a hand through his hair again. I'm getting on his nerves. "You came home so wasted you couldn't even walk straight. We talked, surprisingly enough," he continues in a mock cheery tone, "but I'm not sure if the best part was learning about Maddie and Luke being engaged, you admitting you watched me shower, or that you kept flirting with me."

"What? Why would I be flirting with you? You're—"

"An asshole? Yeah, you told me." That wasn't the end of my sentence, but Adrian doesn't stop long enough for me to respond. "You also said I'm hot, that you liked my tattoo and wanted to touch it." He steps forward with an arrogant smile that I want to slap off his face. "You tried, as a matter of fact."

"That explains how I ended up in your bed, now, doesn't it?" My heart pounds in my chest, head thrashing with pain.

"Do you really think I go for the hardly conscious drunk girl? Even half-naked in my bed I'd never touch you." His glare mirrors his rude tone. "Look, it's not my fault you got so hammered you said things you shouldn't have and don't remember. So hammered that, for all I know, you sneaked in my room to get some, and ended up passing out next to me while I was sleeping."

Shame washes over me, head thumping and throat dry. Our fight could've stopped there, allowing me to calm down and reassess, but Adrian's next words blow like a slap in my face.

"I should've known that in the morning you'd be yourself again." His voice drops and he shakes his head. "Bitter and cold."

"Don't turn this around, Adrian. How am I supposed to react? I wake up half naked in your bed, and you seemed to really enjoy the view."

"Seriously, Eva? You want to put 'ogling people naked' on the table? And lecture *me* about it?"

My mind races for a comeback, but I've already lost.

Adrian sighs and walks closer to me, his body taut with anger. "I'm sick of you, of your arrogance and hostility. It's no wonder you live alone. How would anyone want to live with you? But maybe if I *had* fucked you good and hard last night, it might have lightened you up a little."

"You're fucking disgusting." My throat tightens, my voice low. I shoot back with the first argument coming to mind, the one that will hurt him as much as he hurt me. "No wonder your fiancée sent you back to another continent. How could she even consider marrying an asshole like you?"

I regret it the second the words escape my mouth.

Adrian flinches, pain flashing in his eyes. He takes another step forward and stops right in front of me. He's towering over me, looking down at me with a hateful expression. "You're right, I don't want you here, and I don't want to see you today. I'm going to take a shower, so get the fuck out of *my* apartment before I'm finished. And please try to refrain from opening the door and watching me."

Adrian walks past me and slams the bathroom door, leaving me here, speechless.

My legs wobbling, I crawl to my room and sit on the bed, face hidden in my hands, replaying in my head the fight we just had. Adrian's words ring true, and both Daphne and Madison agree that I've been difficult from the start, even when he tried to be nice. Part of me wants to wait until he gets out of the bathroom to admit that I overreacted. The other part knows he needs space. I should let him breathe.

After changing into yoga pants and an oversized sweater, I head outside, reaching for my phone in my purse to call Madison. In my drunkenness, I'd told Adrian who she lives with. She should hear it from me, before Adrian asks for an explanation.

As I amble toward the Marina, the phone beeps against my ear, and Madison picks up.

"Hi, Eva. Are you okay? My head is killing me."

"Me, too. Um...actually, I'm not okay," I answer. "I need to talk to you. Before you talk to Adrian."

"I don't like the sound of that."

"I know, I'm sorry."

"Oh no...you told him, didn't you?"

"I'm sorry, Madison."

She almost grunts on her end of the line. "I imagine you didn't tell Adrian on purpose." Her tone is soft, understanding, and I let out a long sigh of relief that she isn't too mad at me.

"I don't know, I don't remember much. He just said he knew."

"How did he react?"

"He was already upset with me, we were fighting, so I can't tell. He didn't ask me to explain. I guess he'll want to talk to you. I'm sorry, Madison."

She sighs on the phone. "It's not your fault. I should have told him a long time ago. I hope he'll understand."

"I'm sure he will. And he's so mad at me that he won't have enough anger left for anyone else."

"Eva, why were you fighting again? What happened?"

I take a deep breath to explain as best I can, considering the headache and the state my nerves are in. "Like I said, I don't remember much. The only thing I know is that I woke up half naked in his bed, and I—"

"What? You had sex with him?" Madison sounds more surprised than upset at the idea.

"No. I don't know how I got there, and I was confused and shocked when I woke up—my mouth right next to his morning wood, may I add—"

"Ew, too many details." Madison's voice distorts in disgust.

"Sorry. Anyway, my first reaction was to yell at him, and I think I implied he took advantage of me while I was drunk." I lower my voice as I pass by people on the street. "And that's not even the worst part. We both kept yelling, and I said I understood why his fiancée sent him back here."

She blows out an exasperated breath, so loud it crackles through the phone. "You need to apologize. Both of you. Talk to each other."

"I think I need to apologize for a lot more than just this morning." The tension leaves my body, a weight lifted off my chest. "I'm sorry again, Madison."

"It's fine, I promise. And you're not the only one who made a mess." She clears her throat. "I told my parents Adrian was back. They're expecting us for dinner next weekend."

"He's going to kill you."

"Ugh, I know," Madison whines, and it makes me laugh.

We end the conversation on a comforting note. I shove my phone in my purse and wander along the busy streets, relishing the chilly air of early April and the soft light dimmed by the clouds, delaying the dreaded moment I'll have to talk to Adrian and face the consequences of our behavior. I stop by the closest Starbucks to buy a large caramel macchiato, and stroll until I reach the Palace of Fine Arts, sitting on a bench across the pond, my eyes closed to ease the lingering headache.

No matter how hard I try to focus on the faint sounds around me, my mind drifts back to Adrian, to his cutting words this morning, the fury in his eyes and the pain morphing his features when I hit back. We both went too far.

Behind my closed eyelids, his naked body in the shower appears, the water flowing down his muscular back, following the curves of his toned ass. Now he knows I saw him.

Images of last night flash in my head. I'm pressed against his tall frame, sliding my hand down his bare chest. My heart beats faster. I can't believe I did that. I hadn't realized I wanted to.

I was too focused on hating Adrian for making me relive the most traumatic years of my youth, for triggering the pain, the fear of abandonment I thought I'd buried deep enough. I've blamed him, so much that it's blocked out my attraction to him since the first second we met. The alcohol set it free.

My eyes screwed shut, I search my mind for the memories, and several details reemerge, like holding on to his arm, staring at his tattoo…and telling him he was an asshole.

A swirl of his amber fragrance washes over my memory, so vivid, awakening my senses. I remember the softness of his skin on my fingertips, his body trapped under me. My breathing accelerates, my skin warming. My heart falters when his gaze on me resurfaces. His blue eyes are locked on me, devouring me. The simple memory of it turns me on. Adrian confessed that he thought about fucking me good and hard, and at this second, the idea seems more than appealing.

The cold drizzle falling on my face startles me out of my fantasy. I open my eyes and swallow a big gulp of scorching coffee to help bring me back to reality.

The area isn't as crowded as it is on sunny days, but among the few tourists taking pictures of the monument, my eyes catch sight of a man jogging along the colonnade on the other side of the pond. I squint and sit up straight, as if those mere inches will help me see more clearly. Tall, strong build, light-brown hair and a stoical face — it's Adrian. He runs at a steady pace, the rhythm of his regular strides hypnotizing me as he circles the Rotunda. He slows down as he reaches the front and stops near the water, hands on his hips, catching his breath.

On instinct, I lean forward, my body angling toward him.

His arms reach up, left hand pulling his right wrist as he leans sideways to stretch, his damp T-shirt rising above his waist, and I clutch my coffee cup, silently cursing the blurry distance.

Adrian freezes with his hands up and in a sudden movement, they drop by his sides, his gaze focused in my direction. *He's seen me.*

Before I can decide if I should stand, wave or just look away, he turns around, resumes running toward the other side of the colonnades, and disappears.

I swallow the last mouthful of my coffee with a tight throat and heavy head, torn between too many feelings to process, and too much alcohol still left in my system.

Adrian reappears on my right, at the end of the alley, and my heart skips a beat. He runs toward me, his face peaceful, his footing light, regular, effortless. I struggle not to ogle him, his muscular thighs flexing in his shorts, his strong torso showing underneath the wet T-shirt sticking to his skin.

All of a sudden unsure that he'll stop when reaches me, I stand in the way, my mind set on having a conversation, to be given the opportunity to apologize.

I fidget with the cup in my hands as his sweaty frame slows down. He takes his earbuds out and stops a few feet away from me, breathing labored, loose strands of his hair dropping on his forehead, dripping from the light rain.

"I didn't mean it." His tone is as soft as his gaze on me, apologetic, surrendering, and it takes my breath away. "That you had to stay out of the apartment today...that was a fucked-up thing to say. You have a right to be at home."

His words stun me. I swallow hard, struggling to find my voice under his magnetic blue stare. "Adrian, I—"

He lifts one hand to stop me, shaking his head. "Just... The rain's picking up. Unless you want to get soaking wet, you should come home."

He doesn't wait for me to answer, puts his earbuds back in his ears, turns around and runs back to where he came from. I stand there speechless, my head still clouded from the hangover and my stomach in knots.

Adrian has made the first step, a peace offering to smooth out our chaotic cohabitation. I'll meet him halfway. I throw my empty cup in the closest trashcan and walk home with a whirlwind of emotions and words colliding in my mind, amplifying my persistent headache. I practice the apology I owe Adrian about this morning, about all of it, and fight to keep the memories of his captivating gaze and his naked skin under my fingertips at bay.

Chapter Eleven

Reassess

When I push the front door open, Adrian is already inside, his dirty running shoes kicked off in the entrance and shuffling sounds coming from his bedroom. He ran back faster than I walked, despite the short route I took.

Determined to make amends for my bitchiness and fix this mess, I cross the corridor, stopping by his half-open door. Inside, Adrian has his back turned to me as he puts on a pair of sweatpants with no underwear, offering me a glimpse of his perfect ass. My breath catches, and he spins on his heels, eyes wide in bewilderment.

"Again? Really?"

My hands shoot up in surrender. "I'm sorry."

He takes a few slow steps until he's in front of me, fingers running through his hair. "For what, exactly?"

"It appears that the list is long," I say with a smile to diffuse some of his annoyance.

His face relaxes, his piercing eyes study me, stripping me of the little courage I had. The irritation has vanished from his stare, replaced by a beguiling attention on me.

The right words evade me, but I soldier on. "Mostly, for um...being aggressive from day one, and...about last night, I mean this morning, making accusations, and..."

I stop my mumbling. My mouth drops open, and I breathe louder as Adrian takes a last step closer to me, gaze locked. The soft daylight seeps through the window behind him, shadows dancing over the muscles of his arms and shoulders, framing his strong unshaven jaw. I resist the urge to lick my lips, but I glance at the dark tattoo on his chest, only for a second, only enough to make out some intricate black lines overlapping red slivers. When my gaze travels back to his face, a smile has appeared on his mouth, a teasing glint dancing in his deep blue eyes.

Adrian caught me ogling, and his desirous stare is disarming. I struggle not to peek at the muscles of his torso flexing as he leans on the door.

"That's kind of a half-assed apology, don't you think, Eva?" His slight cockiness brings my focus back.

"Don't be a jerk, Adrian."

"You already said I was," he teases.

"Ugh... I wanted to give you a sincere apology, but you're not helping me."

"Would I be helping if I put on a shirt?" His voice drops to a throaty murmur.

I gape at him. His playful arrogance is frustrating and sparks the urge to wipe that smug smile off his face by either slamming the door in his pretty face again, or kissing the living shit out of him.

Neither of those options is appropriate in the current context, so I turn around and flee to the kitchen, taking a deep breath and releasing it in a long blow. Acknowledging my attraction to him opens the way to sensations I can't rein in, in turns deep exasperation and debilitating lust. Swinging from one extreme to the other is giving me whiplash.

Perhaps Adrian deserved a better apology. Perhaps I deserved one, too. But he seems more interested in flirting than in my apologies, anyway. *Where does that even come from?*

I pull my damp hair into a messy bun with the elastic band I carry around my wrist, grab a diet Coke from the fridge, and reach into the top cupboard for a bag of Cool Ranch Doritos.

As I sit at the table, Adrian enters, now fully clothed in a black T-shirt and zip-up hoodie, his blue eyes standing out even more. He pauses and watches me, the cockiness in his features replaced by the candor I witnessed by the pond.

"I don't want to sound patronizing, but...do you want real food?"

I swallow the piece of Dorito in my mouth, along with the restlessness Adrian elicits in me with a simple look. I'm a grown woman. I should be able to talk to him without either yelling or swooning.

"Shitty snacks are my hangover cure."

"That bad?"

I nod and shove another Dorito in my mouth, and he offers a soft smile.

He opens the fridge, pulls out a bottle of sparkling water that he places on the table, and starts laying slices of bread on a plate before adding mustard, ham, cheddar, tomato slivers and lettuce that I didn't know my fridge contained. I watch him assemble the most mouthwatering sandwich, Doritos bag forgotten, and he chuckles as he pushes the plate in front of me.

"Shitty snacks keep you from puking. This" — he points to the sandwich and sits opposite me — "will give your body the energy it needs to recover." He pours a glass of water and slides it toward me before reclining on his chair.

"You sound like you know what you're talking about." I raise a questioning eyebrow as I pull the plate closer to me and take a sip of water.

A low laugh rumbles in his throat, and the velvety sound warms my entire body.

"I've been close to ethylic coma enough times to know what really helps."

"Well, thank you."

He gives a slight head bow and reaches in his pocket to pull out his phone that keeps vibrating, as I dig into the sandwich in silence.

Adrian studies the screen for long minutes, eyes focused and a small smile on his lips.

"I haven't started working yet, and they already drown me in emails," he says, perhaps to himself.

"You have a job?" My tone sounds more incredulous than I intended, and I clarify to avoid him taking offense. "I assumed it would take longer for you to find one."

"It was..." He pauses and shakes his head. "It's a transfer from the Paris office." He puts his phone on the table and looks at me with a proud expression. "A month of long-distance calls, and four...no, five in-person interviews with HR and senior managers, all crammed into one week. They confirmed yesterday, and I'm starting on Monday."

"Wow. Congratulations, then." I raise my glass to him.

Adrian pours himself some water, and we clink our glasses.

Exposed under his piercing gaze, I divert mine to the table. "What do you do, actually?"

When I look back at him, he's still watching me, his smile in place.

"I'm an investment banker."

"Really?" It appears that we have more in common than I imagined.

He chuckles. "It sounds evil, I know. It is, to most people."

"With your parents and sister in the medical field, I thought you'd be some kind of doctor, too."

"No, saving lives is so overrated," he jokes, and a deep, warm laugh escapes his throat again.

I struggle to stay focused, fight to hold my head high. "I agree. Tapping debt markets or raising equity is a lot more fulfilling."

His mouth drops open, eyes burning as if I had just pronounced the most erotic words. "You work in finance, too?"

"I'm a legal assistant, but I work with Colin, who's a financial lawyer. He teaches me a lot, getting me as involved as possible. The banking field and its ramifications are fascinating to me."

"Hence the shitload of finance textbooks on your shelves."

"Yes. I don't have enough saved up to go back to college yet, and I'm not decided on financial law or banking, but it's definitely a goal."

"That's great." Adrian studies me, silent for a few beats, as if he were trying to solve a mystery. "If you ever need any practical feedback on financial products, let me know."

"Thank you." My voice sounds less and less assured under his intense stare, and I break eye contact to stand and clear the table. "I'll go take a shower," I mumble, almost as an excuse to exit the kitchen.

When I turn around, Adrian is standing behind me. He brushes past me to place his glass in the sink, and a wave of his fragrance engulfs me, the amber note blended with a deep woody undertone, sweetly thick and heady, befuddling my mind. Instead of stepping back, he shifts a little and stops in front of me.

"Eva?" he asks in a low, raspy voice and waits until I look at him. My knees are weak before I even lift my eyes to his. He towers over me, too close. "Eva, I apologize for treating you as badly as I did. I never meant to be an asshole, but I realize I was. I know this situation is hard for you. I'm truly sorry."

His eyes are locked on me, and I drown in them. Wheels turn in my head, straining to find words to answer, but I come up empty. Even breathing is difficult with his body this close.

He leans in, mouth next to my ear, soft breaths blowing in my hair. "Now *that* is an apology."

Adrian pulls away with a teasing spark in his eyes and bites his lower lip. He winks and exits the kitchen, walking straight to his bedroom and closing the door, leaving me behind, breathless.

My brain struggles to process what just happened, my entire body buzzing. In less than a day, we went from barely tolerating each other's presence to smiles, teasing and winks. I withdraw to my room and hide away behind the closed door, hoping the privacy will help sort out the chaos in my head. It doesn't.

I set about cleaning up my room, but waves of images rush over me, drowning my mind and body, overpowering my senses... Adrian's lustful gaze, his fragrance intoxicating me, his breaths tickling my neck. My skin burns as I see his tall frame towering over me. I lie down on my bed, eyes closed and heart galloping.

Firing up my laptop, I try to focus on the latest episode of a random show, but my imagination runs wild. I envision the different turn that our kitchen encounter could've taken, like a scene in a movie. Our bodies close, his arms encircle me, squeezing my ass to push his hard cock against me.

Shaking the vision out of my head, I spend all my energy on keeping it at bay, but when the night comes and I'm alone in bed, my skin still craves his touch.

I cave, allowing my mind to unleash the fantasy. Swept up by desire, I let my hands move on me as I picture Adrian's hand slipping under my sweater, eager, kneading my breast, pinching my hardened nipple. His wet lips and his tongue tasting me send a shiver to course through me and settle between my thighs.

The itch is impossible to resist, overpowering any attempt to reason, to ponder whether I'm crossing a line by touching myself while I think of him — while he's in the next room. But the thought only excites me even more.

My hand travels down as his slips inside my pants, his fingers underneath my panties. I hold back a gasp as I brush over my clit, legs spread on the mattress. Behind my closed eyelids, his muscular arm keeps me in place against the kitchen counter, and his middle finger thrusts inside me.

The sensation is far from enough. I want him shirtless, his skin against mine, his pants shoved down to his knees. My breathing erratic, my hand rubs faster as he lifts me off the floor and against the closest wall, his cock pushing inside me, pounding.

Would Adrian hear me if I let out a moan? Would he join me if I screamed his name?

The possibility of him entering my room in only a towel, muscles flexing and eyes devouring me, drives me over the edge of ecstasy. I bite my lips to keep from moaning as the burst of white bliss overtakes me, hips bucking and breath short.

As my body relaxes and my eyes open, the itch lingers inside me, not fully satisfied. My brain still fails to make sense of it. I resented him for being here and now I want him closer.

Chapter Twelve

Something Different

The restless nights, confusion and tension accumulated over the past days are too much to bear. On Monday morning, I stride to Colin's office as soon as I arrive at work and open the door without bothering to knock.

The worry in his eyes tells me he already knows the mess I've made between Madison and her brother. Luke must've told him. "Are you okay?"

"I'm not sure, to be honest," I answer, failing to find a word that best describes my state of mind.

"Luke called me," he says. "Madison is worried because Adrian won't answer her messages."

"I know. It's my fault."

"Don't blame yourself. She should've told him before it came to this."

I nod, take a deep breath and reveal the one detail he hasn't heard about from Luke.

"I also told Adrian I thought he was hot."

"You want him," he says. It's not a question.

"I can't think straight when he's in front of me. He makes me swoon like a teenager. It's embarrassing. This morning when he was leaving, I got a glimpse of him in a suit. A fucking suit!"

"You work in a law firm. You're always surrounded by men in suits."

"You should see *him* in a suit."

The usual roguish spark is back in his eyes. "Have you told Madison that you're lusting after her big brother like a teenager?"

"No, and I don't intend to."

After relating the details of the fight and Adrian's peace offering in the form of a delicious sandwich, Colin makes me laugh with his dirty jokes about Adrian fucking me good and hard. When I exit his office, the situation doesn't seem so horrible anymore.

Focusing on work all day alleviates the lingering tension from the weekend's drunken debacle. Since our apology, Adrian and I haven't spoken much, only exchanging a few platitudes when we cross each other. Even though the hostility between us has waned, a new restlessness has settled. I don't know how to act around him, and I struggle to hold his ocean-blue stare. My attraction to him is hard to tone down, my body betraying the effect he has on me, and his attitude is puzzling. Is he flirting, or only messing with me because my reactions amuse him?

I step into the office elevator late in the afternoon, ready to leave. Just before the doors close, Patricia follows wearing her usual vain smile.

"Eva, how was your day?"

"Good, as always. And yours?" I ask out of politeness more than true interest. No matter my opinion of her and our lack of basic amity, this is still our workplace, I have to appear cordial, and it's easier to fake it.

"Great. I've heard you've become good friends with the new paralegal…Daphne, over the weekend."

My jaw clenches. I can't have a drink on my spare time without some spy reporting it to our gossiper-in-chief. It's annoying, and a little disturbing, too. "Is that a question?"

"I don't know. Is it a secret?"

I roll my eyes and turn away, ending that joke of a conversation.

"Never mind." Her fake smile doesn't fade as we exit the elevator and cross the lobby, until we step on the sidewalk. "Obviously, you two have a lot in common. You're…that type." Patricia's eyes creep down my body with disdain.

Disbelief stops me in my tracks, and I grit my teeth not to hit back. Nothing I could say would make her reconsider this detestable behavior of hers, let alone apologize, so I turn around without bothering to even say goodbye, and rush to the closest bus stop to put distance between her seeping haughtiness and me.

When I arrive home, the apartment is empty, even quieter than usual in Adrian's absence. I hang in the kitchen, grab a bite to avoid the seclusion of my bedroom and hope for the remaining irritation in my stomach to fade.

I settle on the couch with a notepad, pencil and copy of the case file Colin is currently working on, along with my introductory book on structured finance. I scribble words, outline some notions and draw a rough diagram as I try to make sense of what I'm reading.

The front door opens as Adrian comes home, and the sigh of contentment that escapes my chest almost takes me by surprise, his presence soothing the last remnant of annoyance. Who would've thought that was possible?

"Hi," I call out, lifting my eyes from my books.

"Hi." Adrian trudges through the living room, features gaunt and shadows under his eyes.

I caught only a glimpse of him this morning as he was walking out the door, but up close, even tired, he's still very handsome in the dark-gray suit and lighter gray tie he's wearing.

"How was your first day?"

"Fucking exhausting, but great at the same time," he says in a strained voice, plopping down on the couch, and turning to me with a satisfied smile.

With that smile, in that suit, he is dazzling.

He points to the papers on my lap. "What are you working on?"

His eyes linger for a second on the hem of my skirt rising above my knees, and a tingle crawls on my skin.

"Colin asked me to help out with research on a case." I force my tone to sound confident, hoping it'll help me keep control of my body. "But right now I'm just trying to get a good grip on how collateralized debt obligations work."

He chuckles. "Yeah, those are nasty." He takes off his suit jacket and loosens his tie. "I assume you can't share any specifics on that case, confidentiality and all, but maybe I can help. What do you have so far?"

"That it's a complex and risky structured-finance product, backed by a pool of loans and assets, and created mainly by securities firms and hedge funds to free up capital."

He nods and smiles. "Good, you have the basics. Now, this pool of assets is repackaged, divided into tranches based on level of credit risk, and sold on the secondary market." His eyes study me, deep and inviting.

"Okay, so far, I'm following. This is basically what I wrote down." I turn my notepad to show him the diagram I sketched.

Adrian takes it from me to look closer, then reaches for the pencil in my hand. His fingers brush against mine, sending a shiver up my arm. Our eyes meet for only an electric second before he diverts his focus back to the paper, and I stifle the urge to straddle his lap and kiss him.

He extends the diagram, adding several layers. "From here, you have senior debt, mezzanine tranche and equity, which has the higher risk." In a few seconds, the scribbles on my page turn into a complete blueprint of the entire structure. Adrian's stare is intense, his voice passionate and eager to share his knowledge. "It's called 'collateralized' because it's the underlying asset—"

"That serves as collateral if the loan goes into default." I put the pieces together in a smug voice.

His eyes fire up with excitement and something resembling pride, and his smile widens. "Exactly. You got this."

"Thank you. It helps a lot to hear the explanation out loud. Now I can dig deeper and draw the parallel with Colin's case."

"Anytime. I'll leave you to it, then." He stands, giving me one last breathtaking smile.

I watch him, the fabric of his shirt clutching the strong muscles of his back as he walks away and disappears into his bedroom.

Chapter Thirteen

The Visit

I'm storing just-purchased groceries in the fridge when Eva storms out of her room, bare feet thumping on the living room hardwood floor.

"Thank you so much," she says in the distance. "I'll be there as soon as possible. Thirty minutes tops... All right, yes, twenty."

She appears at the kitchen doorway and stops short of crashing into me, stunning us both.

"Everything okay?" I ask.

Sneakers dangling in one hand, she circles me to grab an apple from the fridge and throws it into her purse along with her phone. "I'm going to visit an apartment in North Beach. The landlord just agreed to wait for me." She sits on a chair to put on her shoes.

She has changed out of the sexy pencil skirt and heels she wore at work, and the skinny jeans and a black sweater she now wears hug her curves like a second skin. Since the night she came home drunk, it's been more and more difficult to rein in the urge to put my hands on her.

I drag my mind out of the gutter and considering how our last conversation about her move ended, I'm careful to keep my tone in check. "At seven in the evening?"

"I insisted. It's the only rental I've found that seems decent. I can't wait, or somebody else might take it. I have to be there in less than twenty minutes." She gives a shy wave and exits the kitchen.

I follow her. "You're going alone?" The question comes out wrong, too cutting, too patronizing, and she stops.

"What?"

Too late for the tone. I'd rather take the risk of her getting upset than being assaulted. No need to add that responsibility on top of the guilt from kicking her out. "North Beach's not a bad neighborhood, but at sunset, to meet some man you know nothing about..."

She props her hands on her hips and sighs. "It's not that far, and I don't have time to call a cab, it's already going to take them ten minutes to get here. Same thing if I ask Colin or Lu —"

She stops mid-sentence, her lips zipping into a tight line as I flinch at the mention of my former best friend. Reality hits me square in the face. They're all a tight group of friends, and I'm the outsider. Getting my life on the right track seems much more complex than expected.

Her face morphs into an apologetic grimace as she takes another step back and opens the front door. I shake the gloom out of my head and get back on topic.

"Do you want me to drive you?"

She blinks a few times, mouth agape, but doesn't answer.

I chuckle. "Maybe it wasn't clear from the start, but really, Eva, I'm a nice guy. And I'm not offering to make sure you'll move out soon." I pause and throw her a teasing smirk. "Not entirely."

She snorts and hesitates.

"Clock's ticking."

"Okay, fine, yes, thank you."

We rush out, I lead the way through the parking lot, and she slows down, eyes wide, when my brand-new white Mercedes-AMG CLA unlocks as I approach.

"*That's* your car?"

"Yes. Impulsive buy. I saw it in the showroom and I couldn't resist."

"Right…"

When she plops down next to me in the passenger seat, her demeanor's changed, posture tense. I curse myself for being such a thoughtless jackass, flaunting my wealth and peacocking about buying a sixty-thousand-dollar car on impulse, as you would with candy at the cash register, when she's struggling to find a nice place she can afford.

Eva was right about me never accepting my part of the blame for throwing her into a difficult situation. I'd put on blinders and refused to see. I ignored the sacrifices she'd have to make in order for me to put the pieces of my wretched life together.

I enter the address she gives me into the GPS then drive. After a few long minutes of heavy silence, I sigh. "You can say it."

"Say what?"

"That I'm an insensitive jerk." I glance at her with a smug smile. I might as well own up to it, at this point.

Her eyes narrow, but the corner of her mouth twitches. "I think I've said it quite a few times already."

The traffic is light enough that we arrive just on time. I park the car, and we enter an old townhouse divided into three rentals. The entrance has fallen into disrepair, paint eroding, the creaky wooden stairs decaying. Eva stays silent, and I follow her without saying a word.

When we reach the second floor, the apartment door is already open. A middle-aged man waits in sweatpants and a suit jacket, as if he changed his mind about his outfit in the middle of putting it on. His face breaks into a smile as he sees Eva, his gaze sweeping over her body for a second too long.

The stench of humidity assaults my nostrils as the landlord leads us around the one-bedroom apartment. Not much furniture can fit in each tiny room. The bathroom is so small it's a miracle the toilet didn't end up inside the shower.

The man doesn't bother highlighting the good points. There are none. And even if there were, Eva's the one who has to sell herself as the perfect tenant in order to get the honor of being picked.

I stand back and watch Eva say nothing when she notices the stain from a pipe leak on the bathroom wall, and others on the ceiling of each room, one covered in what could be greenish mold. Her mouth stays shut, and she swallows hard when she sees the colony of ants along the baseboard, and the cockroach in the kitchen cupboard feasting on a mysterious yellow substance. She doesn't ask why the bathroom door doesn't close all the way, or why the bedroom window doesn't open at all.

My hands shoved in my pockets, I watch her move, nod and give polite smiles to the man who seizes every opportunity to check out her ass whenever she turns around. *Is she really considering living here? Is this what I've thrown her into?* My stomach churns.

The landlord's phone buzzes, and he walks out to answer. Eva turns to me with a flawless poker-face.

"So?" I force out an even tone so as not to sound like a condescending prick.

"I could paint the walls, set some ant baits..." Her voice sounds like a question.

Am I supposed to reassure her, when we're both aware that this place is a dump compared to the apartment I'm kicking her out of?

"I'd be close to work. That's a plus."

"Okay..." Something clicks in my brain when she mentions work. "Didn't you say something about your colleague finding you a place, the night you were...drunk?" I hesitate on the last word, keeping the memories it brings at bay.

"Daphne? Um, yes. She asked her aunt to help me. She's a realtor."

"And?"

She fidgets a little. "She hasn't found anything yet and said that it won't be easy. So I'm still searching on my own." She looks around and shakes her head.

I muster up a wan smile. "Eva, there's nothing I can tell you about this place that won't sound patronizing or offensive."

She nods. "I know."

Her gaze locks on mine, and the pain I witness in her eyes tightens my throat. A pain so raw it stems from something deeper than me asking her to move out. A wound, concealed inside her, that I can only glimpse before she drops her gaze to the floor.

"You could buy some paint." I chance a lighter tone. "Or you could stay at my place until you find something else. Something better."

She blows out a bitter laugh. "I'm not even sure I can afford better. Thank you, Adrian, but — "

"Maddie will kill me if you have to live in a place like this because of me. And I'd like to stay alive for a little longer."

She chuckles, but before she can answer, the landlord comes back.

"I'm sorry, gorgeous. Someone just wired me the deposit, plus six months' rent in advance for this apartment."

"Well, that settles it, then." Her shoulders drop, out of relief or disappointment, I'm not sure.

However, the sigh I hold back is definitely relief. Even though I still long for some quiet solitude to reorganize my life, her presence around my apartment isn't as distressing as I had first thought. I promised her a few weeks to search, and I won't rush her out if it means she'll end up in a dump.

Chapter Fourteen

Closer

Two days pass without Adrian and me running into each other. When I go to bed early at night, he isn't home yet, and when I wake up in the morning, he has already left. Considering the tornado of emotions Adrian's return unleashed on me, the distance is a pleasant respite.

After a grueling day at work, Madison calls while I'm walking home.

"Eva, I need your help." Her stern tone doesn't leave much room for refusal. "Adrian is still ignoring me. Can you talk to him? Please."

I grimace. "I'm not sure it's a good idea. Talking to him is what put you in this position."

"Colin said you two were starting to get along. Can you please ask him to call me?"

My resolve is fading, even though I know I shouldn't accept. "Maybe give him more time. I don't think harassing him is going to help."

"Please, Eva. I'm begging you here. I need my brother not to hate me."

I can't refuse her. I revealed the secret, so the least I can do is help her reconcile with him, hoping I don't make it worse, or ruin the fragile peace between Adrian and me.

"Fine, I will."

"Thank you." She sighs. "By the way, Mom invited you, too, Saturday night."

"Saturday..." The distant memory of Madison mentioning it resurfaces. "Adrian still doesn't know about that, right?"

"Which is why I need him to either call me or answer his goddamn phone." She pauses, and I can imagine her rolling her eyes. "Anyway, we'll sleep over, as usual. Luke is relieved that Colin will be there because he was worried about facing Adrian alone. Ask Daphne, she has to come, as well. Mom's going to love her. And she shouldn't spend all her weekends alone in that hotel room."

I stay stunned for a few seconds. "Madison, do you even realize the situation you're throwing your brother into? Facing your parents, and Luke, and you, surrounded by other people he doesn't even know."

"Oh, look at you, defending him now." Behind the surprise in her voice, a strange undertone I fail to recognize seeps through. *Is she upset?*

Words catch in my throat, not sure how to answer. "No, um... If you think it'll be fine... I'll tell him you want to talk to him."

I barely give her time to say goodbye before I hang up, hoping she didn't notice how flustered I got. My opinion of Adrian has evolved, yet I'm not sure how to define our relationship. We're not becoming friends — we crossed that line when we started flirting. What could I tell Madison? She wanted me to be nice to her brother, not thirst over him. This whole situation is enough of a mess without me displaying my lustful whims.

* * * *

When I arrive home, Adrian is sprawled on the couch in a dark blue shirt, his jacket and tie taken off, a beer in hand. He lifts his arm in a drowsy greeting gesture.

"Tired?" I ask as I hang my trench coat then take off my stilettos.

"Worse than that." He rubs his eyes with the base of his hand. "Thank fuck, tomorrow's Friday."

"I don't want to bother you, then..."

"What's going on?" He straightens on the couch and sips his beer.

Hesitant, I take a seat next to him, not sure how to broach the subject without upsetting him. Madison's secrets wounded him, and coming from me, it could be even worse. I don't want to go back to fighting with him.

"I talked to Madison today," I start with caution, waiting for his answer, and he arches an eyebrow.

"And?"

"She's worried about you."

"No, she's worried about me not talking to *her*. There's a difference."

"Probably, yes. Still, she'd like you to call her."

"If I wanted to, I would have already. I..." He stops and sighs. He seems annoyed, and I don't know whether I should say more or leave him alone.

Adrian swallows a big gulp of his beer and slaps the bottle on the coffee table. He opens a second button of his shirt, undoes his cufflinks, and rolls his sleeves up to his elbows. I observe him in silence, not wanting to leave and end this conversation myself. The thin band tattooed on his forearm catches my attention. I had forgotten this one, the other on his chest absorbing all my focus.

Adrian clears his throat when he notices me staring, and I open my mouth to apologize, but he's faster than I am.

"What is it with you and my tattoos?"

His teasing tone of voice and suggestive gaze disarm me.

"It's just curiosity, I guess. I'm never close enough to see them properly."

The words are out of my mouth before I can choke them back. A small smile lifts his lips, a mischievous glint in his eyes, studying me.

"Let's get closer, then." Adrian's voice is low, the underlying meaning to his sentence rendering me speechless.

He slides on the couch until he's an inch from me, and I don't venture to move, my heart speeding up. His left side brushes mine as he shifts to hold his right arm in front of me. His fragrance envelops me, hypnotizes me. I clear my throat in a vain attempt to stay focused, and from the corner of my eye, I notice his smile widen.

"I had this tattoo done years ago."

The brutality of the design positioned halfway between his elbow and wrist is astonishing. The drawing makes it appear as if his skin were slashed all around the arm to reveal a small band of flesh, both sides held together by several little safety pins. Its realism is remarkable. I stare at his arm for the longest time, observing all the details.

"It's amazing."

Unable to restrain the urge to touch it, I move my left hand before I can ponder whether it's a good idea, my fingertip running along the pretend wound. His breath hitches, but he doesn't move. My finger prickles at the electric warmth of his skin as I trace the lines of the tattoo. When I reach the side, Adrian turns his arm, palm up, so my finger can continue its journey. His fingertips brush the underside of my forearm, barely touching, sending a shiver over my skin.

"It was during a trip to Los Angeles." A sudden tinge of pain veils his voice. "We went on vacation there. With Luke."

I remove my finger from his skin, breaking our connection. "You cared a lot about him, didn't you?"

"I still do." He pauses. "I thought I'd never see him again, and now, I have to deal with him marrying my baby sister." Adrian moves to grab his beer on the coffee table before swallowing a mouthful. "I don't want to fight with her. If I call her, we'll fight because I'm mad at her for keeping this a secret. But I don't want to fight, not with her."

His eyes are downcast, his voice sad. I would drop the topic if there weren't a detail that he needed to know.

"Adrian, you have to call her. Before this weekend."

His head snaps up in my direction. "Why?"

"I'm not the one who's supposed to tell you this."

"Come on, Eva, just tell me," he urges.

"Your parents know you're back."

"Fuck! When is this going to end?" He jumps from the couch and starts pacing the living room. His hand runs through his hair, like every time he's upset.

"I'm sorry."

"Don't be." He plops down at the end of the couch and sighs. "Why this weekend specifically?"

"Your mother is expecting you for dinner Saturday night." I pause, take a deep breath and continue with a cautious tone. "She invited all of us, as a matter of fact."

"Who's 'all of us'?"

"You, Madison, Luke, Colin, me and Daphne, too."

"Fuck me…" He sighs again, takes a big swig of his beer then drops his chin to his chest, remaining silent for a few beats. "Can you tell Maddie I'll be there, and that we'll talk then?" Adrian raises a pleading gaze to me.

I recognize the same begging expression I've seen so often in Madison's eyes, the one I can't say no to. "All right, I'll tell her."

"Thank you." He smiles and stands up. "I'm going to bed."

"Good night," I answer as he exits the living room.

After texting Madison to confirm Adrian's presence this weekend, I invite Daphne, who accepts without question.

This dinner promises to be nerve-racking, given that Adrian is mad at both Madison and Luke, and my relationship with Adrian is still bewildering, at best.

Yet, as I fall asleep, the only thought on my mind is Adrian. His fragrance, his wrist tattoo and his pleading blue eyes.

Chapter Fifteen

Fitting In

When I wake up, rested as if I'd slept for an entire day, the clock shows it's in fact past three in the afternoon.

In the living room, Eva watches TV, lounging on the couch in dark-blue skinny jeans and a loose V-neck T-shirt with just enough cleavage to reveal the tops of her breasts. Her feet are perched on the coffee table, the thin straps of high-heeled pumps clasped around her ankles. Her slim legs could only look better naked and locked around my waist as I thrust into her.

Eva brings me back to Earth with a light giggle. "Hi." The smug smile on her lips gives away that she caught me ogling.

"Coffee?" I ask, fleeing to the kitchen to regain some focus.

"No, thanks."

In the last few days, something has clicked between Eva and me, and the mood has shifted. Our late evening chats have been pleasant, and teasing her is even more enjoyable. Her body reacts, her breathing accelerates whenever I approach her, and it's electrifying to witness. On top of the sexy secretary outfits she wears every day, her hungry eyes and velvety voice now complete my fantasy.

I can't control my reactions, the effect she has on me. I'm deliberately playing with fire. My body aches to touch her, and I haven't felt that debilitating draw in months. Long before Pauline and I broke up, before we started fighting all the time, that attraction was already gone.

Eva awakens every cell in me, and I'm not sure what to do with it. Perhaps I should force myself to ignore it, at least for now, until I put my life back together.

Her voice from the other room snaps me out of my musings. "I thought about waking you up. We're supposed to leave in half an hour."

"Shit, that's right!"

My brain got sidetracked by the mere sight of her. How could I forget? Even though my stomach turns as I dread facing Luke after all these years—his resentment and disdain, with Madison by his side—this is another essential step to getting my life back in order.

"You should pack a bag, too," she says.

As I lean on the doorframe with my coffee in hand, Eva answers before I even ask the question.

"We always sleep over when we go to your parents, even though it's not that far away. Jill's Sunday morning brunches are the best." A pretty smile graces her lips, and her eyes sparkle. Only a week ago, she seemed a different person. She's fucking glowing.

"Do you do that often?"

"Twice a year, at least." Her face contorts in a sympathetic grimace.

The weekend hasn't started yet, and I'm ill at ease. Finding my place back in my family is daunting. They moved on, new people coming around, without me.

I go back to my room to pack a bag that I drop in the entrance next to Eva's. On my way for a second coffee that won't help settle my nerves, Eva is no longer on the couch. My mind registers her absence only a second before I pass the doorway to the kitchen, and it's a second too late.

In my haste, I bump into Eva's bent frame from behind, making both of us tip over. I circle her waist with one arm to keep her from falling headfirst, reaching over to the table with my other hand to steady myself. We both freeze, my body touching hers, my junk pressed against her tight ass, for long seconds.

In my head flash images of fucking her in this position. My cock reacts, pushing against my boxers and the thick fabric of my jeans. I grit my teeth, conjure up some scraps of self-control and release Eva before she can feel it.

"Sorry..." My voice comes out low and hoarse.

She keeps her back to me, hands on her stomach. I circle her, bringing her to face me. When she lifts her gaze, her wet lips parted, my cock grows even harder. Her green stare locks on mine, burning with pure lust. Fucking sexy. There's no doubt left in my mind that she's attracted to me, turned on by me. Her mind clearly just pictured the same thing mine did. Fuck, her eyes are begging me to take her, and I love it.

With one step closer, my body brushes against hers. This may not be a wise idea, but I want her too fucking much to think it over.

Her hand yanks the neckline of my T-shirt to pull herself up against me, and I lose control. I grab her ass and lift her off the floor, crashing her against the closest wall. My lips barely reach hers before voices echo from behind the front door, and we both freeze again. The door opens and Madison calls out to us, followed by Colin's and Luke's voices. Panic flashes in her eyes, probably in mine as well, as reality catches up to us. *What the fuck just happened?*

I put Eva down and step back as she casts her eyes to the floor.

"I dropped the towel. I was just picking it up." She crouches in front of me to retrieve it, her face level with my crotch, driving me even crazier, and she throws the towel on the counter before exiting the kitchen without another look in my direction. This woman drives me wild, renders my brain useless, igniting my body like a horny teenage boy.

But there's no time to ponder over what Eva and I just shared, or what it meant. I have to deal with my family, and with Luke.

After a few deep breaths for my heart—and my cock—to settle down, I follow her to the entrance with a knot in my stomach. When I join them, Eva has already greeted her friends. I force myself not to glance at her, afraid that our attraction will show in front of everyone. One issue at a time.

Colin steps forward and offers a friendly handshake with a grin on his face as if we already know each other, yet not mentioning the drunken context of our first encounter.

Madison comes closer to me, her eyes down, and before I can say a word, she snuggles in my arms, face hidden against my chest. The last time she did that, she was no more than nine, I think, and had just broken my Han Solo action figure. I couldn't stay mad at her then, and even though we still need to have a grown-up conversation, I can't now, either.

Holding her close, I plant a small kiss on the top of her head, and she moves away, her eyes still avoiding mine.

The last person I must greet is Luke. My stomach cramps, sending a violent pinch in my chest. He stands with his hands in his faded jeans pockets, posture tense, muscles taut, jaw clenched. My throat constricts, blood rushing, pounding in my ears. I want to launch at him, scream at him for being such a lousy friend. I want to hit him, hurt him for not being there when I needed him most. But I'm paralyzed.

He doesn't move either, our inflexible stare on each other. Luke's here, in front of me, six years after I lost him, after I had to make peace with his absence, thinking I'd never see my soul brother again.

Next to us, Madison lets out a long, desperate sigh and, for her, just as I lift my hand, Luke reaches out with his, almost like in a mirror. His strong grip crushes my hand, and I squeeze harder. His eyes don't leave mine, unwavering. We have issues to settle. Whether with a conversation or in a fistfight has yet to be determined.

Luke and I drop our hands when Eva's phone beeps as she receives a text.

"Daphne says she'll meet us downstairs in five minutes. It didn't take her long to walk here."

"Let's go!" Colin claps. "But the six of us won't fit in my car."

"Hadn't thought of that," Luke says in his typical Californian surfer drawl. "My car's parked eight blocks away. If I run, I can be back in ten, if needed."

"I'll take mine." I intended a casual tone, but it comes out awkward, and Luke gives a slight nod.

Eva throws me the quickest glance, too quick for me to decipher her expression, whether she's uncomfortable, regretful about what transpired in the kitchen a few minutes ago or just still too aroused to look me in the eyes without the others noticing. Her evasive gaze makes uneasiness creep inside my guts.

Assuming Luke and Madison will go with Colin, the prospect of being in a car for half-an-hour with Eva and her friend, unsure how to behave, overwhelms me. This is too much. The weekend isn't starting well.

I grab my bag on the floor and walk out, trailing behind the group down the stairs, the guys' awkward silence only broken by the ladies' light chatter. We meet Daphne in the parking lot, wheeling her tiny black suitcase behind her. Madison and Luke follow Colin to his car, and Eva tags along, perhaps out of habit. My unease grows, because she could be avoiding me on purpose.

After a glance in my direction, Daphne switches directions and walks next to me. She answers my puzzlement in a firm voice contrasting with the fragility of her appearance. "I'm coming with you." She opens the passenger door without a word to the others.

I don't argue, since she might be the only person in this group I'm not uncomfortable with.

We drive in silence for a few minutes before she speaks in a relaxed tone. "You seemed more than ready to drive by yourself. How come?" There's a slight edge to her voice, revealing she already knows. *No point making excuses.*

"Because I'm avoiding a difficult talk with Madison, I haven't spoken to Luke in six years, and being next to Eva is…" I trail off, unsure of how much I should share.

"What?" she asks, this time truly waiting for me to clarify.

Except I can't tell Daphne that her friend is so fucking hypnotizing I can't think straight every time she's near me. "I have no clue what it is, but it's not simple, that's for sure."

"It's not simple because you don't really talk to each other. You should." Daphne sounds as if she had the answers to all our problems. Perhaps her external point of view allows her to see more clearly. *Or Eva confided in her.*

"Eva mentioned your aunt was helping her find a place," I say, but it sounds like a question.

"She's trying, but she hasn't come across anything yet."

"That's…good. That she's helping, I mean." My voice sounds hesitant, tainted by the guilt of putting Eva through this.

Worried that I might appear too eager for Eva to move out no matter where, I shift the conversation away from us. "Why did you get in the car with me?"

"You looked so fucking miserable I took pity on you."

My breath catches in my throat at her brazenness, and I laugh. Her blunt honesty is refreshing. I understand why Eva likes her so much.

"That's a pretty good reason. Thanks."

I relish the moment of lightness, but the knot in my stomach returns. I shift in my seat, and my sweaty hands squeak on the steering wheel. The closer we get to my parents' house, the more nervous and less capable of focusing on the conversation I become.

"Adrian, it's just dinner, you know. You'll survive." Her voice is a little standoffish, but I bet she means well.

"I didn't tell my parents I was back, or that I broke off my engagement, or for what reasons. I feel like shit."

"Take tonight as an opportunity to come clean," she advises as if it's the easiest thing to do.

We remain silent for the rest of the drive to the outskirts of San Francisco until we arrive in Orinda. I park behind Colin's car in the driveway of my parents' home, a two-story modern house design.

"Fuck, that's a big house."

"Dad's a surgeon, Mom's a shrink."

She nods. "That explains it."

My mother waits on the front step, leaning on the doorframe in jeans and a gray T-shirt, her light-brown hair tied in her usual ponytail. Her eyes light up as soon as she sees me. My heart breaks a little. I've missed her very much.

It's astounding how Madison looks more and more like her as they hug each other. From a few feet away, they could pass for twin sisters.

She greets us one by one as we enter, taking everyone in her arms. Luke is without a doubt considered the ideal son-in-law, lifting my mom a foot off the floor when he hugs her, earning him her beautiful crystal laugh. Eva and Colin seem to be part of the family, too.

I come in last and hold my mom for a long moment. A strange feeling of being a little boy again, protected and safe, submerges me, and I hug her even closer. I never imagined I'd need it as an adult, and I was wrong.

"I've missed you, sweetie." Her voice is soft as she pulls back from my embrace, her eyes full of pride. I can't grasp what in my behavior could have made her so proud.

"You, too, Mom. I'm sorry for not coming home sooner."

"I don't need to hear any of that. You're here now, that's all that matters." She places her hand on my cheek and with a simple nod, motions for me to follow inside. "Go see your father out back, and ladies with me in the kitchen, old-school-style. If you thought I was going to cook for eight people all by myself, you're clearly mistaken." She pushes me down the hallway while Madison, Daphne and Eva disappear into the kitchen, protesting at the misogyny of the arrangement.

With Colin behind me, I follow Luke as he walks through the house with confidence, as if it were his home. Perhaps it always was, spending most of his time here since we were teenagers after his parents pushed him away because of his sexual orientation. In any case, it has been his home more than mine these past few years. I've become the stranger here.

We move to the patio where my father waits for us with a beer already in hand. He welcomes Luke in his arms, tapping him on the back.

"Good to see you."

"You, too, Daniel," Luke says. "I finalized the floor plan for your pool house. It's in Madison's bag. Remind me to give it to you before we leave."

My father nods and turns to me.

"Adrian, still alive? That's great news!" He drags me into a big hug and holds me for a long moment. Some tension leaves my shoulders, relieved that neither of my parents is too disappointed in me, even though I know I can't avoid explaining my return indefinitely.

After giving Colin a warm handshake, my father retrieves a beer from the cooler and hands it to me, doing the same for Colin and Luke. He sits back in a lounger near the pool, and we gather around him.

As the women's laughter chimes from the kitchen, the conversation between us flows. My father acts as if I'd never left, as if it hasn't been six months since I last called.

Colin, too, makes big efforts to include me in the conversation. My self-consciousness must show more than I think. He steers the discussion toward sports and asks me about soccer, the Tour de France and Roland-Garros.

Luke speaks with natural ease with my father and Colin, but never addresses me, never replies to something I say. He never looks at me in the eye, and every time I open my mouth to speak, his jaw clenches. I fight the urge to clench mine.

The last time Luke and I talked face to face, it turned into a fistfight, so I wasn't expecting friendliness today. But I didn't expect outright anger in front of my family, either, especially since flinging himself at my sister as soon as I left should call for less condescension on his part.

His behavior annoys me. I breathe in deep, focus on Colin and my father, forcing my irritation into silence. The more relaxed I act, the more edgy Luke gets. I disregard his knee jolting up and down, as if his body can't restrain the need to come at me.

When my father leaves for a moment to fetch some peanuts, Luke's restraint snaps.

"You're really not going to say anything?" He stares at me, eyebrows arched.

"Excuse me?"

"You heard me." He straightens on his chair, leaning toward me. "You're *really* going to act like you never left? No explanation, nothing? And we're just supposed to indulge you, is that it?"

"What the fuck is wrong, Luke? Does it bother you that much that I'm here? That I'm talking to my father?"

Luke snorts and shakes his head. The disdain flares in his eyes as he stands up from his lounger. "If you wanted to talk to your dad, you could've picked up the phone sometime in the last six months."

"Fuck you! I don't owe you anything." I thump my beer bottle down and stand, taking a step closer to him.

"What's going on?" My father's strong voice booms from behind me.

Colin stands. "Settle down, guys. Come on."

"You blow everyone off," Luke shouts at me. "You don't visit. You don't call. And now you reappear and act like nothing happened? You owe your family an apology, don't you think?"

"I don't remember blowing you off. *You* did that to me, all of you," I yell louder, ignoring my father who tells me to calm down. My heart races, my fists tighten. "And what explanation do you want to hear, exactly? That I got fucking hurt, that I feel worse than shit? That she was just a two-faced slut, and I only realized it when I caught her being fucked by some other man, in my own bed? I know it's burning your lips, Luke. Come on now, fucking say it!"

"I fucking told you so!"

Anger combined with humiliation overcomes me, my muscles tense up, and my fist hits him square in the jaw. Luke's arm lifts into position to punch me back, but Colin grabs him by the shoulders as my father pushes me backward, his hands flat on my chest while I resist and prepare for a second blow.

"Adrian!" My mother's voice snaps me out of fury. "Go inside, now!"

I know I have no choice but to obey.

"Get your shit together, boys. I won't have this in my house," my father adds.

Luke retreats, pushed away by Colin, but his eyes still throw daggers at me. Madison rushes to him, and the rage on his features only softens when he looks at her.

I cast my eyes to the ground, avoiding Eva's gaze and the possible repulsion on her face at my humiliating confession and violent outburst, before isolating myself inside the house. I find refuge in my father's office, like I used to when I was a child, and as expected, he comes in after me. The door clicks shut, and he leans on it, hands in his pockets, blue eyes locked on me.

"How's your hand?"

"Fine." I stand in the middle of the room, struggling to hold his imposing stare.

"Let me see."

He walks toward me and examines the hand I punched Luke with, making sure I didn't fracture a bone. It isn't the first time he's had to check, but I thought I had grown up. I imagine he did, too.

"Not too bad," he says, flexing each finger. "But it's going to swell. Put some ice on it."

"I will."

His stare lifts to my face again, and he waits.

"Are you going to tell me what's going on with you?"

"You've heard the key points. You want more details?"

"Don't be smart with me. Do you want me to set your mother on you? She *will* wrestle every detail out of you."

His hands slide back in his pockets, his stance relaxed, in complete contrast with my restlessness.

"I don't even know what to say."

"Anything. You could've started with the simple fact that you were back in the States and gone from there."

"I'm sorry." I look away, run a hand through my hair out of habit and wince at my harmed fingers.

"You're sorry... That's it?"

"No... I don't fucking know. I just needed some time. It was too painful, too humiliating. And you were all so ready to throw it in my face. Like Luke just did."

"So you had to punch him?"

"He had it coming. He was asking for it."

My father stares at me, one eyebrow raised, incredulous. When he speaks again, his voice rises. "Are you really that egotistical, Adrian? Can't you see how much *you* hurt this family? Not everything is about whether we liked Pauline. Have you taken a second to look at your own behavior? Get the fuck over yourself!"

I plop down on his desk chair in defeat, elbows on my knees, face hidden in my hands. "I'm sorry, Dad."

"You say you're sorry, but you don't get it. How many hours, days and nights do you think we've spent with your mother talking about you, worrying? How guilty do you think your mother felt for not liking Pauline enough and driving you away? How sad do you think your sister was that you left without looking back?"

I recline on the chair, lifting my eyes to meet his hard gaze.

"I..." My voice catches in my throat, trembling. My chest tightens, my head throbbing, overwhelmed by too many thoughts to process.

"Take some time if you need." His tone returns to comforting, paternal. "We're here for you, but you have to accept your share of the responsibility. And stop punching Luke. He's the one who missed you the most."

Before my mouth opens to respond, my father turns on his heels and exits his office. The door doesn't close, and Madison steps in, a furious stare hardening her features.

"Can we talk?"

"Now?"

She arches an eyebrow. "You just punched my man. I think you owe me one."

My stomach churns. I can't wrap my head around them being engaged. Not a full hour has passed, and this day is proving to be more draining than I thought possible.

"I was on your side, Adrian. I defended you from the start. At least, I tried, but you just went over the line."

"Because I punched *your man*?"

"Don't you dare attack me on this."

"Why didn't you tell me it was him? You took off your engagement ring when you came to see me, for fuck's sake!" I point at the diamond on her finger.

"Do you think it's the most important issue here?" Her voice rises, her chin up, feet firmly planted on the floor as she stares down at me. "You came back and you still haven't talked to anyone. I mean, really talked. What's going on with you?"

"Where do you want me to start?" I raise my voice, too. "My life was a complete wreck, wedding canceled, relationship over, friends, job, home... all gone. My baby sister has a life I knew nothing about, my apartment is occupied by someone I've never met. Oh, and I just hit my best friend who actually hates my fucking guts. So, please, Maddie, tell me what's the most important, because I'm completely lost."

"You weren't here!" She throws her arms up and lets them fall with a loud slap on her hips. With a slight shake of her head, eyes closed, she sighs, sitting down on my father's couch, on the other side of the room. "I didn't tell you about Luke because you weren't here," she repeats with more calm. "At first, I thought maybe Luke and I were just a fling, or that he'd prefer dating a man more than a woman, so it'd end, and there'd be no need to tell you. The more time passed, the harder it became to broach the subject. I should have told you, though. I'm sorry."

The anger in her eyes has subsided, but they don't leave mine. Taking a deep breath, I move from my chair and around the desk to sit by her side on the couch.

"Maddie, I know I wasn't here. Dad just said I was selfish, and he's probably right," I say, and she smiles. "But I never meant to blow anyone off. You all ditched me because you hated Pauline. I felt alone, I couldn't talk to any of you. You weren't interested if it involved her."

"She wasn't the right woman for you, Adrian."

"It wasn't your choice to make."

"Maybe, but you were different with her. Blind, subdued. We tried to protect you, but you had to make your own mistakes. It was just too hard to pretend."

"I never felt I had the right to be happy with her. To all of you, it didn't even matter that I was. That's why I took some distance."

"Were you?" she asks. In her eyes, the annoying glint of *we were right* is still there, and I don't answer, words evading me.

Indeed, they were right.

Silence stretches between us. Maddie is giving me the opportunity to get my feelings off my chest, so I push further.

"Why Luke? Why did it have to be him?"

"Come on, Adrian." She tilts her head to the side, a small smile on her lips. "Luke has been your best friend for…what, twenty, twenty-two years? You of all people should know why I fell in love with him."

"He hasn't acted like a friend for a while."

"One could argue that you haven't either. In any case, this is a discussion you need to have with him, not me. Preferably without punching each other," she says, amazing me again with her maturity.

"Does he make you happy?"

"He treats me like a queen." Her eyes water with tears, and her lips turn into a pleading pout. My heart swells, all anger vanishing. I take a deep breath and release it loudly.

"Then I'm happy for you."

"I love you." She launches in my arms and holds me as tight as she can.

Whatever reason I thought I had to be angry with Madison seems irrelevant now. "I love you, too."

Madison drags me out of my hiding place and to the kitchen where they all have gathered. She enters first, and I stop in the doorway to watch the family portrait in front of me. Madison scurries to Luke to help him with the bruised jaw, courtesy of my right fist, holding a frozen steak to his face. I can't hold back a snigger at the sight. His eyes snap in my direction. The fury I expected to find in them has disappeared, replaced by a glint I've often seen — he's testing me, challenging me. Madison wants us to talk like adults, but we just might settle it like immature morons. It wouldn't be the first time. If Luke comes at me for a second round, I'm ready for it.

Colin helps my mother retrieve the porcelain plates from the top cupboard. They seem close, almost like mother and son, and my heart pinches. Daphne and Eva are baking cookies, and my father keeps leaning over them to steal chocolate chunks. Eva laughs every time he does, and Daphne pretends to elbow him in the ribs.

"Cut the crap, Daniel. I'm not as nice as Eva. I won't let you ruin the cookies."

My father bursts out laughing and steals another chunk, winking at Eva who smiles and winks back.

Jealousy arises in me at the evident bond between them. She seems to belong here, just like the rest of them. The only one who doesn't fit in is me, out of place again, left out. I lean on the doorframe and observe them, until my father brings me out of my musings.

"Come on, Adrian. The ladies are being mean to me, and you're just standing there. Come defend your old man."

"Sorry, Dad. You're on your own." I laugh. "I'm not rising against Eva. I'd rather keep some peace at home."

The words spill out of my mouth before I realize how much they sound like we're a couple. A fleeting moment of silence passes, my family taken by surprise. Myself, as well, to be honest. Eva glances in my direction with the hint of a smile on her lips.

I join them as we finish preparing dinner, moving around the kitchen, following my mother's directives, joking with my father and Colin. Maddie and I share an affectionate smile when our eyes lock, but I avoid meeting Luke's gaze.

Every time I pass by Eva, the urge to imitate my father and steal some chocolate chunks to win that cute fucking wink from her is difficult to restrain. Among all the erratic issues I must straighten out this weekend, I never thought that it would be her attention I'd crave so much.

Chapter Sixteen

Rebound

I enter the dining room with a bottle of wine in hand. The family is already gathered around the table crammed with three large dishes of lasagna. My parents sit at each end, presiding. I take the last available seat next to Eva, with Daphne on her other side. Colin sits across from me, next to Luke then Madison. Luke plants a small kiss on her lips, as a natural gesture, a common token of affection between two lovers, but then he glances at me and squirms on his chair. He isn't enough of a jerk to use my little sister to get to me, so I ignore it and focus on pouring the wine instead.

Colin lightens the mood with jokes and easy conversation. Eva's attention swings between her friends or my parents, but never me. No doubt now that she is avoiding me on purpose, but I'm still clueless whether she worries her reactions will betray her attraction to me or she regrets our kitchen encounter. As the uncertainty causes a creeping strain along my nerves, Eva acts very cozy among my family. The crude jokes she exchanges with Colin elicit several loud laughs from my dad. This carefree and laid-back, she's glowing.

I must have scrutinized her with too much insistence because Colin kicks me under the table. He throws me quirked eyebrow, inquisitive, along with a lopsided smile. *Fuck, I'm busted.* With a pointed look, I beg him not to comment, and before he can even say a word, we're both startled out of our silent chat when my father asks me about job hunting.

"I don't have to, actually." I sit up straighter at the one piece of good news I can announce. "I had applied for a transfer from the Paris office. I started last Monday already."

Eva imitates my change of posture, with a content expression. She's the only one who knew.

"That's great." My mother smiles. "So your return wasn't completely out of the blue, then..." She reaches my shoulder and squeezes once before picking up her fork again, not expecting an answer from me. She knows me well enough to understand I'm not ready to talk about it yet.

"What do you do, actually?" Colin asks as he fills his second plate of lasagna.

"I'm a senior investment banker at Morland Stanwell," I answer with my usual hesitance, accustomed to derogatory comments about the evilness of my job.

"No shit? I'm a financial lawyer." His face lights up.

"Yes, Eva mentioned it."

"Man, we'll have so much to talk about."

Luke almost pouts like a child at Colin and me getting along so well, and I throw him my best smirk.

"Wasn't it difficult working in finance in France?" Colin asks, not caring that it could be a sore subject. His forwardness is appreciable. Tiptoeing around me only makes me feel pathetic.

"Not really. The big firms hire many English native speakers for international transactions. Anyway, it wasn't an issue because I'm fluent in French."

"You are?" Eva's head snaps in my direction, desire dancing in her green eyes as it has many times lately. How I've missed it, all evening long.

"*Bien sûr, Mademoiselle.*" My voice is soft and warm.

We keep our gaze locked on each other for probably too long since I receive another kick from Colin. Breaking the spell, I turn away from Eva and reach for my glass of wine to take a sip. The whole table studies us, and discomfort creeps up on me. Eva shifts her focus to her plate, pushing food around with her fork, and Colin resumes the discussion about work, rescuing me by deflecting attention.

Our dialogue centers on international markets, capital assets and liabilities, and becomes rather technical. My family remains silent as they listen to our unintelligible financial gibberish. Eva chips in with eagerness, asking for more details on concepts she's not familiar with and bringing up very insightful points. Her natural knack for finance is evident, and the confidence radiating from her when she speaks is inspiring.

For once, having a conversation with people who understand and are as enthusiastic as I am about financial markets is enjoyable.

Luke steers the discussion toward the new wing for Saint Francis Memorial Hospital where my father works, since the project could be granted to Luke's architectural firm. The discussion is turning into a pissing contest, both of us showing off and wanting to get the last word in. It seems we're both choosing the 'immature morons' path instead of acting like adults. Soon, we'll be arguing over whose dick is bigger, and having shared a room with him at Berkeley, I know for a fact that mine is.

With everyone jumping in, the conversation drifts. When our plates are empty, we all clear the table before dessert is served.

I head toward the bathroom and cross Eva in the hallway. For the first time since we arrived, she's alone with me.

"How's your hand?" She gestures toward the fist I hit Luke with.

"It hurts a little, but it's okay." I flex my fingers to emphasize my words but cringe at the lingering pain. I should've listened to my father and put some ice on it.

"That punch was quite the display of toxic masculinity." She raises an eyebrow, eyes sparkling with mischief, making me chuckle.

"I know. You're right." How could I contradict her? Hitting someone — let alone a friend — is never a source of pride.

Our eyes lock for a few beats, a hint of desire emanating from her, and I give my cockiest grin, the one that has made her lose her focus several times. The one she brings out of me so easily.

Even though defining what Eva and I feel for each other still escapes me, I want to trigger her lust-filled stare that drives me crazy. We spent the evening acting like nothing happened between us, probably for my family's benefit. Now we're alone, isolated, and I need that connection with her, whatever it is.

"Eva, about earlier, in the kitchen…" I search for my words, ready to apologize if needed, if I went too far, too fast. "I feel you've been avoiding me since."

"I have, a little, because…" She pauses, fiddles with her nails, her lips sealed in a tight line. She's clearly fighting our attraction, trying to remain composed, but her eyes twinkle.

My heart speeds up, and my voice drops. "You look stunning tonight."

"How much wine did you have?" She laughs, but I don't feel like joking.

"Not enough to say things I wouldn't want to." My gaze sweeps down along her legs, then back up, slowly, marveling at every inch of the luscious curves of her body. "And you're so fucking beautiful."

Eva rewards me with the hungry spark I was aiming for. I step closer, and she doesn't move, waiting for me to continue. I take another step toward her, inches from her.

"What truly hurts my hand, more than the punch, is having to refrain from touching you."

The words are out of my mouth before I can ponder whether I should have said them. My hands clench at my sides, itching to feel her.

Her breath hitches, lashes fluttering. "Who said you had to?" Her voice is a low murmur, seductive. She's the fucking sexiest woman I've ever met, bar none.

My entire body is tense, my muscles quiver, ready to pounce on her, to ravish her. I push forward, making her retreat inside the bathroom. "You're driving me crazy."

Eva's stare becomes more erotic each second, making me lose the little self-control I'm clinging to. With my hands on her hips, I push her against the wall and kick the door closed behind us. My body presses against hers, my cock growing hard. Her warm hands lift to my shoulders and slide down my chest until they rest on my waist, my muscles flexing under her soft touch.

"Adrian," she whispers, pulling me closer as I lean in, my lips brushing her cheek. The stubble on my jaw scrapes the delicate skin under her ear, and her head lolls back. "Tell me, is it true, then?"

Eva keeps me in place as her knee rubs up my thigh and hooks on my hip. My heart gallops inside my chest. I slide my hand to her knee then back up her thigh, fingertips kneading her denim-clad legs, until I reach her tight ass.

I pull back to watch her. "What?"

"What you said... That you wanted to fuck me good and hard." The sinful smile on her lips elicits a low growl in my throat, unleashing the wildest part in me, and I tighten my grip on her ass.

"Fuck..." I'm panting. "Feisty, smart, beautiful and fucking naughty. That's a deadly mix."

Her smile turns into a victorious smirk. She won't let me make her swoon without a fight. She isn't holding back, and I love it. With her back pinned to the wall, I pull her hips to mine and press the hard bulge in my pants between her legs, desperate for her to feel it. She gasps, eyes burning with desire, devilish.

"Fuck yes. You have no idea how true it is." My lips graze hers, touching but not kissing yet, because I really fucking love playing this little game with her. My breathing is labored, and her temperature rises, heat radiating from her body in a whirlwind of her sweet flowery fragrance. My tongue licks my lips, swiftly touching hers. "Do you want it, Eva? Do you want me to fuck you hard?"

She answers with a roll of her hips, grinding against me as a soft moan escapes her mouth.

A strong knock on the door makes us both jump in shock, and my mother calls out to Eva in the hallway. I push away from her just as the door opens. My heart beats so fast I might have a heart attack. My mother throws a suspicious glance toward Eva, and if a look could kill when she turns to me, I'd be dead.

"Eva, sweetie, can you go help Madison in the kitchen, please?" Her voice is kind, but her death glare never leaves me.

"Sure," Eva mumbles before exiting the room without a peek in my direction.

"Mom—"

"Shut up, Adrian." Her eyes narrow, and I close my mouth. Her tone, calm and cold, is the most menacing I've ever heard. "I'm only going to say this once, so you better listen. I adore Eva, so if you use her as rebound sex, and she gets hurt, I'll have your father kick your ass so thoroughly you won't be able to fuck anyone, hard or otherwise, for a very long time. Am I clear?"

"Yes, Mom." I'm frozen in shock. And to be honest, fear.

"Good. Time for dessert," she adds before walking out.

I lean on the sink, struggling to get my breathing and heartbeat back to normal. Several minutes pass before my mind registers what my mother said. The fact that she heard my words to Eva is as traumatizing as her throwing them back at me. I need fucking therapy.

I've let myself float on the electric current between Eva and me, refused to pause and contemplate what it means. With her, no more disgusting images of betrayals assail my mind, no more sense of failure or damaged ego. Whenever she's close to me, my mind is clear, my cock is hard, ready to fuck her into oblivion, her intoxicating presence silencing any self-doubt.

Is it why I want her?

My mother's words echo in my head, *"use her as rebound sex…"* Is that what I'm doing? I try to erase them, but they're carved in my brain, pricking, letting guilt and doubt seep in.

After splashing some water on my face to calm down, I trudge back to the dining room. Eva toys with the slice of cake on her plate, avoiding my gaze.

When I sit at the table, Colin's brow furrows. He mouths a silent "You okay?" and I answer with a meek nod, but it's not enough for his face to relax.

As we eat dessert, the awkward silence surrounding the table becomes heavy. Maybe they guessed what occurred between Eva and me in the bathroom. Eva's posture is tense, to the point that Madison and Daphne glance at her with worried frowns. She may have heard my mother's scolding, and I can't blame her if she believes I'm using her. I was a jerk to her when I returned, and now I'm almost jumping her.

Even though light conversation has picked up, the atmosphere is still oppressive when dinner is over. The table is cleared, my father and Luke step into his office to review the plans Luke designed for my parents' pool house while the women sit for a game of Hearts. With a kiss on my mother's cheek and a wave goodnight to the others, I retreat to my old bedroom that I'll share with Colin, according to my mother's sleeping arrangements. Eva and Daphne will share the guest room while Madison will sleep in her room with Luke, as usual. Bile rises in my mouth. Adjusting to them being together won't be easy.

Colin downs the last mouthful of his bourbon and follows me. The initial wave of relief to be paired with him abates as he watches me. He already proved his insightfulness during dinner. If he pries, how can I tell *him*, Eva's friend, what happened earlier?

Colin enters the bedroom and turns to me as I close the door. "That's lame, man. I used to sleep in your bed, but now all I get is the sofa bed." His attempt to lighten the mood falls flat. He isn't fooled by my forced smile as I struggle to hide my nerves, and he sits on the edge of the bed in a sigh. "All right, what's up?"

"Nothing," I answer, and he raises an eyebrow. "I don't want to talk about it."

"It's about Eva?" he asks as if he already knows the answer.

"Which is why I don't want to talk about it."

"With me, you mean? Come on, Adrian, she'll probably tell me anyway. And from where I stand, you barely made up with your sister, and you just punched your best friend. It sounds like I'm all you've got."

He has a point. I have no one else I can confide in.

I drag the desk chair closer and sit in front of him. "Eva and I are attracted to each other."

"No shit!" He scoffs and waits for me to continue. Colin caught me ogling her, but he doesn't seem surprised that *she's* attracted to me, too.

"We kind of…made out, earlier." I edit the truth and choose my words with caution, not sure how protective of her he might be. "And my mother caught us."

A boisterous laugh booms from Colin's throat, so loud that I'm concerned the neighbors might hear him from down the street. His guffaw is infectious, and I join him.

"You're not sixteen, man. It's not a big deal," he says when he settles down.

My laughter fades, and I take a deep breath, knowing the next part might upset him. "Mom assumed I'm…using Eva, that she's only a rebound." I wait for him to get angry, maybe punch me, too, but he just studies me for long seconds.

"I'm going to say something because I'm Eva's only family, so it's my duty." He sits straighter, serious. "I'm twice your size. If you hurt her, I'll fuck you up."

I hold his stare and nod, aware that he *could* kick my ass without much effort, although I doubt he would.

"You'll be happy to hear that my mother also gave me a similar warning, with a distinctive threat aimed at my balls," I say, and he laughs again.

"Seriously, though, is it what you're doing with Eva? Is she a rebound to you?"

I run a hand through my hair and sigh. "I have no fucking idea."

"My opinion is biased. Eva acts like a tough girl but she's fragile. She's been through some rough shit." His voice is calm, poised. The enthusiastic man he was all day is replaced by a sober, serious adult who exudes maturity. In the man in front of me, I recognize what a great lawyer he must be. "You're a decent guy, Adrian. I'm sure you don't want to hurt her. If you don't know what you're doing, maybe you should leave her alone." Colin isn't giving me a warning. He's asking for a favor, for her.

"Maybe you're right. Thank you for letting me unwind."

"No problem." He nods and stands up, rummaging through his bag to pull out his toothbrush, and we remain silent until we get to bed.

Colin's advice doesn't appease my mind, I'm still lost, but confessing to him relieves some of the worry.

After tossing and turning for almost an hour, sleep brings a restless storm inside my head, assailed in turns by Luke's thwarted glare, and Eva's body trapped against a wall, moaning, her sweet lips on mine.

Chapter Seventeen

Recovery

I struggle to get out of bed, my head still a mess from yesterday's chaos, when a knock on the door startles me. Colin is folding away his blanket as I put on some clothes then open it to find Luke on the other side, head high despite the bruise covering the left side of his jaw, already growing purple.

"Can I come in? We need to talk."

Dumbstruck for a few seconds, I sigh and spin on my heels, leaving the door open for him to enter. No escape possible.

"Can I leave you two alone, or do you need a referee?" Colin teases.

"We should be fine." I sit on the edge of my desk, resigned, facing Luke. "Unless you're here for round two?"

Luke lets out a long, exasperated breath, shoves his hands in his pockets, and nods to Colin who exits with a worried frown.

"Try not to break anything, including your noses," he says and closes the door behind him.

As Luke stands in the middle of the room, the anger I carried for years vanishes. Punching him liberated the outpouring resentment, and his familiar presence fills a void in my chest more naturally than I anticipated.

Even though Madison must have pushed him to make the first step, I'm glad he did.

He inhales and releases the air through his nose in a loud blow. "I've been mad at you for so long, but now that you're in front of me, I don't even know where to start. I've imagined this conversation so many times, so many versions of it."

"And how did they go?"

The hint of a smile twitches the corner of his mouth. "You were usually the one who ended up with a bruise on your face, but since we already covered that..." He trails off and shrugs.

"I don't know what to say, either." I push my hands down my pockets and avert my gaze.

Luke moves around the room, scanning the memories of my childhood still on display, almost all of which we shared. Sports trophies, rock band posters, a large dent in the wall from a heated indoor basketball game gone wrong, plus burn marks on the carpet my parents pretended they never noticed, from dropped ashes when we were smoking weed in secret. He chuckles and turns back to me.

"When did you ask her? When did you tell Pauline you wanted to move back here?"

My eyes flash to his in surprise. "That's what you want to know?"

"Yes. I imagine that was the turning point in your relationship, so how long did you wait for her to accept before you decided to come back, no matter whether she followed or not?" His voice is lenient, concerned, brotherly. "How long have you been brooding over this, all alone?"

"It was about a year ago. A whole fucking year of discussing, negotiating, fighting... I caught her cheating only two months ago, though." I push my voice not to sound pathetic but fail, and Luke breathes out a low "fuck."

"Yeah, you told me so..." I mumble, halfway between miserable and a tinge of remaining annoyance.

His hands leave his pockets to rub his face in exasperation. His manners haven't changed much. "Adrian, six years ago, I witnessed you make the biggest mistake of your life. I tried to talk to you, and you basically told me to fuck off."

"I didn't tell you to f—"

"Maybe not in those words, but admit that was the idea." He steps forward and waits. I don't respond, so he continues. "I may not have reacted the way I should have, but you expected me to encourage you to jump off a cliff and just wait to see how fucked up you'd be when you'd reach the bottom. I couldn't do that."

"How fucked up do you think I am?" I mutter, almost in shame.

"I'm guessing it's pretty bad." His stare is locked on me, cornering me.

The sense of failure, of powerlessness I hadn't felt since my return twists my stomach, and my voice rises. "What do you want me to say? That you were right, and that it was reason enough for not being there when I needed you? That I'm sorry for choosing her over you?"

"You chose her over *yourself*, not us! You still don't get that?"

Some part of me recognizes the truth in his words, but there's an edge to his tone that still bothers me, a trace of superiority because he knew all along what took me years of relationship to discern.

My mouth opens to respond, but Luke doesn't stop, his patience fading. "And if I wasn't there for you, it's because you wouldn't let me be. I loved you like a brother, and it fucking killed me that my opinion didn't matter enough. That *I* didn't matter."

"Is that why you started banging my sister?" I snap at him and regret it the second the words come out.

He takes a quick step closer, his fierce hazel glare level with mine, his stance menacing. "Say that again, and *I'll* fucking punch *you*, this time." He shakes his head and continues in a dejected tone. "Do you really have such a bad opinion of me? That I could use Madison to get back at you? I've known her my whole life, too. Do you think I could do that to her?"

One hand running in my hair, I breathe in deep. I took it too far, and we both know it. "No, I don't."

"Then, what? Is it that terrible? Am I really the worst guy she could be with?"

"You're not exactly Prince Charming, either, Luke." I scoff. "You've fucked more people than you can remember."

He snorts. "Look who's talking! Apart from your collection being women only, you were just like me."

"I was, a long time ago."

"Precisely. And yet, you're not the one who cheated." He pauses, resuming his position a step away, his voice more peaceful. "I fell in love with your sister, Adrian. We've been together for more than four years now. I want to marry her and spend the rest of my life with her." His eyes shine with happiness while mine open wide in astonishment. As he pronounces the words in front of me, resolute and confident, somehow it all makes sense.

"If you want permission, you're supposed to ask my father." I let a smile spread on my face, and he smirks.

"I've had your father's blessing for a while." He throws me his cockiest grin, making me laugh. He's still the same arrogant bastard. But his joyfulness weakens, and his confidence wavers. "I'd like to have yours, too." The obvious sincerity in his statement leaves me speechless, the importance he's granting me overwhelms me, and my throat tightens. In this moment, I can't see any reason to refuse.

"You have it."

The most vibrant smile lights up his face. His hand reaches out to shake mine, gripping a little too hard no doubt on purpose, and I wince. With a smug laugh, Luke pulls me into his arms and holds me, freeing my chest from remnants of bitterness. We grew up side by side since we were twelve, both flawed and stubborn, and no matter our mistakes, we need to move past them, for ourselves and for Madison.

"I'm sorry," he says. "And I missed you."

I pull back from his embrace and say in earnest, "Thank you for taking care of her."

"Fucking finally, something smart coming out of your mouth!" He laughs and hits my shoulder.

"Stop that, or I'll throw you another one." I point at his bluish jaw, and we both laugh.

Luke and I join the rest of the family in the kitchen for a most copious brunch, acting as if we don't notice their expectant gapes on us as we enter, neither of us willing to launch into a dramatic retelling of our discussion. Luke walks to Madison, leaving a small kiss on her lips while her stare moves back and forth between him and me, and I wink at her. I sit next to Colin, thank my mother for the coffee cup she hands me, and clear my throat to catch Eva's attention. She mouths a distant "hi", face impassive, and shifts back to Daphne. My chest constricts at her detachment.

My parents eat in silence, clearly pretending not to be aware of all the drama in their children's lives.

Daphne explains she'll move into her apartment next weekend, and that she has asked Eva to be her roommate. Yesterday, that offer wasn't even on the table, but now it seems resolved and well planned. Our encounter in the bathroom must have pressed Eva's decision. It's obvious that she regrets it.

Even though her presence around the apartment has felt nice this past week, she had to move out eventually. Perhaps it's for the best, for both of us.

Luke passes behind me and, with a hand on my shoulder, leans on my back to reach for the fruit salad on the table.

"You're staring at her like a lost puppy," he whispers in my ear low enough that nobody can hear amid their conversations and taps my shoulder before returning to his seat.

They may not have heard, but the whole group saw his gesture, and gapes at us with the same questioning expressions they had when we entered. I clear my throat, trying to regain some composure under their scrutiny and Luke's pesky insightfulness.

"So, when is this wedding, anyway?" I ask in a teasing tone. "Am I even invited?"

Luke grabs a waffle and throws it at me across the table, hitting me right on the forehead. "You jackass!" He laughs.

In a guffaw, I retrieve the waffle-weapon to throw it back at him with force, but he dodges, causing it to stick on the wall behind him and slide down to the floor.

"Hey, hey, no playing with food, kids!" my father scolds as if we were children, and the rest of them stare at us, baffled.

"Sorry, Daniel," Luke says, cleaning up the mess.

"Suck-up." I wink at him, and he chuckles.

"*This* is their normal behavior?" Colin asks, incredulous, and Madison nods.

Luke and I exchange a glance. We understand each other in silence at Colin's words. After years, a simple conversation was all it took, and our bond is strong enough to slide back into friendship without effort.

"To answer your question," Madison says, "we haven't set a date yet or started planning."

"Are you throwing a big engagement party?" Daphne asks.

"Ugh, no, we don't really want to. The wedding in itself will be hell enough to organize."

"Your father and I took a trip to celebrate our engagement," my mother says between two sips of her coffee, seated on the counter to leave us space at the table. "It was just us, with our closest friends. Sara and her then-husband Will, you probably don't remember him, and your uncle Henry and Quinn."

"I didn't know that," Madison says. "That's cool. What did you do?"

My father shakes his head. "Sweetheart, it was the seventies. We're not telling you that story." He places a hand on my mother's mouth to keep her from revealing inappropriate and disturbing details about their youth, and she laughs against his palm.

My heart pinches as I witness with envy their adorable connection after so many years of marriage. Pauline and I never came close to sharing this, but as I shift to Maddie and Luke, that same effortless devotion shines through.

"Let's go to Vegas!" Madison claps, startling us.

"Yes! Vegas, baby!" Eva and Daphne yell at the same time, high fiving each other.

Colin and Luke burst out laughing and accept with enthusiasm, both then turning to me, waiting for my answer. My heart swells as I'm included in the group without reservation, although unsure that I deserve it, and I nod.

Brunch drags on in a good atmosphere, but I can't shake the distress creeping inside me, caused by Eva ignoring me. She never left my mind last night, at times pressed against the bathroom wall with her bright green eyes begging me to touch her, then silent at dinner, her face hidden from me. Every ticking second heightens the guilt of treating her this way.

Too soon, it's time to head back home. I hug my mother once more before walking to my car, and the rest of the group follows. Just like the outward journey here, Madison, Luke and Eva move to Colin's car while Daphne walks toward mine. Unlike yesterday, Colin doesn't agree with the arrangement.

"No fucking way, I'm sick of this shit. Eva, you go with Adrian. Daphne, get your ass in my car so they can talk like adults."

We all watch him, dumbstruck. Daphne and Eva exchange a disbelieving look, frozen in place, hesitating. My parents, sister and Luke laugh quietly, but no one counters his instructions. My heartbeat accelerates, both out of panic to discuss with Eva last night's bathroom session, and out of excitement to just be alone with her.

"Smooth, man. Real smooth," I say, and he shrugs.

With a similar silent gesture, Daphne follows Colin, and Eva takes the passenger seat next to me.

We remain quiet as I drive away from the neutrality of my parents' home, the atmosphere growing awkward and my palms getting sweaty. Eva clasps her hands together on her lap, her breathing controlled, her head averted to the side window. I'm lost, nerves prickling, not sure if I should mention what occurred last night or lighten the mood first with small talk.

Eva speaks before I can decide. "I heard what your mother said to you. I was in the hallway. I couldn't help but listen."

My heart drops, my throat dries and words evade me.

"Eva, I'm sor—"

"You don't need to apologize, or even explain." Her voice sounds detached, as if none of it mattered, anyway. "I'm moving out in a week. Let's just make it through these few days, and everything will be easier."

I can't grasp the meaning of her words. Will it be easier to figure out our attraction, or just to move away from it? I'm too scared to ask, too confused for any reply to assuage my doubts. Even if she wanted me, what could I offer her, be for her? My head is a mess, and I can't reason.

The silence becomes suffocating. I switch on the radio and push the volume loud enough to give us a reason not to speak. Eva's body doesn't relax, fiddling with the hem of her jacket. The fragile side of her I'd glimpse during the filthy apartment visit resurfaces. Colin was right. I wish she would yell at me, make a snappy comment, even insult me. But she doesn't, and my chest tightens.

The mood the entire drive is heavy. I park the car, and we make our way to the apartment in the same smothering silence.

Eva trudges toward her bedroom. "I'm going to lie down, or...read a book or something." The misery seeps through her voice.

I stand there, helpless. My mother's threats and Colin's advice spin in my head. The best thing for her may be that I leave her alone. I've hurt her enough. Watching Eva walk away and lock herself in her room, believing I only used her to make myself feel better sickens me.

Our relationship has been fucked up since the second we met, in turns explosive, uneasy or plain wild. We never managed to act responsibly around each other. This needs to be fixed, even if only for one week.

I stride to her door and knock. "Eva?"

"Yes?"

"Can you open the door, please?"

After a few rustling sounds inside, the door cracks open. A small smile graces her lips, although not very convincing.

"I want to start over." My hand reaches out for her to shake. "Hi, my name is Adrian Hensley. Nice to meet you."

Chapter Eighteen

The Right Decision

My head spins, exhausted from the near-sleepless night spent attempting to make sense of my relationship with Adrian, confiding in Daphne and planning my move after her very generous offer to share her place. I need to escape this situation with Adrian.

His mother's comments hurt, tearing through my chest every time the words echo in my head. Adrian suffered with his ex-fiancée, and perhaps I'm indeed nothing more than a rebound.

The hope for a true, meaningful connection with Adrian had crept into my chest, settling deep inside me, taking roots without me realizing it.

Whether Adrian's behavior with me is deliberate doesn't matter. I don't want to be trapped in the middle of his issues. If only I could control my attraction, but his stare was locked on me with such intensity during the entire dinner that my skin tickled. His firm touch set me on fire, his lips on my skin had me panting. With a whisper in my ear, uttering the dirtiest words, he aroused me like I have never been before.

Yet, I have to resist him until I move out of his apartment.

After only a moment of solitude in my room, a knock on my door brings me out of my reverie. Adrian asks me to open in a pleading tone, and when I do, he stands there, determined. I swallow hard, helpless as the shadows in the corridor dance on his square jaw, his eyes bright, and I force away the reckless need to pull his strong body to me until we're lying naked on my bed.

"I want to start over." He holds his hand out for me to shake. "Hi, my name's Adrian Hensley. Nice to meet you."

My stomach drops, and the floor gives way under my feet. Is he proposing that we erase everything we've shared, no matter what it was?

"Adrian, I don't understand."

The hopefulness on his face doesn't falter. "We keep fucking this up. I keep treating you like shit and I don't mean to. You say it'll be easier after you move, but we're bound to see each other again. So let's start over."

My heart pinches. Having friends in common seems to be what motivates him to fix our bewildering connection. I push aside the disappointment, shake the hand he's still holding out, and force my voice to be as cheerful as his. "I'm Eva Duncan. Nice to meet you, too."

"Do you want some coffee?"

His effort to reach out warms my heart. I nod and follow Adrian, settling on the couch while he prepares two mugs before joining me. He reclines against the armrest, cross-legged, watching me.

"How did you meet Maddie?"

I mimic his position, gripping the hot coffee mug with both hands on my lap, and some of the apprehension subsides. His idea might not be to forget it all, but to start where we should have.

"We met at a bar, about five years ago. A little bit more, maybe."

"Soon after I left, then."

"I guess. We fought over the last vacant table. I was waiting for Colin, and she for Luke. Neither of us was willing to give up, so we both sat down and agreed that the first guy to arrive would determine who got the table. Luke and Colin came in at the exact same time, so we shared and spent the evening all together. We've been friends ever since."

"Sweet story. Maddie and Luke, they weren't dating yet, were they?"

"No, they were just friends at the time."

He nods and sips his coffee, eyes unfocused for a fleeting moment. "It's so weird, seeing them together. She did have a crush on him when Luke and I were seventeen, maybe eighteen. She was about thirteen, and always giggling like an idiot when he was around, acting kind of jealous when he was dating someone. But back then, she was just my annoying little sister to him."

"Madison would say that she knew all along. That it was meant to be. So sentimental," I mock.

He lets out a quiet laugh, the warm sound invoking a surge of thrilling shivers in me. "How did you end up living here?"

"I'd just broken up with my boyfriend and needed a place. Madison had a spare room, so she let me move in for a very cheap rent."

He raises an eyebrow, a hint of a smile arising, and tilts his head to the side. "You know she never paid any to me, right?"

"Are you serious?" I almost choke on a mouthful of coffee as I burst out laughing. "Well, it's still a good deal for me, but she's made money off your back for two years."

"Quite the businesswoman." His smile widens.

"I don't want to pry, but how could you afford a place like this, then, on top of your life in Paris?"

"Indecently big bonuses. I love what I do, and I'm good at it." He shrugs. Unrepentant confidence radiates from him, giving him a raw magnetism that I struggle to resist.

I take a sip of coffee, hiding behind the mug, and he continues.

"But also, I inherited this place from my grandmother, and Madison got enough cash to start her veterinary clinic. It makes life easier." That warm laugh again makes me shiver. "So, you broke up with your boyfriend and landed here... It looks like I'm not the first jerk kicking you out of your home."

"You're right, although the first wasn't my ex. We ended it on good terms. It was my stepfather, and his jerkiness reached a whole other level." I pull my knees to my chest in a shielding impulse, feet on the couch.

Adrian frowns. "Sorry, I didn't mean t—"

"It's fine." I clear my throat along with a dismissive wave, gathering enough strength to expose the origin of the bitterness he's had to endure. "When I was five, my father left with another woman, never to be seen again. My mother remarried. We moved to Cloverdale for her husband. He despised me, the simple fact that I existed. I was a constant topic of dispute between them, sometimes violent fights, but in the end, my mother always took his side. Somehow, it was always my fault. He didn't want me in his house, he made it clear that it wasn't my home, and he couldn't wait for me to be old enough to move out. I ran away a few times, and he kicked me out for good the minute I graduated high school. I don't think they even wondered where I went." I swallow the lump in my throat, a remnant of rage and hurt that hasn't completely healed after all these years.

Adrian's soft gaze studies me in silence, attentive, so I continue. "Luckily, I had Colin. We were in school together since first grade. He was my playmate, my brother and later my bodyguard against insistent pricks, my guardian angel. No doubt my life would've taken a wrong turn, if I hadn't had him to keep me on the right track. I followed him to San Francisco when he went to USF. I found a job and a room to sleep in, although I sneaked in his dorm quite often. He's not only a friend, he's my only family."

"Fuck, I'm so sorry," he murmurs, tugging at a loose strand of hair. "I never wanted to make you feel this way when I asked you to move out."

"I know. The situation is different, but these old wounds reopened, and I lashed out. I'm sorry." Giving him the apology he deserves, at last, alleviates the weight on my chest, and I blow out a long breath.

Adrian gets up in a swift movement before snatching the mug from me. "Fuck coffee. We need alcohol." He balances my mug with his in one hand and holds out the other to help me off the couch.

My hand in his, I stand and follow, the warmth of his fingers spreading up my arm to the nape of my neck, and he doesn't release his grip until we're in the kitchen. He places the mugs in the sink as I grab two beers from the fridge and hand him one.

Adrian leans back on the counter, head down, a sudden spike of distress and anxiety rolling off him, his muscles quivering.

I remain silent and sit on the table, feet perched on a chair.

He pulls at his hair, harder than usual, and downs a big gulp. "I came home early one day, almost…two months ago now. As soon as I walked in, I knew. I heard Pauline, her fake, porn star moans." He shakes his head, eyes screwed shut, as if he could still hear her and wanted to make it stop. "I'd had doubts before. We had problems, so it wasn't really a surprise, but I needed to see it, to have the truth right in front of me." His gaze unfocuses. He's lost in his thoughts, not speaking to me anymore but to himself, perhaps saying it aloud for the first time. "I followed the trail of discarded clothes to the bedroom, cracked the door open and she was there. She was…" He inhales a sharp breath, jaw clenched. "She was on all fours in our bed, wrists fastened to the bedpost with one of my ties, with some guy fu…" His breathing catches, his lips shut tight for a second, and he swallows hard. "Some guy fucking her from behind. And the dickhead smiled at me, so proud."

"Shit…" I let out, my entire being aching for him, yearning to comfort him.

Adrian swallows a few mouthfuls of beer and drags his sad stare back to me, back to reality. "I'm sorry, that was *way* too much information."

"It's okay. You had to get it out."

"When Pauline saw me, her first reaction was to ask me what I was doing there. The same question, the same words you pronounced when we first met, and I think that's why I snapped at you. Sorry, I'm not trying to find excuses for my shitty behavior, but—"

"No, I get it. It explains a lot."

The tension oozing from him eases, and he sighs, offering me a genuine smile. "Thank you. I never told any of this...to anyone. I didn't even tell my family that my wedding was supposed to be six weeks from now."

"Why is that? I mean, they knew you were engaged. Why not tell them the date?"

"It took Pauline and me a while to set a date. We kept postponing, there was always a good reason. When we finally chose one, it was under the implicit condition that we'd move back to San Francisco after the wedding. It was to me, at least. But she never really agreed, so part of me, deep down, knew we wouldn't go through with it." Sadness taints his voice as he tears the label off the bottle, and finishes it in one big swallow, while I sip mine with more moderation. "I applied for the job transfer—not even sure I'd take it. But when I caught her in bed with that guy, I packed my bags. Almost ten years of relationship, of commitment and compromises, all down the drain."

"You made the right decision coming back."

"I shouldn't have left in the first place." An acerbic chuckle escapes him as a self-deprecating grimace distorts his features. He throws his bottle in the trash and opens the fridge. "I need a snack. You hungry?"

I slide off the table and point toward the jelly as I pass behind him to retrieve the bread and peanut butter from the cupboard. "You can't see it now, but there has to be something positive that came from this experience."

"I doubt it."

We move around the kitchen as we prepare sandwiches, his body relaxing with each passing second, the dark clouds in his eyes making way for a lighter glint.

"You learned French, that's positive."

"Not really. I never spoke French with Pauline, never felt comfortable doing so. I started studying it in high school, and I was almost fluent before I even met her." A slight cockiness reappears, a beguiling impudence, as he gathers the sandwiches and walks to the living room.

We settle back on the couch in our original positions, with the plates on our laps, and start eating.

"Seriously? I took French, too, and I'm definitely not fluent."

"You know a few words, then?" His features brighten.

"The basics, and a lot of swear words, like any teenager learning a foreign language."

"Well, *I* was studious. Our teacher had us read *Les Liaisons Dangereuses*," he says with a flawless accent that makes my heart flutter. "In retrospect, it was very inappropriate, but I fell in love with the culture and never lost interest."

"And I'm sure it helped with girls."

"I'd be lying if I said no." He throws a tiny piece of bread into his mouth, confidence back in full force, and breathes out a velvet laugh that envelops me, heat creeping up my neck.

My focus wavers, my mind drifting as I lick the peanut butter on my thumb. The spark of lust igniting his pupils as he glances at my tongue overpowers me. My body craves his touch, and I almost cross the space between us to straddle his lap, tear apart his clothes, and feel his tongue on my burning skin.

But my good sense pins me to the spot, hammering the hurtful words again, *"use her as rebound"* like a stab in the chest.

I avert my gaze and take a deep breath, putting my plate on the coffee table. Silence stretches between us, and without any explanation from me, Adrian answers my doubts.

"Eva, I'm not using you. I'm sorry if it feels that way. I understand why it might."

"What are we doing, then?" My eyes search his, but instead of reassurance, all I find in them is confusion and uncertainty.

With a trembling hand in his hair, he sighs. "I have no fucking clue. My head is such a mess."

My heart drops, torn between pain and gratitude for his honesty. "You need peace to digest what you've been through and get your life back on track. I think you need to be alone for a while." My voice cracks at the end as I can't hold back the unexpected wave of sorrow washing over me. *Why does it feel like we're breaking up?*

His face falls, head bent for a second, as if he wished for a different outcome, as well.

"I'm sorry that you have to move out." He tosses his plate on the table and chances a teasing smile. "If it makes you feel any better, I would've kicked Maddie out, too."

I giggle, and we stand to clean up the table and the clutter we left in the kitchen, moving around each other in an easy silence before returning to the couch. Adrian switches on the TV and flips through the channels, stopping on a criminal legal show, and laughing as I comment on the unrealistic lawyers yelling "Objection!" every two minutes.

* * * *

Late in the evening, he's fallen asleep on his side of the couch.

"Adrian," I whisper, crouched in front of him.

He squints as he wakes. "Eva?"

"You should go to bed."

He stands up, still half-asleep, and heads toward the bathroom as I stay behind to shut off the TV and straighten the cushions. I cross the corridor after he exits the bathroom and pause.

"Good night, Adrian."

Clutching his bedroom door handle, he spins and observes me without responding.

"Good night," I repeat.

Immobile, he murmurs, "I didn't even kiss you. Not the way I should have."

My heart skips a beat, and I just stand here, stunned. The soft light beaming from the bathroom graces his side, the deep blue of his eyes shimmering. He releases the handle to step toward me, and I don't move, hypnotized by his piercing stare.

It's a bad idea. I should stop him. We agreed a few hours ago that nothing should happen between us, but he takes another step, only an inch from me, and I want him even closer.

My heart races as he leans in, studying me. His palm lifts to my neck, fingers tangling in my hair, and he pulls my face to his. His breathing is as ragged as mine. "Eva, I'm dying to kiss you." His desperate voice, rumbling in his throat, echoes through my core.

Words evade me. As an answer to his plea, I reach for his waist, lift on my toes, and push myself against his muscular chest. His mouth ghosts over mine, his other hand gripping my hip, and my eyes flutter closed. I float on the electric current running between us as his lips press on mine, his kiss languid and sensual. My heart pounds and my skin ignites under his touch. His tongue grazes my lower lip, the tip caresses mine, gentle, tender, dancing in a slow rhythm. I melt, intoxicated by his heady fragrance, his thumping heartbeat resonating against my breasts. His fist clutches my hair harder, his grip on my hip tightening, his tongue slides inside, stroking mine with passion, and a moan escapes me, pleading for more. Then he closes his mouth on mine, leaving a last kiss, delicate, almost chaste. When he pulls back, his gaze drowns in sadness.

"Goodbye," he whispers and lets go of his hold on me.

My heart sinks as I grasp the finality of his choice of word. Adrian didn't say 'goodnight'.

Before I can react, he turns around and walks to his bedroom, closing the door behind him.

I totter to my room on weak legs and slump down on the bed, my heart still hammering, a flow of images whirling in my head—the desperation in his look, his velvety voice, the intensity of his kiss. It meant more than a rebound.

But Adrian said goodbye to what we could've been.

Chapter Nineteen

Wicked and Irrepressible

Eva's place, nine p.m. as planned. I've got gossip!

Daphne's mysterious text to Madison and me offers a much-needed distraction after spending two days musing about Adrian's kiss. He came home late from work last night, long after I went to bed, and the loneliness worsened the chaos in my head.

I'm alone again when my friends arrive right on time, and their visit lifts my spirits in a second. They settle on the couch, their bubbly chatter like a fresh breeze blowing through the room, allowing me to breathe.

"So, what's going on?" I ask from the kitchen while I pour three glasses of white wine before joining them.

"I was at the office late last night," Daphne says, reaching for the glass I hand her. "I thought I was the last one. The building was practically empty, except on our floor."

"Was Colin still there?" Madison asks.

"Not that I know of," Daphne shrugs. "However, when I came back from the archives room, I heard peculiar noises coming from one of the lawyers' office." Her eyes narrow, her tone suspenseful.

"What kind of noises?" Madison leans forward, engrossed in the story.

"The kind a despicable receptionist would make while being fucked on a desk."

"Patricia? You're kidding? After all the rumors she spread about us." I lean back in disgust. "And with whom?"

"Um...don't remember his name. Senior partner in Intellectual Property, I think. Tall, creepily white, with a weird pointy beard?"

"Joseph Miller?"

"Yes! The door was ajar, so I peeked inside and saw them."

"Did you take a picture?" Madison points at Daphne's phone on the coffee table.

I cringe. "Why would you want to see this?"

"And that would be illegal," Daphne adds in a laugh.

"Sorry, sorry, I got caught up." Madison waves a dismissive hand and grabs her glass with the other.

"I actually wish I hadn't looked. It wasn't a sexy sight."

A shudder runs down my spine "This guy is...peculiar. I mean, he makes my skin crawl just by speaking, sometimes."

"Me too." Daphne brings her glass to her mouth to take a sip. "Yet Patricia seemed to really enjoy his dick."

"Whose dick?" Adrian asks as he comes in through the door, startling us. "Sorry to sneak up on you. I guess I wasn't supposed to hear that."

He gives a quick hug to Madison before taking off his jacket, then his eyes land on me. In their blue depths, the intensity showing when we kissed is there, hypnotic, and he offers me a soft smile.

Daphne's cringe is still plastered on her face. "I saw a colleague screwing our receptionist on his desk."

A low, appreciative chuckle resonates in Adrian's chest. "Well, I see lawyers have the same habits as bankers."

"Really? Does that happen a lot in your field?" Daphne asks.

"Of course. People fucking in their offices, in conference rooms, bathrooms. Corporate Christmas parties are particularly wild. But I think it's a rather widespread fantasy for a guy to bend a secretary over his desk."

A loud huff sound escapes my mouth at the unpleasant idea of Adrian fucking his secretary, and his gaze flashes to me.

The corner of his mouth lifts. "You don't think it's true, Eva?"

"No... Maybe... I don't know." My defensive tone amplifies his smug smile.

"I imagine it's the same for women with firefighters or..." He trails off, hesitant, but his smoldering gaze locks on me. His long fingers trace the silky gray fabric of his tie as he loosens it.

...or bankers. In tailored gray suits with chest tattoos peeking out.

I keep that thought to myself and break eye contact, fighting to suppress this consuming draw to him. I clear my throat to regain control of my voice. "I guess so. But I thought the secretary fantasy was a sexist cliché these days?" My tone comes out more teasing than I intended, my treacherous body luring him, as if I can't control it.

His smile widens. "It doesn't have to be. Even if high heels and pencil skirts are hard to resist, secretaries can be fierce and headstrong, and in control." He winks at me, and he's so fucking handsome I can't look away.

A sudden sadness veils his eyes, pinching my chest, and he casts his gaze down with a slight shake of his head. We're slipping down the wrong path again and we both know it.

"I still have some work to do. Good night, ladies." He picks up his laptop and steps backward out of the room before I can collect my thoughts and answer.

Madison's head spins in my direction. "What was that about? Did I miss something?" she asks in a low, hushed voice.

"What are you talking about?" I respond in a tone that I intend to be casual but isn't.

"Come on, Eva, what's happening between you two?" She shifts in her seat to face Daphne. "Do you know anything?"

"I'm not answering that question." Her hands shoot up in self-defense.

Spending even one evening not thinking about Adrian proves to be impossible, but their opinion might help. Perhaps I was too quick to push him away, even though he didn't challenge the decision. His kiss might not mean as much to him as I think. His goodbye could be less definitive than it sounded. It's all too confusing.

"Okay, fine." I pull their attention back to me. "You were upset that Adrian wouldn't talk to you. I didn't want to bother you with this."

"It's fixed now. Bother me."

"Since last week, I've been feeling…" I stall, but her stare is unyielding, and she doesn't blink. "I'm attracted to him. And he is to me, too." Judging by the smile creeping on her face, I can continue without the worry of her reaction. "We kind of made out when we were at your parents' house last weekend."

"Is that why you were all weird when you came back from the bathroom?"

"Your mother caught us and yelled at him for using me as rebound sex."

"Oh shit!" She winces.

"Anyway, Adrian and I spent Sunday afternoon together. We both apologized for our shitty behavior. We shared a lot about our past, and…" I pause for a second and sigh. "He's a mess. We kind of agreed that it would end there, whatever it was."

"Really?" Daphne's mouth turns into a frown. "And that's it?"

"Well, that night, before we each went to bed, he admitted that he wished he had kissed me."

"You just said you made out?" Madison interrupts, brows furrowed.

I clear my throat. "Um…dry-humped might be more accurate, then."

Daphne giggles, and Madison shakes her head with a momentary grimace.

"What did you answer?" she asks.

"I didn't, and he kissed me. So passionately, it was insane. Then he said goodbye."

Apprehension rises in my stomach as I wait for their comments. Adrian's words and kiss have haunted me for two days, and even after turning them in my heads for hours, I'm still lost. Both of them observe me with eyes wide in anticipation.

"And then?" Daphne presses.

"Then, nothing. We haven't seen each other since, until just now."

"And he's flirting with you. And you're jealous when he makes a comment about some random fantasy of a hypothetical woman bent over his desk."

"He wasn't flirting. And I'm not jealous," I screech in an awkward half-whisper.

"You should've seen your face." Madison laughs. "And yes, he was."

I sigh again, not willing to admit it. "Adrian needs time alone. He ended a ten-year relationship two months ago. Nothing else is going to happen between us. I shouldn't dive into something with him too fast, or maybe at all. I don't want to get hurt."

They remain silent for a moment and nod in agreement. No matter how much I wish the situation were different, easier, keeping some distance is best for both Adrian and me.

An hour later, after exhausting all gossip and relationship topics, Daphne has just left and Madison stands from the couch.

"I'm leaving, too." She grabs her jacket and purse on her way to the door. "Eva, Adrian has been through a lot. I think you're both doing the right thing," she says with affection and hugs me before walking out of the apartment.

With our glasses cleared from the table, I head straight to bed. I won't sleep well again, tonight. Images of Adrian flash before my eyes, the sound of his voice resonates in my head. I still feel his lips on mine, his hands on my skin.

As hard as it will be, I have to stay away from him, for both our sakes. Only one week left, and it won't be a problem anymore. I can't wait to move out of his apartment.

Chapter Twenty

Piling Up

As I walk through the front door coming home from work, three cardboard boxes stuffed with bubble wrap lie open on the floor. I bend down to peek inside, push one corner up and discover Eva's wrapped-up belongings. I follow the trail of boxes to the living room and study my surroundings. Every object and trinket that used to adorn the apartment is now packed. My place seems cold and empty.

Shuffling sounds echo from Eva's bedroom, and she's mumbling to herself as I reach her doorway. A dozen empty boxes surround her, with the entire contents of her closet piled on the bed. She turns to me, hands sliding in the back pockets of her loose jeans, an unruly lock of hair that has escaped her messy bun now covering one eye. "I'm packing."

I throw a playful glance at the mess she's made. "I'd offer to help, but it looks like you have it under control."

On the first night we'd fought, when I forced her to move from my room like a jerk, she managed it with a lot of efficiency. How can she be so disorganized now?

"It's not as bad as it looks. I just need to throw all of this"—she gestures to the pile of clothes—"into the boxes. And the shoes, too." She points to the twenty-something pairs lined up on the closet floor.

Our eyes lock, but after only a second she averts her gaze, leaving me wondering if she's more self-conscious about potentially asking for my help, or about us being secluded in the intimacy of her bedroom. I shake that last thought out of my mind. We can't go back to letting our attraction bring us down the wrong path. I can't have the same conversation leading to her telling me again I should take some time to be alone, even if she's right.

"Let me get changed, and I'll give you a hand."

Before she can refuse, I stride to my room, change out of my suit into jeans and a T-shirt and return to help.

While we pack, her loud sigh breaks the silence.

"What's wrong?"

"I didn't realize how much stuff I have. I don't even know if it will all fit in my new room. It's much smaller."

A tinge of guilt pinches my chest for inflicting this on her, but I endeavor to keep the mood light and change the subject as I spot a huge textbook on her nightstand. "*The Fundamentals of Finance: Markets and Investments*. Is that your bedtime reading?"

She peers at the book and nods. "Boring, right? I'm a nerd."

"First of all, it's not boring. This book is a gold mine. It was my go-to resource throughout my MBA. I could talk about this book all night." I smile and reach over to grab it, studying the dozen sticky notes in flashy colors poking out from between the pages. "And second, there's nothing wrong with being a nerd. It means you're passionate about something."

"Yet, it's still boring to most people." She crunches her nose in the cutest way and shrugs.

I'm not most people. And I'm fucking impressed at the amount of detail and dedication she puts into her work as I flip through the pages and read her annotations. "I bet finding this on your nightstand has scared at least one guy away." I chuckle and put the book down, smothering the sudden prickle of jealousy that creeps inside my gut at the thought of another man in Eva's bedroom.

She laughs. "Literally, it has."

"Are you serious?"

"He was clearly disturbed by it, started babbling nonsense and tried to mansplain the book to me, which didn't go down too well for him."

"I can imagine," I tease, stifling a laugh as I finish gathering her towels and linen. "Glad to hear I'm not the only man who can trigger your wrath."

"I didn't even bother getting upset." She shrugs. "I just sent him on his way before he could even try to take off his clothes."

"Good call." I wink at her, and she throws me a mischievous smile.

Our eyes lock again. The sparkle in her bright green eyes echoes through my core, and I almost launch forward to kiss her. This time, I'm the one who averts my gaze.

"What's next?" I ask.

"There's only that dresser's top drawer left, but — "

I don't let her finish before opening it, and I should have. The end of her sentence would've been for me not to, considering what's inside. A floating awkward moment passes as I stare at the contents, speechless in front of the different colors and fabrics of her underwear.

Fuck. Me.

Visions of Eva in those pieces assail my mind, sun-kissed skin naked except for her round breasts covered with one of these black lace or red silk bras, the matching panties on her tight ass. I try my best to keep myself, or more precisely my cock, in check.

"I can do this one by myself, thank you." Her voice is stern, but her eyes dance, and she doesn't budge from her spot.

"Are you sure? I'd be happy to help." I offer my best cocky grin, because I simply can't refrain from teasing her. When I glance back into the drawer, a set draws my attention. "I didn't picture you wearing this kind of hot pink flouncy stuff." I pick up the ruffled thong between my thumb and index finger and hold it in front of me.

She snatches them from my hand with a playful smirk, lust firing up her eyes. "What did you picture me wearing?"

"I imagined black or dark colors. A deep purple, maybe, but certainly not hot pink."

She giggles, and I fucking love that sound.

"I have a lot of those, too, as you can see." She moves in front of the drawer and pushes it shut with her back, the fire in her eyes burning bright.

My body brushes against hers, heart hammering. I have her trapped between the dresser and me, and her body language invites me in closer. Shallow breaths escape her parted lips, back arched a little, breasts inching toward my stomach and nipples hardening as she's braless under her T-shirt.

Her resolve fades, almost giving in to this attraction, as I fight my instincts to keep from lifting her up and fucking her senseless on that dresser.

There's a line we agreed we wouldn't cross, and she seems determined to keep it that way as she casts her gaze down and steps aside.

I clear my throat. "I guess you can handle that last part without me."

The fire in her eyes has dimmed, and her voice dulls. "Thank you for your help."

"No problem." I walk out of her room with a smile, but a gnawing void in the pit of my stomach.

Chapter Twenty-One

The Last Night

After a typically stressful Friday at work, I leave early to make sure I arrive before our friends invade my apartment to surprise Eva. Colin was worried she'd spend the evening mulling over the details for tomorrow's move and had organized an impromptu get-together.

Eva comes home not long after me and before joining me on the couch, she changes into loose jeans, for which I'm grateful. Reining in my attraction to her is a real struggle when she parades in tight dresses and high heels, my favorite fantasy in the flesh.

"No plans for tonight?" I ask as she sits next to me.

"No, I don't want to be too tired tomorrow. What about you?"

"I do have plans, actually," I reply with a small smile, yet not letting the secret out about Colin's plan.

"Oh?" Her voice sounds halfway between surprise and annoyance.

For the second time, a hint of jealousy shows in her reaction, and I enjoy it more than I should.

Our friends arrive with six-packs of Guinness and warm hugs for Eva. As Colin explains the reason for their presence, she spins toward me, hands propped on her hips, a teasing glint in her eyes.

"You're actually celebrating me moving out of your place?"

"Yes. *Finally*," I say in a slight grunt with the same playfulness.

I throw her a wink, and she giggles. That fucking sound, again.

The ladies gather on the worn-out leather couch, Colin on the big armchair, leaving Luke and me on kitchen chairs we dragged to the living room. Daphne and Eva bubble with excitement as they organize the move. Daphne and Madison will go straight to the new apartment to unpack the first incoming boxes that Luke will bring from Daphne's storage unit. Colin will meet Eva here to move her belongings. I'll help however I can.

When Colin's stomach screams for dinner, Eva gets up to order pizzas, passing by me on her way to the kitchen. My gaze follows her and lands on her ass, only for a second or two, but long enough that when I turn my head back to the group, they're all staring at me.

"You're so obvious, man." Colin chuckles.

I don't bother responding, no point pretending they're mistaken. I can't keep my eyes off her.

Eva comes back with beers in hand, and the pizzas arrive twenty minutes later as the conversation flows with ease.

When we've finished, Luke and I clean the table. He follows me to the kitchen with the empty pizza boxes, and I retrieve a second six-pack from the fridge.

"Now that we're alone, tell me," he says in almost a whisper. "Are you settling back all right? How are you feeling?"

"Better every passing day." The downbeat undertone in my voice is evident even to me.

"You don't seem entirely convinced by what you just said." Luke leans against the counter with his legs crossed at the ankles, hands in his jeans pockets and stare fixed on me.

I put the beers down and mimic his stance, propped against the table, and blow out a loud breath. "Some things are getting better. Others are only more and more confusing."

"I know. Madison told me about your conversation with Eva. And your *insane, passionate kiss*, quote-unquote."

"Eva said that?"

My heart races at the memory of her lips on mine, but an unexpected wave of doubt washes over me. What we shared, what she felt was evident, but Luke's confirmation reassures me more than I thought I needed.

"You seem surprised. Do you doubt the effect you have on her?" His usual smirk appears. "Come on, you know women can't resist you."

Words evade me, and Luke's amused expression morphs into a worried frown. My chest constricts as I strain to reason. The unease overpowers me. My throat tightens, and self-doubt creeps back into my stomach.

Luke steps toward me, hands on my shoulders. "Adrian, talk to me. I don't like what I see on your face right now."

In my mind swirl all the explanations I could give, the confessions I could make. Luke has always known every detail about me, every thought my brain comes up with. Perhaps I should spill it all.

I breathe in deep and swallow hard. "I don't know that I'm irresistible. I couldn't even..." I choke, eyes screwed shut, unable to say the words...*save my engagement, satisfy my fiancée so she wouldn't fuck someone else...*

Even to my best friend, my brother, I can't admit that. I can barely admit it to myself. That sense of failure hadn't overwhelmed me this much since my return.

Luke pulls me into a hug and taps his hand on my back. "Hey, don't go full-on panic attack on me, bro. You're going to be fine now," he says, almost as if he could read my mind.

I relax and let the tension wane. Luke pushes back from the embrace and grabs me by the neck with one hand, his grip firm. "You're a hot motherfucker, and when you're not acting like a jackass, you're the greatest guy I know." He plants a hard kiss on my cheek.

"What are you—?" Eva stops mid-sentence as she enters the kitchen. "Am I interrupting something?" She bends through the door, laughing. "Madison, your brother's stealing your boyfriend."

"We're having a moment here." I grab the towel and throw it at her.

She laughs louder and throws it back before exiting the room. The huge grin she brought to my face remains in place when I turn back to Luke, who observes me with a strange look.

"Adrian, I know you better than anyone else. You were wrong once, but don't make another mistake now because you're too scared."

"What do you mean?"

"Why the fuck are you letting Eva move out?"

Our friends laugh in the other room, calling us, and Luke walks away before I have time to answer.

What can I say, anyway? The truth is I'm not sure that I want her to go anymore.

I snatch up the six-pack and follow him, still confused.

Daphne has moved to one of the chairs, which leaves me a spot next to Eva. Luke perches on the armrest of the couch with Madison cozying up to him.

"Are you going to dump me now that you got the other Hensley sibling back?" Madison asks Luke.

"No way, you do things to me that he never wanted to." His tone is bordering on indecent.

"For fuck's sake, can I please not hear this about my baby sister?"

"Wait." Madison's eyes widen at Luke. "Did you actually try? Did something happen between you two?"

Luke chuckles. "Adrian's like my brother. Nothing happened, and I never tried. I would've told you."

"Good." Madison sighs in relief. "That'd be too weird. I don't want to have to compete with my brother on that level."

I cringe. "This conversation is horrifyingly gross. Please stop."

The whole group laughs, and Luke leaves a tender kiss on the back of Madison's hand.

The evening flies by, and the more time passes, the harder it becomes not to touch Eva sitting next to me. She throws glances at me from the corner of her eye, turning her head to me every few minutes even when I'm not the one speaking.

When Daphne suggests we play poker, Luke sits up straighter with a smug smile. "Yes! I haven't kicked your ass in a long time, Adrian."

"True, but I kicked yours last week already," I reply in the same tone, motioning at the greenish remainder of a bruise on his jaw.

His eyes narrow but he can't hold back his smile. "Game on, bro."

As instructed, Colin reaches for a deck of cards stacked in the bookcase behind him. "I haven't played in years. It was strip-poker, actually."

Luke snorts. "Nobody wants to see you naked, dude."

Eva laughs and throws a naughty glance in my direction. The look in her eyes drives me insane. It's too tempting not to seize the opportunity to tease her.

I lean to whisper in her ear. "Am I reading this wrong or are you partial to the idea of me stripping?"

"Come on, Adrian." Her voice drops. "When I want to see you naked, I just peek while you're showering."

The last time she hit on me so forwardly was while drunk, and I wonder how many beers she's had tonight.

"Are you drunk again?"

She shakes her head, points to her beer bottle, still not empty, and inches closer to me, pushing herself against my shoulder for her mouth to reach near my ear. "Not enough to say things I wouldn't want to."

A shiver runs along my neck as her breath blows on my skin, but I stay still until she moves back, away from me.

All eyes are on us, and I get a very pointed look from Luke. Nobody says a word, though, and we start the game.

After playing for more than an hour, Eva, Madison, Daphne and Colin have lost, leaving me facing Luke, who has returned to his chair. Madison reclines against his legs, plopped on a cushion on the floor.

Eva has slid closer to me so that she can peek at my cards. Concentrating has become difficult — her thigh presses against mine, her long hair brushing against my arm, sweet flowery fragrance enthralling.

Luke glances at his cards. "We should make this more interesting. Let's bet for real."

"What do you have in mind?"

If he wants to raise the stakes, it means he's sure to win.

A roguish smile crosses his features. "Like our trip to L.A. If you lose, you get another tattoo, and I get to choose what and where, this time."

"Oh, I want to hear that story." Eva perks up.

Luke chortles. "We took a trip to Los Angeles together back in college. It was spring break, sophomore year. We played poker —"

"Drunk and high as fuck," I add as justification to what happened.

"Right," Luke continues. "We bet that the loser would get a tattoo, but the winner would decide the design and on what part of the body."

"That's a risky bet," Colin says.

Daphne scoffs. "*Stupid* is the word you're looking for."

"Well, yes, but I won." I smirk, even though it was the only time I'd ever won against him. "And Luke got a cute little pink heart tattooed on his left ass cheek."

"You actually did it?" Colin asks between two bursts of his boisterous laugh.

"He did. And it *is* cute," Madison says.

I still can't wrap my head around her being in a position to confirm that.

Luke shrugs. "A bet is a bet. And don't laugh, bro. I've heard about that butterfly with a girl's name that you had to get covered."

Colin sobers up. "I was drunk. And my brothers from Pi Kappa Phi were douchebags."

"Like I said...stupid," Daphne mumbles.

"Plus, you can't prove anything. All I have on my lower back now is a majestic dark phoenix." He shrugs, and we laugh again.

Luke turns to me. "So, are you in?"

"I'm in, as long as you promise not to ruin my other tattoos."

"Of course not."

"How many do you have?" Colin points to my forearm. "This one, and I remember seeing another on the ladies' drunken debacle night."

"Only those two. It goes from my left shoulder blade, over the shoulder and around the ribs to my chest. It's biomechanical."

"What is *'biomechanical'*?" Daphne asks.

"Basically, it looks like some of the skin was ripped off to expose a metal robotic skeleton."

"It's freakishly realistic," Madison says, and Colin nods in appreciation.

Eva has remained silent, and when I turn, a cute pout graces her lips. "So that's what it is?"

I chuckle. "You could have just asked, if you wanted to know so badly."

Her pout morphs into a smug, teasing smile. "It would've meant asking you to take off your shirt to let me look."

I'm helpless under her irresistible eyes. My body aches to touch her, kiss her, take my shirt off and let her hands roam over my skin.

"Fuck," I let out in a groan, and tear my gaze away from her to Luke. "Let's play, man."

We play the last hand and as expected, Luke wins, beating my flush with a full house.

"Yes!" He fist-bumps Madison. "I'm not going to be too hard on you, though. I think a cute little pink heart on your left ass cheek should do just fine."

They all laugh again, and I accept my defeat with a graceful bow.

He stands, bringing Madison up with him as she yawns. "All right, babe, let's get you to bed."

"Same for me." Daphne grabs her jacket. "See you tomorrow, roomie." She hugs Eva before they all walk out.

Daphne's words scrape my ears. Tomorrow, Eva will be *her* roommate.

As we clear the remnants of the evening, Eva's behavior toward me shifts—more distant, less confident. Now that we're alone, teasing her, playing with her isn't as easy. The context is different, and so are the consequences.

I clear my throat almost awkwardly. "Tonight was fun."

"Yes, it was."

The look in her eyes takes my breath away. She flirted with me all night long, making sexual innuendos, but what I discern in her gaze is not only lust anymore.

I follow behind her, observe her as she walks to the bathroom, my hands itching to reach out to her, to hold her back.

The reality crushes me. She leaves tomorrow. This is her last night here, the last night I go to bed with her in my apartment. The last day I came home to her smile. I don't know when we'll see each other again, how often. I pace back and forth between my room and the hallway, panicking.

Luke is right. Why the fuck am I letting her get away?

It's too late now to change her plans, and maybe we made the right decision, but I can still hold her, I need to, even if only for tonight.

Eva comes out of the bathroom, and I must stop her before she retreats to her room and closes the door.

"Eva?" My voice is hoarse, my throat tight.

"Yes?"

As I stand in front of her, the hint of hope in her eyes is all I need to spur me on. I reach for the hem of my shirt, pull it over my head, and drop it to the floor. Her breath hitches. Her eyes fix mine, and my heart races. I fucking crave her gaze on me like never before.

"Look at it."

A small smile adorns her lips, and she steps closer. Her stare lowers to my torso, the urge to feel her skin on mine growing stronger, but I stay still and watch her while she focuses on the drawing on my chest.

Eva studies the details, slowly. The silence is only interrupted by the steady rhythm of our breathing. She moves around me, following the design along my ribs. Her fingertips graze my back as she traces the drawing, electrifying each dark line, setting my body on fire. Her left hand rests flat on my skin and slides over my shoulder, the fingers of her other hand hook in the waistband of my jeans, lifting on her toes to pull her body flush against my back. My fists clench, I fight to remain immobile and let Eva set her own pace, but when her soft lips plant a kiss on my shoulder blade, I give in.

I spin, grab her neck and pull her to me, crashing my lips to hers, kissing her with passion like I've wanted to for days, and the feeling surpasses anything I'd imagined. I bend my knees so she can press her whole body against mine. Her fingers tangle in my hair and tug hard. Eva is as frantic as I am, tongues thrusting, teeth grazing our lips. Sliding my hands down her back, I squeeze her ass, and she shoves her hips against me, pressing against my hard cock through the denim, igniting every cell in me.

I guide her backward to the bed without breaking the kiss and lie her down on the mattress, her small frame under me. My mouth devours her, my hands wander all over her, impatient, almost tearing the fabric of her clothes to feel her. I get lost in the sensations, in my desperate need to taste her, to take her, and she pulls me even closer. With my lips on her jaw, down her neck, I nibble at her skin. I barely resist biting her to leave a fucking mark as she writhes under me, hands grabbing my ass, feet planted on the bed to lift her hips to meet mine when I rub my cock between her thighs. Sweet moans escape Eva's lips, the sexiest sounds I've ever heard, awakening the deepest, wildest rawness in me.

Before I let myself plunge into that fierce desire without restraint, I pull away to look at her. The intensity of her stare is breathtaking, tantalizing. More than lust, more than sex, more than anything I've felt in a long time.

I bring my lips to hers again, not willing to waste a single second of this smoldering bliss.

Eva might be gone tomorrow, but tonight she is mine.

Chapter Twenty-Two

Mine

Tomorrow I'll leave him alone, but tonight Adrian is mine.

My head had been spiraling in doubt and desperation, but Adrian holding me now keeps me grounded. No matter how lost my mind gets about our chaotic relationship, his skin, his kisses enliven me more than I have been in ages. How can such a reckless and wrong decision feel so right?

Every cell in me yearns for his touch, and I pull his body closer on top of me, let his weight crush me. Our lips devour, tongues battling. The warmth of his palm scorches my skin as his hand slips under my shirt, grazing the underside of my breast. My back arches, nipples hardened against the lace of my bra, my heart hammering.

The world outside disappears, our reality forgotten, reason be damned.

Adrian breaks the kiss to grab the hem of my shirt, and I wriggle out of it as he lifts it over my head to throw it aside. His intense gaze burns with desire, and my blood boils from the need to feel him closer, on me, inside me.

I reach down to the buttons of his jeans, but he seizes my wrists, pinning them above my head, a mischievous glint in his eyes.

"You've seen me naked already," he whispers, his lips ghosting over mine. "It's my turn."

As he sits on his heels between my legs, his hands release my wrists and travel down my arms, over my breasts, igniting every inch of my skin on his way to my waist.

Arms still stretched above my head, I let him set the pace, and I give in to the thrill he provokes in me.

He unbuttons my jeans, his fingers sliding inside to peel them off my legs in one swift move. With my feet resting on the mattress on either side of him, my knees slightly drop to offer him a perfect view of my lace-covered pussy as his hungry eyes roam over my body.

His tongue darts out to lick his lower lip. "You're so beautiful."

The softness of his words, the velvet in his voice envelops me, and all I can do is smile.

His hands trail down my thighs, fingers spread wide, gripping, greedy. And back up again, his thumbs tipping toward the inner side. My breathing speeds up. I observe him, the devoted focus on his face, his lips parted. His stare follows the journey of his thumbs, and he throws a few glances at my breasts heaving with each ragged breath I take as I struggle to remain immobile, clutching the pillow above my head. When he reaches my pussy, I surrender and tilt my hips to meet his fingertips pressing through the thin fabric, just for a second until he drags them away.

I gasp. "You really enjoy playing with me, don't you?"

"I really fucking do." His shameless arrogance excites me even more.

His feral stare is locked on me as he unbuttons his jeans, abs flexing, his movements unhurried and controlled, clearly intended to tease me. The brutality of his intricate tattoo, skin ripped off over metal pieces, flesh and bones showing underneath, gives him a powerful aura, dominant.

Adrian stands to take off his pants then kicks them aside. When he crawls back on top of me, the weight of his body trapping me, the heat of his skin sets fire to mine. I capture his mouth in a fiery kiss, grip his hair with one hand as the other travels down his back, slipping under his boxers, grabbing his ass to pull him closer. His hard cock presses against my pussy through our underwear. My legs lock around his waist, his length pulsing, his hand holding my hip.

And he breaks the kiss.

"Shit..." he whispers, hidden in the crook of my neck, panting. "Please tell me you have a condom."

"You don't?" My voice sounds more amused than I intended.

"I actually threw them away in a fit of anger, a couple of weeks ago." He shakes his head. "I hadn't anticipated this. I hadn't anticipated you." The intensity in his gaze takes my breath away, and he leaves a tender kiss on my lips.

I swoon. How can he be so erotic and affectionate at the same time?

"I have a pack...somewhere in one of the boxes." I grimace.

"Fuck." Adrian closes his eyes, stock-still for a moment before breathing in deep through his nose and releasing it loudly as he stands from the bed.

The loss of his warmth brings a shiver to my skin, but the sight of him walking backward as he exits, eyes on me, muscles flexing and cock bulging in his boxers, is enough for the fire in me to keep burning.

Shuffling sounds of cardboard boxes echo from my bedroom. "Any idea which box they're in?"

My body is restless. My mind runs wild. I contemplate touching myself and moaning loud enough to drive him crazy in the other room. But as satisfying as it would be to tease him, I want *him* to make me moan.

I take off my bra and panties, scurry to the next room and find him crouched on the floor among the boxes. I strike a pin-up pose with one hand on the doorframe, the other propped on my hip, and drop my voice to a sultry murmur. "Probably the one on your left. I threw the contents of my nightstand in it."

His head snaps in my direction, eyes wide and dark, hungry. He stands, takes a swift stride, and slams me against the wall.

A smug smile on my face, I bask in the power I have over his reactions.

Adrian lets out a wild groan, and his mouth crashes on mine with passion. His hand pinching my nipple sends an electric shock through me. His fingers reach between my thighs. My body is desperate, my pussy wet. Holding on to his broad shoulders, my nails scratch his back as his middle finger thrusts inside of me, eliciting a deep moan muffled by his mouth on mine. I'm breathless.

His finger moving in and out mimics the languid rhythm of his tongue, and I melt against him, knees weak, supported by his tall frame pinning me against the wall.

"You're extremely unhelpful. You know that?" He teases against my lips, making me laugh. "Which box did you say it was?" His tongue slides inside my mouth once more, his palm pressing against my clit.

I inhale, battling to remain focused enough. "That one." I motion with a head tilt.

With frantic haste and determination, Adrian steps away from me, searches through the designated box and retrieves a condom from the half-empty pack without saying a word. He prowls back to me, lust darkening his wild blue stare. With a commanding hand on my waist, he guides me backward to his bedroom, switching the lights off on the way.

In the soft glow of his bedside lamp, his chest lifts with each heavy breath. Neither of us utters a word, neither of us is playing games anymore, both aware that tonight might be reckless, but craving this connection too much to care.

I snatch the condom from his hand and tear it open. When he takes his boxers off, I reach for his thick cock, my movements assured.

His breath hitches and he watches me with awe as I stroke him, then lifts his thumb to my lips, meeting the tip of my tongue. I suck it into my mouth as I roll the condom onto his length.

The teasing is unbearable, and we both fall over the edge of self-control, losing ourselves in each other. Adrian's movements become more forceful. He lifts me off the floor, wrapping my legs around his waist. I cling to him, nails digging, feverish. He keeps me flush against him as he lays me back on the bed.

Propped on one elbow, one hand in my hair, he reaches down to my pussy. Two fingers thrust inside with urgency, earning a throaty whimper from me. A smug dirtiness radiates from him, and it drives me crazy.

Adrian shifts on top of me, and his fingers are replaced by the head of his cock. His hand grips my hip tight enough to keep me in place before pushing inside of me until he's buried deep. A low grunt rumbles in his throat as I moan, and he crushes his lips on mine.

Our tongues mingle, our hands, eager and adventurous, explore every inch of our skin. My hips sway to meet his every thrust. Our fragrances blend in a heady whirlwind of amber and white flowers. A thin coat of sweat covers our skin, both of us out of breath, yet both clearly wanting more. Adrian hooks my leg higher on his waist, his cock boring deeper inside me, but it's still not enough.

With one hand flat on his chest, I push him so that I can lift one leg over his arm to rest my ankle on his shoulder. The expression in his eyes morphs to obscene. He rests his hand on the back of my thigh, pulls out his full length and slams back into me, the overpowering sensation bursting out of me in a loud pleasure cry.

Adrian almost growls. "You're so fucking naughty."

It's my turn to throw him a smug smile.

His pace quickens, hitting hard. I reach above to the headboard for support, my leg trapped between us, knee almost next to my ear. The muscles of his chest tense up with each harsh movement. The shadows dance over the flawless lines of his raw tattoo.

Adrian's untamed lust awakens a primal thrill deep inside me, an unashamed obscenity that overpowers me, loud moans breaking free, filling the silence around us.

His arms on either side of me quiver under his weight, sweat dripping down his temples. He slides his hand beneath my lower back to pull me with him to a sitting position with his cock still inside me.

Our hips rock in a slower rhythm, in perfect sync. His mouth trails down to my breast, tongue swirling around my nipple then moving to the other. With his hands on my ass, he guides me, picks up the pace, lips ghosting over my neck, grazing the skin, licking.

"*J'adore ton petit cul*," he says in French, the sounds husky in his throat.

His velvet voice echoes through my core, my pussy pulsing around his cock.

He smiles against my neck. "Do you like it when I speak French, *ma puce*?" His hands on my ass urge me to take him deeper.

I whimper. "Fuck, yes."

A tingle crawls up my feet, a wave of heat coursing through me as my orgasm builds. His mouth trails along my jaw to my lips, his indecent smile never fading.

"*T'es tellement belle*," he whispers against my lips.

The sensuality in his voice drives me over the edge, and a wave of pure bliss washes over me. I scream his name, head thrown back, eyes screwed shut. My heart gallops in my chest. Breathless, I relish the ecstasy.

Adrian tightens his grip, pulling me down as his hips roll up.

"You're mine, *ma puce*," he groans, coming inside of me in one last deep thrust.

His lips reach mine, hungry and frenzied before slowing down to a drowsy kiss, our wet lips brushing and tongues licking. He falls to his side, taking me with him, and we lie there panting until our bodies relax.

Adrian pulls out, and after discarding the condom, he tugs the sheets to cover us.

He runs his fingers through my hair with affection as I snuggle in his strong arms, my face buried in his chest, the salty taste of his sweat on my lips, not willing to lose this mind-blowing connection with him just yet.

This intimacy, his tenderness brings a twinge to my stomach. This wasn't just sex. I don't want it to be.

As if he senses my sudden distress, his hold tightens around me. "*Bonne nuit, ma puce,*" he whispers in my hair.

My body melts against him, sheltered in the warmth of his skin, of his words, and I fall asleep, already dreading tomorrow.

Chapter Twenty-Three

Uncertain Tomorrows

Adrian and I are startled awake by a loud bang on the front door.

"Fuck, we overslept." Adrian sits up straight in bed.

"Shit! It must be Colin."

We jump out of bed and get dressed as fast as humanly possible, both silent. Three more bangs vibrate from the door, and Adrian rushes to the entrance.

Colin's voice echoes from the hallway. "What took you so long? Were you guys sleeping?"

"Yes, um..." Adrian says. "Neither of us thought about setting the alarm clock, apparently."

As I join them, Adrian manages to remain casual, or at least appear so. I follow his lead, but Colin throws me a suspicious look.

Colin always reads me like an open book. I could never hide my thoughts from him, nor would I want to. However, Adrian and I haven't talked about what last night meant. I'm not sure what I'd even tell Colin.

My chest is heavy. Was it only one night, only sex, for Adrian? The intensity of his eyes on me, of his words, meant more, without a doubt. Does it change the decision we have made? Should we chance something, or listen to reason and move forward as planned?

While my mind whirls with too many questions, Colin already walks to my room to take the first boxes. I follow in a panicked haze as Adrian slips away to the bathroom, gaze down.

I freeze when I enter my bedroom, and Colin turns to me with a cheeky smile. The bed is perfectly made, and it's obvious that I didn't sleep in it.

"Are you still moving?"

To him, spending the night with Adrian results in me staying. Words escape me, I struggle to hold his optimistic stare, and his face falls.

"You don't know. You didn't talk about it." Colin understands without me having to say a word, as always, and I release a loud breath.

As Adrian exits the bathroom, his phone rings, and he pauses in the hallway. After a quick peek at the screen, he mumbles *what the fuck*. Apparently sending the caller to voicemail, he shoves the phone in his back pocket and joins us. Before any of us has a chance to speak, the phone rings again. Adrian cuts it off and runs a nervous hand through his hair. His behavior is strange, and it deepens the worry settling in my stomach.

"Okay, what do we do here?" Colin asks.

The tinge of discontent in his tone might be imperceptible to others, but I recognize it. The distress must show on my face more than I think.

Adrian opens his mouth to speak, turning his distracted gaze to me, but his phone rings again.

"Fuck!" he shouts and this time, he picks up. "What?" His voice is curt, harsh, and he walks back to his bedroom, slamming the door behind him.

Colin and I stay silent, staggered. My doubts about our night are pushed into the background by this call, my chest constricting when we overhear him yelling on the phone.

"Are you fucking kidding me? Why are you here? I don't want to see you. Go the fuck back to France!"

Adrian's ex-fiancée is here. The floor gives way under my feet, and darkness tears a void inside my guts as Colin and I stare at each other in silence, eavesdropping without shame.

"I don't give a fuck, Pauline. What do you want us to talk about? There's nothing else to say," Adrian yells then pauses, leaving us waiting for him to respond to what she's saying. "What? An hour? I can't fucking believe that you'd do that." Another pause. "Yeah, fine. Looks like I don't have a choice," he quips before it goes quiet.

"This is so fucked up," Colin mumbles, shaking his head. "You should get the fuck out of here. Don't put yourself through this, Eva. You shouldn't have to face her, or him with her, or whatever the fuck this circus is going to be."

I never wanted to be stuck in the middle of his issues. And no matter what, I don't want to see Adrian with her. I swallow back the confusion, the ache, the tears menacing to spill and put on a brave façade.

"Grab the boxes. Looks like I'm moving out." I tug the sheets off the bed and shove them in the last open box.

Adrian comes out of his room just as Colin and I pass with our arms full.

"We'll be gone in an hour," I say, not daring to even glance at him, too afraid that I'll cry.

Adrian stops me with a gentle hand on my elbow. "Wait, Eva, please."

He takes the box from me and places it on the floor, waiting for Colin to exit the apartment.

"I'm sorry, I'm..." Nervous hands tug at his hair, and he exhales a loud breath. "This is a fucking nightmare."

"I shouldn't be here when she arrives." Dejection and resignation seep through my voice.

"I'm going to tell her to go away. You know that, right?" He chances a step toward me, hand reaching forward, but stops before touching me, hesitant.

I take a deep breath and swallow my delusions. "This is exactly what I didn't want. To get dragged down in the middle of some drama I have no part in."

"I'll make her go away, Eva." His voice pleads, his eyes blurred behind a gloomy veil.

"This is not about me, Adrian. No matter how you decide to deal with her, this is between you and her. Clearly, whether you want it or not, this Chapter of your life isn't closed, far from it. And I'm not a part of it. I refuse to play a part in any of this."

He sighs and takes one step backward to lean on the wall, head down. "I don't want you to leave like this."

I clench my teeth to keep from answering that I didn't want to leave him *at all*.

"You understand why I have to talk to her, right?" His piercing blue eyes beg me to understand, to not be mad at him.

Deep down I don't think I am. They spent years...maybe a decade together. We knew it could end up like this. I knew.

"I get it," I say and pause, my gaze on him, blinking back tears. "Do you understand why I need to protect myself and step away?"

He just nods and casts his eyes down again, pushing his hands into his jeans' pockets.

After a few silent beats, listening to his slow and deep, controlled breaths, I pick up the box at my feet. "I'll see you around," I say in a strangled voice, and it sounds like a question.

His stare meets mine, blue as deep as an ocean storm, his jaw clenched. "Yeah, see you around."

I fight my own body, resist the need to bury myself in his arms one last time. And walk away.

Colin fetches almost all my belongings in record time with some unexpected and lucky help from River, as I wait downstairs to stack the boxes in his huge BMW.

Even without explanations, River senses the tension and tries to lighten my mood with jokes about not having the most awesome woman as a neighbor anymore. I force a feeble smile, but I guess it doesn't look convincing.

Adrian helps by bringing the boxes halfway down, but I never see him. It's better this way, I imagine.

Soon, Colin and I drive in a crammed full car to Daphne's apartment — *my* apartment — leaving behind the few boxes we couldn't take, along with my delusional hopes that my blissful night with Adrian would lead to something more.

My throat tight, my brain struggles to rationalize the situation, but tears still roll down my cheeks.

When we arrive, Madison and Luke are already helping Daphne unpack her belongings, and they drop what they had in hand to rush to me.

"What's wrong, Ev'?" Luke asks.

"I... Adrian and I... We spent the night together."
My tears have dried but my voice is still choked. "We
didn't talk. We didn't take the time to talk. His ex called
this morning, she's here, and I left before she arrived."

"No fucking way," Luke yells. "What the fuck is that
bitch doing here?"

"Calm down." Madison places a soothing hand on
his chest.

Witnessing this simple tender gesture pinches my
desolate heart.

She turns to me. "He's going to throw her out,
right?"

I swallow the lump in my throat. "I think so."

"It was clear he didn't want to see her," Colin says,
one hand on my back, guiding me to sit on the couch.
"He was fuming."

"You ended it," Daphne says, her tone only half a
question.

"We knew it wasn't the right moment for this, for
us." I shake my head, still trying to make sense of what
happened. "I didn't want to get stuck in his unresolved
relationship with her. So, yes, I ended it."

They nod, but I can sense they don't entirely agree
with me. What else could I do? Asking her to leave is
his decision to make, not mine. Is it even what he wants,
deep down? If so, he still needs closure from her, and
time to heal.

The day passes in a daze, swinging between doubt,
sadness and irritation. My friends allow me some
much-needed space to breathe and organize my
thoughts. I need to be alone.

By the end of the afternoon, we've unpacked, and I
pretend to be tired as an excuse to escape to my room.
None of us have heard from Adrian since this morning,
to my knowledge.

My head throbs, my imagination overflowing with the different possible outcomes to his conversation with his ex. Maybe he threw her out and sent her back to France. Maybe they're still talking. Maybe she convinced him, reassured him, and they decided to move past her betrayal. Years spent together and an engagement aren't that easy to discard and forget. The mere thought of Adrian holding her in his arms hurts more than I imagined possible.

I rummage through my purse until my hand comes in contact with the key to Adrian's apartment. I ran out so fast I forgot to return it.

Determined, silencing the disappointment smothering me, I join my friends who are drinking coffee in the kitchen.

"You okay, Ev?" Luke asks.

"Could one of you give this back to Adrian for me, please?" I place the key on the table.

They nod in silence, and I ignore the glances they exchange. Whether they agree is irrelevant, but at least they respect my decision.

I walk back to my bed, struggling to hold back the tears prickling my eyes. As soon as I close them, images of Adrian swirl back in my mind. His fiery blue stare devouring me, his hands burning my skin. And his voice resonates in my head.

"You're mine, ma puce…"

Chapter Twenty-Four

Without Her

I pace my room like a caged lion, waiting for Pauline to arrive. *What the fuck is she even doing here?*

The pounding of my heart thumps in my ear, my breathing gets more and more erratic as the minutes pass, the knot in my stomach pushing bile up to my throat. I fight back the urge to scream or break the first object within reach.

Pauline cornered me, decided to travel across the world without asking beforehand, without giving me a choice. As if it were a proof of love. As if it'd change anything between us at this point. I have nothing more to say to her. If only she didn't know where I lived, but she's using the last string she can pull.

I need something to settle my nerves, although nine a.m. seems way too early for the rum shot I'm craving. Coffee will have to do.

I venture out to the hallway without daring even the smallest glance into Eva's empty room. I can't shake her dejected expression when she walked out of the apartment. I fucked up. We had agreed that we shouldn't let our attraction to each other lead us to that point. I should've taken the time to get my life in order, and Eva wouldn't have been hurt.

The coffee burns my throat as I swallow too fast, but its warmth helps to calm me down. By the time Pauline knocks on the door, some of my fury has already waned.

I breathe in deep, clutching the handle for a moment, then open the door. Pauline stands there, chin down, eyes puffy and red, blond hair lifted in a messy bun. She looks awful, tired, distressed. She deserves it, yet I don't like seeing her that way. Ten years loving her, caring for her... Old habits fucking die hard.

"Hi, baby," she says in a weak voice, her eyes as imploring and innocent as she can fake it.

"Don't call me that," I spit out.

She drops her head, and I sigh in capitulation, moving to the living room, letting her enter then close the door behind her.

"What the fuck are you doing here?" My voice is as cutting as I can make it, and *I'm* not faking.

I slump down on the couch while she just stands there.

"I came for you." Her voice cracks.

I can't tell whether her distress is genuine, or if she's pretending just to soften me. I learned too late how manipulative she can be.

"We haven't spoken in almost two months. Why now?"

"I went to Amélie and Gaston's wedding last weekend. I was sure I'd see you there. I thought we could... I don't know. Reconnect. But Amélie told me you left Paris. I had to see you, talk to you."

"And say what?"

"That I miss you. So much. I miss your smile, your kindness and attention." Tears well up in her blue eyes, her chin trembling, and I look away to quell my growing pity for her pain.

"Please, don't cry."

She wipes the tears from her eyes with the sleeve of her jacket before taking it off, then sits on the couch next to me, too close. The revulsion I expected to be overwhelmed with, the rage I've grown accustomed to these past two months at the thought of her are somewhere in the pit of my stomach, but barely there. Being with her in this apartment feels strange. We haven't been here together in a very long time. Although I'm beyond angry at her, having her next to me feels familiar.

"Talk to me, please." She sounds desperate.

It changes nothing. The resentment over what she put me through weighs more than the distant impulse to comfort her.

"I've already said to you what I had to say."

"No, you yelled, you cursed, you insulted me, and I deserved it. But we never talked." She sniffles and wipes a tear. "You just packed your bags and moved out—and yelled some more whenever I tried to reach out. I never had the chance to apologize. You never gave us a chance to talk."

My mouth zips in a tight line, fury flares up, but I remain silent. There's no point yelling at her again. I've done that enough, she still doesn't get it, and we are past that point anyway.

We stay there for the longest time, her eyes on me, waiting for me to speak as I'm looking out the window.

"I thought that if I gave you time, you'd come back to me, eventually. But you left the country, so I made this grand gesture, travelled across the world for you, because..." she says in a strangled voice, "we were supposed to get married next month."

"I don't know what kind of reaction you're expecting from me," I snap, turning my seething gaze to her. "Yes, we were supposed to get married next month. The main reason we won't be is because you fucked someone else."

"I know." A tear rolls down her cheek. "I made the biggest mistake of my life, baby. I was just—"

"Don't fucking call me that!" My voice rises, disgusted by the sound of that pet name in her mouth. "And you were just what? Bored? Amnesiac? Or just too fucking horny? Do we really need to have that conversation?"

"You were never there," she cries, fat tears spilling from her swollen eyes and trailing down her face. "You were always working, you were distant, and I was lonely. And your family...you refused to understand that's why I didn't want to move back to San Francisco. They hated me, and that was always there, in your mind, over us and our wedding, like a shadow. It hurt, I felt unworthy of you, and—"

"Well congratulations, you proved them right." I sneer, and her eyes close.

Silence drags on again, only punctuated by her sniffles and muffled whimpers.

"Please, don't do this," she pleads between sobs. "Don't end this. We can talk about moving back here if you want. We can work this out. We used to be happy, remember?"

I take a deep breath and, as I observe her, the full weight of reality dawns on me. Our relationship is over, it already was long before she even cheated, and there's nothing left to recover.

Spite and anger subside. She needs to understand that this is definite.

But I take too long to answer. Pauline rests her hand on my thigh, and my stomach churns.

"Get your hand off me!"

She complies as tears smear her soaked mascara down her cheeks. "I'm sorry. I just need to be in your arms again."

"Did you ever think about what *I* needed? Just once?" My tone is cold. I pause to give her the opportunity to answer, but she doesn't, so I continue. "I gave it all up for you. My family, my friends, my job, my fucking country. I forgot myself for you. And when I pleaded to get some of that back, for fucking months, you just refused. What *I* needed was to be with someone I could trust, who would respect me, but you couldn't be that person for me. There were a thousand ways for us to work through our problems, or for you to walk out of this with your head high. You chose the only way that broke us beyond repair."

"I'm so sorry..."

"I don't give a fuck. You talk about moving back, but I already have. Without you. What I need *now* is for you to leave because you ruined everything, you ruined us, and there's no coming back, and the person *I* want to hold in my arms right now is certainly not you."

The words are out of my mouth before I realize.

A hint of surprise crosses her features. "What does that mean? Is there somebody else?" Her tone is halfway between panicked and angry.

I shouldn't have brought Eva into this, but now that I have, I might as well make it clear. "No, there isn't somebody *'else'*. There's just her."

Saying those words aloud, allowing myself to admit it, lifts almost all the weight that was crushing my chest.

Pauline drops her head to her hands for a moment then wipes the tears from her cheeks. She turns her face to me, and she seems lost. She brought this on herself though, and I won't budge.

"Get the fuck out of here, Pauline."

With a sharp sniffle and a slight nod, she stands from the couch, grabs her coat and walks to the door.

I don't bother following her.

She opens it but stops before exiting. "You got your revenge. Fine. Now if you want us to move past this, I'll be in town for a while." And she closes the door behind her.

I stay stock-still on the couch, turning her words in my head. Once again, from an external point of view, Eva seems to be nothing to me. My mother worried that she was a rebound, and Pauline assumes that she's just a revenge fuck.

Thinking of Eva in these terms constricts my chest. Eva means more to me than either rebound or revenge, but I'm still in a bad place in my life, and all I managed to do was hurt her. I never intended to, but I did. I don't want to see the same expression on her face she was wearing this morning and know that I caused it. It's time that I stop acting on impulse and get my shit together for real.

Eva is gone now and probably mad at me. I owe her some space to breathe, settle in her new apartment and step away from the drama I dragged her into. We both got lost in our attraction for each other, and maybe we made a mistake.

I spend the rest of the day cleaning, storing the few boxes Eva left behind in her haste to escape and rearranging the furniture in my room. Tidying the apartment helps me organize my chaotic thoughts.

Standing up to Pauline was a giant step in the right direction for me to heal. I don't want to be with her anymore. I never will. In hindsight, I think I hadn't truly wanted to be with her in a long time.

I find my bearings again in my apartment now that I live alone, but my mind drifts back to Eva. In the kitchen while making myself a snack, I remember the voracious look in her eyes as I prepared a sandwich for her. Passing by the couch, I see her pained expression when we shared our life stories. When I enter my bedroom, I'm submerged by all of her—her voice, her fragrance and the blissful feeling of her body under me.

I go to bed early, my head throbbing from the whirlwind of emotions. I imagine my friends spending the evening together after taking her boxes to Eva's new place. Maybe they talk about me, about Pauline coming back. They might think she's still here with me. Maybe they understand that I need some space to pull it together, at last.

* * * *

On Sunday morning, the soft rays of the rising spring sun warm my body as I run to Land's End Trail, my favorite spot in all San Francisco. I hike down the steep coastline to Mile Rock Beach and let the salty fresh air of the ocean fill my lungs. The hypnotic rhythm of Apparat's early songs fill my ears, my gaze on the horizon. The area is deserted at this hour, and I take my time to rest before running back home.

When I walk in, Luke and Colin are waiting for me on the couch with a beer in hand.

"Please, make yourselves at home," I joke.

"How are you doing?" Luke asks with a worried frown.

I take off my shoes, grab a water bottle from the fridge then join them in the living room.

"I'm fine, I guess. How did you even get in?"

Colin gestures to the key on the coffee table. "Eva gave it to me. Asked me to give it back to you."

I freeze, eyes locked on the small piece of metal, and my stomach cramps.

Colin continues. "She thought I'd probably see you before she did." His voice is soft, sympathetic. He doesn't even try to sound casual.

It might not be the real reason why she gave him the key. She's walking away for good. She might not want to see me again, at all. I just nod in response, shocked into silence, confused. Fucking terrified, also.

Luke snaps me out of my stupor. "So, where the fuck is Pauline, anyway? Back to France?" He throws me a defying look, watching me sideways as he takes a swig of his beer.

I shake my head, slouch on the armchair and let out a grunt. "No, she's staying in town for a while."

"What? Why?"

"I..." I pause, rubbing a hand over my face. "I mentioned something about Eva. Not on purpose, it just came out. Pauline assumed I used Eva to get my revenge, and that now we could move past this. Together."

Luke opens his mouth, his eyes narrowed, but I speak before him. "Which is *not* going to happen."

Colin leans forward, elbows on his knees. "That's not what you've done with Eva. Right?"

He's asking for reassurance, and I can't blame him. We only met a few weeks ago, and what he'd heard about me before wasn't pretty.

"No, of course not." I finish my water in one gulp and crush the bottle in my hand. "I can't believe how badly I fucked this up. How is she?"

"She'll be fine," Colin says. "I don't think she blames you for this. She knows you need to be alone right now."

His own opinion is barely veiled. He warned me once before that I should keep my distance before I end up hurting her. I should've listened the first time.

Better late than never, I guess.

Chapter Twenty-Five

Engage

"I thought you weren't throwing an engagement party?" Colin asks as Madison retrieves another plate of various avocado-based appetizers from her fridge.

"This is *not* an engagement party." She points her finger at him in warning. "It's just a small gathering. To celebrate our engagement. With a few friends." She grunts. "Eva, back me up here."

I laugh and snatch a cheesy avocado bite off the plate. "Don't contradict her. She's already having anxiety attacks every time we talk about planning the wedding."

"Sometimes I think we should just get married next weekend while we're in Las Vegas." Plopping down on a stool at the kitchen island, she throws a longing look at Luke.

He's chatting with his friends from work in the living room. As if he can sense her gaze on him, he turns his head and winks at her.

My heart is torn between swooning over their adorableness and breaking from the stab of jealousy.

She smiles and sits up straighter, her eyes sparkling. "Did you guys book your plane tickets?"

"All done," I say.

"Yes, and the hotel rooms, as well," Colin adds.

Madison claps her hands. "It's going to be *epic*."

The awkward glance Colin and I exchange contrasts with Madison's enthusiasm, and I squirm on my seat. An entire weekend with Adrian...in a hotel in Vegas... The mere thought causes more angst than excitement. Colin's retelling of his conversation with Adrian the next morning appeased some of my worries. I know his ex-fiancée left, and that he blames himself for hurting me. But Adrian and I still haven't spoken since I moved out of his apartment a week ago.

Madison pauses and watches us with a frown. "Okay, maybe not epic. Maybe it's just going to be awkward and weird." She shakes her head and turns to me, her face soft with concern. "I've seen you check the front door every two minutes." She raises an eyebrow. "Adrian's stuck at work, but he'll come."

I open my mouth to protest but stop myself. There's no point pretending I haven't been watching that door hoping to see him enter since the first second I arrived. Trying to imagine the possible outcomes of our next encounter is nerve-racking. I need to know Adrian and I are on good terms, at least.

"How have you been this past week?" Madison asks.

"Fine." My voice doesn't sound convincing even to my own ears. "Don't get me wrong, living with Daphne is nice. She's awesome and she manages to make me laugh."

"But?"

"I don't know. I guess it doesn't feel like home there yet. And..." I pause and swallow back the words I don't want to utter.

...and I miss Adrian.

I miss his smile, the spark in his eyes whenever we'd talk about work. I miss his natural kindness, even though it took me a while to see that side of him. And his deep velvet voice, his laugh, his amber-wood fragrance that lingered in the air after he left in the morning.

Every time I close my eyes, his hypnotic blue stare haunts me. The touch of his fingertips still burns my skin. My nights are restless, my body igniting at the thought of him, his warm lips, his tongue. My hands moving as I imagine his, uncontrollable, reaching between my legs. Lost in the memory of the sensations, my fingers playing as I remember him sliding in and out of me. But on my own, I don't even come close to what he elicited in me.

"You and Adrian, you're both so dumb." Madison snaps me out of my thoughts.

"Thanks, I'm so glad I have a comforting friend like you," I deadpan, and Colin laughs.

However, Madison seems almost upset. "Seriously, what's wrong with the two of you? Look, I don't want to meddle —"

"Too late," Colin says, still laughing.

" — but the way he looks at you..."

I shake my head in defeat. "He's a mess. He keeps hitting on me then pushing me away. What else am I supposed to do?"

She hesitates, then sighs. "I'm sorry, but I don't agree with you. You're both too stubborn and scared to admit how you feel. And you're both too dumb."

Stunned and a little lost, I turn to Colin for his opinion, his support, as usual. He offers me a small smile but remains silent, the look in his eyes almost apologetic because he doesn't agree with Madison. He's seen me too hurt too often to push me into Adrian's arms only to get hurt again. His gaze flashes to the living room. "Speak of the devil..."

My breath catches. Any words my brain had prepared as a reply to Madison evaporate when I turn around.

Adrian makes his way through the few gathered friends in a perfectly fitted charcoal-gray suit, with a burgundy tie loosened around the neck and top button of his shirt undone. The edge of the tattoo on his collarbone peeks out when he moves.

If forgetting him was already close to impossible from a distance, now seeing him, it's not even conceivable.

Madison squeezes my shoulder. She grabs the plate and exits the kitchen to join Luke as he introduces Adrian to his colleagues.

Adrian's smile is polite, warm, business-like. I'm catching a glimpse of what he must be like at work. When he walks over to Luke's college friends, his face lights up, his smile brighter. He knows them. His posture changes, he's more laid-back, and his usual assurance radiates.

"Don't drool on the table," Colin whispers in my ear as he passes behind me.

When I wipe my mouth as a reflex, he bursts out laughing.

I narrow my eyes. "Not funny." I swallow a gulp from my glass of white wine to hide my smile.

"It is, though." He grabs my hand to drag me out of the kitchen. "Come on, don't hide in there all evening."

As I walk behind Colin, Adrian notices me across the room. Our eyes lock, his face unreadable, controlled. His friends pull his attention back to the conversation, and I force myself to look away.

I settle next to the appetizer table, my back turned to Adrian to avoid ogling him.

"There you are." The familiar voice of Madison's colleague Diego brings me out of my daydreaming. "You disappeared for a while."

"I was in the kitchen, digging into Madison's private stash of white wine." I raise my glass before taking a sip.

He peers down at the greenish fruit punch in his hand and looks back at me with his nose scrunched up, lips pursed. "You mean there's decent grown-up alcohol at this party?"

I let out a laugh, relishing the unexpected lull in my ever-present tension.

Diego joins me but after a quick glance over my shoulder, his laughter dies down, and he angles his body closer to me to whisper. "Don't turn around. Madison's brother is staring at you."

"Wh—?"

"Don't turn!" He chuckles. "He's chatting with Stuart and Lee, but he's been checking you out for the past ten minutes. Do you know him?"

"Yes. It's complicated." I clutch my glass harder and fight the urge to turn around.

Diego nods. "I see. So that's why he looks so jealous."

My heart skips a beat. "What?"

Diego's smile widens, and he steps back to lean on the wall, shifting to hide from Adrian's view. "He looks at me like he's going to kick my ass any second now. Which is fair. He doesn't know me, or that my beloved husband is waiting for me at home with our six-month-old baby girl. To him, I'm just a handsome man chatting with his...what? Girlfriend?"

I flinch. "Like I said, it's complicated."

He gives me a sympathetic smile along with a nod, and we change the subject as other acquaintances join us. I struggle to stay focused on the conversation. My mind wanders back to Adrian, the hair on my neck prickling as if I can sense his intense stare on me.

I can't resist shifting sideways to glance at him. He's standing across the room, jacket taken off, sleeves rolled up to his elbows. His eyes travel back to me between each answer to his friends. He mouths a simple 'hi', his lips remaining slightly parted, a small smile dancing on his lips.

My heart races, and my mouth dries. I flee to the kitchen for a refill of wine. One look from him was all it took. I can't control myself.

I sit on a stool and pour a glass when Adrian enters, stopping on the other side of the kitchen island with his hands in his pockets. I fight the urge to wrap his loosened tie around my fist to pull him closer to me.

Some of his confidence has faded, and his eyes avert from mine when he speaks. "I wasn't sure you'd want to talk to me... How are you?"

Tired because I spend every night thinking about you, about your body on mine, your tongue licking my skin...

I hold back the words, and instead I just give a meek "Fine. And you? You seem to be having fun with your friends."

He grabs a beer in the fridge then sits two stools away from me. "Yes, I hadn't seen them in a while. And they don't know much except I spent a few years abroad, so that's nice."

Silence stretches, both of us looking down at the drinks in our hands. I sip my wine while he takes a mouthful of his beer.

Our friends chat and laugh in the background, the noise almost covered by the pounding of my heart beating too fast. My palms are sweaty, my brain is blank, unable to find what to say, how to act. I breathe in deep to regain some focus, but his heady fragrance overflows my senses. It takes all my strength not to go to him, kiss him, tear his shirt apart to feel his skin on mine.

"I was thinking..." He shoots out a bitter chuckle. "Or actually *trying* to find something fucked up to say so you'd make a snappy comeback. Anything to break this awkward silence."

He keeps his eyes on his beer, his fingertips tracing lines on the mist of condensation covering the bottle.

"I'm surprised you can't find anything," I joke.

The warm laugh rumbling in his throat and the teasing glance he throws me make my skin tingle.

But his smile fades. "There's something I want to ask. It's beyond fucked up though, so I'm worried you'll throw your drink at me instead of a snappy comment."

I angle toward him. "Now I'm curious. Ask anyway."

A knot twists my stomach. Adrian isn't joking. His knee jerks up and down so fast that it makes him tremble. He pushes his beer in a sharp move, rests his elbows on the counter and lowers his head in his hands, gripping his hair, pulling, nervous. He keeps his face hidden from me. "Who's the guy you were chatting and laughing with earlier?"

"Who, Diego?"

"Don't know the dude's name," he mumbles.

I'm stunned. "So you *are* jealous."

His stare flashes to mine, drowning in a dreadful panic. He's terrified.

My breath catches in my throat, and I get lost in the stormy blue of his eyes.

"I'm not jealous, I'm…scared, I think. I'm sorry," he says. "It's none of my business. You don't owe me anything. I just…" He diverts his gaze again, grabbing his beer to drink a mouthful.

My heart sinks. "She really broke something in you, didn't she?"

"More than I thought, apparently."

"And she wants you to get back together?" My voice is hesitant, feeble, as if the question were too hard to pronounce, because the answer could be too hard to hear.

"I won't." His stare holds mine, unwavering. "I told her that. And she can wait in town all she wants. It doesn't change a thing."

I nod and pour myself a third glass of wine to drown the lump in my throat with a big gulp.

"I'm sorry for putting you through this." His voice is a soft velvet tainted by sadness. "And…" He hesitates, peeling the label off his beer. "I know it's unfair to expect of you to wait around until I get my past in order and my nerves under control, but…"

Hope bubbles inside my stomach. "But?"

He must find some reassurance in my eyes because a smile lights up his face, and he laughs softly. "But if you could keep all the Diegos out there at a distance, just for a little while, I'd appreciate it."

His focus on me, deep and burning, sends a shiver all over my skin. I'm lost, my body overwhelmed by his presence, my brain swirling in all the contradictions I can't make sense of.

"Then what?"

Adrian reaches over to me, his strong hand envelops my wrist, his thumb caressing the inner side of my arm, and my heart falters. He watches his hand clutching me, as if unable to let go. I don't want him to.

He stands up without releasing me and pulls me to my feet. My legs are wobbly, either from the wine or Adrian's magnetism, I'm not sure.

"Then I'll make it up to you."

With his body inches from mine, he brings my palm to his chest, his heart hammering inside his ribcage. The words catch in my throat. I drown in his pleading stare.

He opens his mouth to speak, but Luke clinks a spoon on his beer bottle to grab the room's attention before throwing it back on the table.

Adrian grunts, letting go of my wrist. "Fuck." He casts his gaze down. "We better go listen to this." He tilts his head toward the living room with a smile.

I nod, struggling to come back down to earth as I follow him.

Luke stands in the middle of the room, and he takes a deep breath before speaking. "Thank you all for being here."

"Yeah, thanks for *not* inviting us to Las Vegas next weekend," Stuart jokes, and everybody laughs.

Luke's mouth turns into a repentant smile, and he shrugs. "Most of you have known for a while that we've been engaged — "

Adrian snorts, making some of his friends laugh again, and the others look puzzled. "Sorry, don't mind me." He waves at Luke, who chuckles and continues.

"So I'm not going to make a long speech about how lucky I am that I've found shelter in Madison's arms, and that I hope I'll get to stay there, and keep her safe in mine, for the rest of our lives."

My heart swells. The women around the room let out envious gasps, and Madison grins, hands clasped over her chest.

Luke smiles at her then turns away. "It's also traditionally the best man who makes a speech about the groom, but, as I haven't done it yet, I wanted to take this opportunity to officially ask, um…" He clears his throat. "The other person who offered me shelter when I needed one, who accepted me for who I am when even *I* wasn't sure who that was." Luke pauses, his gaze on Adrian who listens with a hopeful attention. "It was fucking time you came back, bro. Because I need a best man."

Everyone cheers as Adrian remains immobile, eyes wide. Without a word, he takes a swift stride and grabs Luke in a big hug, keeping him there long enough for people to stop clapping and get back to their conversations.

Daphne sneaks up on me as I observe them. "You've put on a brave face for the entire week. And I pretend I don't know you're full of shit." She raises her eyebrows, and I roll my eyes. "How do you feel now that he's in front of you?"

"He's so fucking handsome I want to cry. Or rip his clothes off." I groan in frustration. "I hate this situation."

Daphne guides me to a corner of the room where we won't be heard. "Ok, so what's the plan?"

"What plan? What do you mean?"

"You want to be with him, right?"

I take a deep breath, opening my mouth to speak, but Daphne doesn't let me say a word. "Yeah, yeah, not the right time, don't want to be collateral damage, blablabla... Bullshit."

I lift my hands and let them drop at my sides. "First Madison, and now you?"

"I never said that I agreed with you in the first place. And you're both too miserable." She shakes her head.

"Maybe we are, but..."

"But what? Can you look me in the eye and tell me that you're done? That the one night you spent with him was enough?"

"Not even close." The weight that has settled on my chest for the entire week suffocates me.

"I'm not trying to pressure you, but I hate seeing you like this, and from my *very insightful* point of view" — she winks before becoming serious again—"you're both trying to do what you think is right for the other, but you don't talk to each other. Not really. Not about what you feel. You should. See past your fears, both of you."

"He, um...he just asked me to wait for him."

"And? Are you willing to risk not being around when he's ready to date again?" She pauses and snorts. "I bet there's already a waiting list of women ready to swoop in the first chance they get. I mean look at him, for fuck's sake."

My eyes can't move away from him, studying every line in his body, his muscles stretching the fabric of his shirt as he moves, the most mesmerizing smile spreading on his face as he laughs with Luke. The electric spark lighting his eyes whenever he glances at me.

"You're right."

"*So...* What's your plan?" A devilish smile lifts one corner of her mouth.

The wheels turn in my mind, at a loss for words, for ideas, for the right way to get back into his strong arms before we both slip away from each other for good.

I don't want to rush it and ruin it. I need more time.

And it hits me. "Next weekend. In Vegas."

Chapter Twenty-Six

Under My Skin

"Vegas, baby!" Colin claps his hands, and the loud bang carries through the entire lobby of the Mirage Hotel.

Eva laughs. "Please don't get us thrown out yet."

She walks among our friends in front of me in tight jeans and a T-shirt, her ponytail rocking from side to side with each step. I force myself not to ogle her or invade her personal space by staying too close, but it's a challenge.

Since the party at Luke's, the quiet in my apartment hasn't brought any rest to my chaotic thoughts. The consistency of my daily routine hasn't brought any peace. Being away from Eva didn't dull the need to be with her.

When I asked her to wait for me, her reaction made it impossible for me to envision any future without her. She didn't say a word, but her eyes, hopeful and eager, answered for her. The attraction between us is too strong to walk away from. Sometimes I can't remember why I thought I had to.

Racking my brain, torn between finding a way to get her back and forcing myself to make good decisions, my head is still a mess. Worry creeps inside my stomach that the more time we spend apart, the easier it will be for her to move on.

At the hotel reception, my friends and I go through check-in before we each settle into our rooms. Every minute spent away from Eva is more painful than the previous one.

We all meet at the High Card Café. Luke orders a magnum of champagne for us to toast to their engagement. The group is bubbling with excitement, and I allow myself to be lifted by the vibe, enjoying their energy. The heavy guilt on my chest lessens as I watch Eva, a magnificent smile spreading on her luminous face when she looks at me.

To prevent being hammered in the middle of the day, we temper the effect of the alcohol with tacos and mini burgers. The ladies plan their afternoon at the hotel spa for an *"aromatherapy desert stone massage"*, whatever the fuck that is. Luke watches me with the biggest grin on his face. I know that look, roguish and defiant.

I hate that look.

"Okay, tell me what fucked up idea you have in mind."

He smiles wider. "You didn't see it?"

"See what? Come on, spit it out."

He reaches inside his back pocket and hands me a flyer.

Sixth annual Nevada Ink Fest, this year at the Mirage.

I let out a grunt. "A tattoo convention."

If I hadn't lost that bet to Luke, I'd be thrilled about it. I'd rather spend two days among tattoo artists than casino slot machines. However, this time, it means getting a pink heart on my ass.

"I swear I didn't know before we got here." Luke can't wipe that triumphant smile from his face, and Colin slaps me on the back.

"Fuck," I mumble.

Eva giggles next to me, her eyes sparkling with amusement mixed up with something else, something naughtier. My throat dries. I haven't seen that sparkle in her eyes in a while. I thought I'd never see it again.

We down our second glass of champagne amid growing excitement and laughter. As soon as the ladies leave for their massage, Luke, Colin and I skip the casino and head straight to the tattoo convention. Humiliating me can't wait, it seems.

We spend almost an hour talking to several artists as they explain the origins of their particular style. My pink heart almost forgotten, I gather a few ideas for my next big piece. The buzzing sound of the tattoo machines surrounding us makes my skin itch. Getting tattooed is like a drug—as soon as one is finished, there needs to be a next one.

The anticipation is almost enough to erase from my mind the idea of Eva getting her massage, half naked, her skin glistening with oil.

Luke pulls me out of my thoughts. "Come on, man. It's time."

He's beaming, and I can't blame him for being thrilled. I was too, when the situation was reversed.

Colin and Luke follow me back to the artist I've chosen and let me explain what I want.

"I'd like a little pink heart on my left butt cheek." I keep my tone as serious as I can manage.

"You lost a bet, didn't you?" he asks with sympathy.

I nod, and he offers me his hand to shake. "My name's Jax."

He's old enough to be my father, tall and lean, full rockabilly style with thick blue jeans, white T-shirt and suspenders, hair slicked back and a perfectly trimmed gray beard. Apart from his face, every inch of visible skin is covered with tattoos.

He points to my forearm. "I see you already have one, so you know the drill. And this is a convention, so the goal is for people to see what we do."

"Which means no privacy whatsoever." I sigh in defeat, ignoring Luke and Colin chuckling behind me.

Jax shrugs with a smile and turns to prepare the sterilized equipment. We step inside the booth, Luke and Colin crammed into one corner.

People passing by slow down to watch. I unbutton my jeans with unease at first, until Luke's teasing whistles remind me that this moment is meant to be fun. That I never used to be so insecure before.

Taking a deep breath, I force my brain to silence this debilitating self-doubt and let myself be carried by my friends' excitement. I play along, pushing my pants down a few inches, and earn appreciative glances from bystanders. Colin joins in the whistles as I do my best impression of *Magic Mike*, sliding my pants all the way down with a suggestive hip thrust, turning my ass to the few people who have stopped by for the show. Luke, Colin and even Jax burst out laughing.

I climb on the chair and lie on my stomach, lowering my boxers, my ass bare for everyone to see.

Jax pulls the tray with the needles and ink closer to him. "Do you want something specific, or I can just let my imagination take the lead?"

Hesitating for a second, an idea pops in my head, and it's too tempting to pass. "I *do* want something specific." I turn to Luke with a grin. "I want the exact same one as my best friend here."

Colin claps once and lets out his boisterous laugh as Luke jumps from his seat.

"Oh, come on, man, that's unfair."

"If I have to be bare-ass in public, so do you. It wasn't part of the original deal."

His mouth opens and closes, his eyes threatening me with revenge for this, yet his lips are unable to contain his amusement. "Are you sure you want us to have the exact same tattoo on our asses?" he asks, eyebrow raised.

I think it over before answering. "To be honest, I do."

After what Luke and I have been through, what our friendship has survived, nothing could seal this journey better than matching tattoos. Although a more masculine design would've been nice.

Luke just smiles and shakes his head as he pulls his pants down.

"Fuck," Jax mumbles. "Why does this never happen with hot chicks?"

Colin snorts. "Women are way smarter than this."

We all nod in silence, and my mind drifts back to Eva, wondering what she'll think, if she ever gets to see it.

"I can take a picture if you want to put your pants back on," Jax says.

"Fuck no," Colin yells. "He stays bare-ass. Let them enjoy the show." He points to the people approaching the stand with smiles on their faces.

Jax shrugs again and brings the needle onto my skin.

Every muscle in my body contracts under the unexpected sting. "Motherfucking shit!"

"Yeah, surprisingly enough, that's one of the most sensitive parts of the body."

More people gather around us and laugh at the situation before moving along. Lounging on a chair in the corner of the booth, Colin chuckles each time I wince from the pain and jokes about Luke who stands there, his ass showing as he clutches the front of his boxers to keep his dick hidden.

"Dude, you're laughing, but I'm sure you're just jealous of that amazing piece of art," Luke teases.

Colin sobers up and hesitates. "Honestly? Maybe a little bit."

I turn to Colin, alone in his corner, watching us but not participating. "You feel left out or some shit?"

For the first time since we met, I witness another side of him, less exuberant than his rowdy laugh and crude humor, less assertive than his professional expertise. It hadn't occurred to me before, yet at this moment, I realize that Colin may be Eva's only family, but she's also his. He has no one else outside of our group of friends.

Colin hesitates again, and Luke turns to me. "He has to get that tattoo, right?"

Jax lifts the needle from my skin for a second to let out a laugh. "Seriously, are you guys drunk?"

Colin shakes his head. "I'm not doing it. One of us has to be the adult here."

Luke snorts. "What's the fun in that?"

"Okay, I'm done," Jax says, straightening on his seat.

Luke sighs in relief and slides his pants back up. I stand from the chair in an awkward maneuver, holding the front of my boxers as Luke did a minute ago, keeping my ass bare. Jax holds a mirror for me to see his work. A chubby, hot pink heart on the upper side of my left cheek. For the rest of my life. We really are morons, but I love it.

Jax covers the tattoo with a thick layer of Vaseline and gauze. I put my jeans on and turn to Colin.

"You're doing it."

"Like we're the three fucking Stooges?" He laughs.

Luke taps him on the shoulder. "Let's say the three Musketeers. It has more panache."

"Come on, you know you want it," I say.

"I already had one dumb tattoo covered, and you want me to do this?" Colin pretends to argue, but we can tell he's already caving.

"This one, you're choosing to do it, at least," Luke says.

Colin pauses, deliberating, and he smiles. "All right, I'll fucking do it. But I'm sure it's only because you want to see my ass."

Luke and I high five each other. I haven't had this much fun in a long time, haven't felt so carefree.

Jax laughs too as he prepares the equipment. At least it makes up for having to stare at our asses for half an hour.

People watch us and laugh as Colin gets his skin inked, maybe thinking we're stupid. We must look like three irresponsible boys, making rash and dumb decisions without thinking twice. Nobody would guess that the men getting the same pink heart tattoo on their asses are in fact a lawyer, an architect and an investment banker.

Once it's finished, we apologize to Jax for taking so much of his time. After all, most of the artists come here to show off their work and their skills. Yet he assures us that he's had the most fun in a long time at that kind of event, and he'll be telling this story to a bunch of his friends tonight.

We make our way back to Luke's room where we agreed we'd meet, with shit-eating grins on our faces. When we enter, Eva, Madison and Daphne are already here, all dolled up.

As Luke runs to Madison to kiss her more passionately than I care to witness, I breathe out a low "*fuck*", my body frozen in place but my blood boiling at the sight of Eva leaning on the small corner table. She's wearing the tightest dress she could possibly fit into, held by only two thin straps over her shoulders, and the hem reaching the tops of her thighs. If that wasn't enough to awaken the primal need to rip it off her body, the dress is red. Fucking candy-apple red. I want to devour her.

The dark makeup on her eyes accentuates her green stare. Her long hair falls down her back, straight and shiny, and I ache to wrap it around my fist. Her black stilettos are clasped with a thin strap around her ankles. And those fucking legs — slender, silky.

My gaze travels up and down her body several times, marveling at every inch of her, and when I reach her face, Eva watches me with a victorious expression. If this is a trap to capture my attention, I'll walk into it without protest.

Before I can force my body into motion, Daphne speaks. "Close your mouths, boys. We know we look hot." She winks at Colin, and he bursts out laughing.

Madison extracts herself from Luke's grip. "So, Adrian, did you get that pink heart on your ass?"

"I did." I nod with a proud smile.

"We did," Colin says in the same tone.

A moment of silence lingers between us.

Madison frowns. "What?"

"All three of you got the same tattoo?" Daphne asks, eyes wide.

Luke holds up his hand. "I already had mine. But yes, they did."

Colin and I tap each other on the back in a semi-hug, still amped up on the fun we'd had.

Madison, Daphne and Eva exchange a disbelieving look before laughing.

"But you didn't lose any bet," Eva says.

"I know, but... It was a beautiful bonding moment," Colin says with an overly soft voice, one hand on his heart. "Don't ruin the bromance."

Daphne snorts. "I'm not often surprised by men's stupidity anymore. Yet, you amaze me."

Colin chuckles and straightens his back. "I'll take that as a compliment. Thank you."

He blows her a fake kiss as she shakes her head, and we all laugh louder.

We discuss our plans for tonight, which include winning a jackpot, getting dinner, partying all night in a club, and drinking more champagne. Not necessarily in that order. I struggle to keep my eyes off Eva leaning on the table in that dress that rises so high I could see her pussy if she just spread her legs a little.

As we move to leave the room, Eva steps closer to me, her body brushing against mine, and she whispers. "So again, you have a hidden tattoo that I haven't seen..." She tilts her head to the side, eyes lustful. "...yet."

My breath hitches, heart racing. She walks out of the room, glancing at me over her shoulder, and it takes me a few seconds to move.

The last time we saw each other, she seemed determined to stay away from my fucked-up relationship issues, at least for a little while. One week later, she's wearing that red 'fuck-me' dress, no doubt for my benefit, and flirts with me. *What did I miss?*

We make our way to the casino, and spend a few hours alternating between roulette, craps and slot machines. We win some money that we lose right afterwards, but we're having fun regardless.

I focus on keeping my instincts in check as Eva moves closer to me from time to time. Too close and too often for it to be a coincidence. Her fragrance bewitching me with every hair flip, her hand on my arm whenever she walks past me, her ass brushing against my cock and the way she whispers "*sorry*" with batting eyelashes, as if she didn't do it on purpose.

The game she decided to play with me tonight drives me crazy. My top five fantasies now feature fucking Eva senseless on a poker table in the middle of a crowded room.

For once, I don't care what it means, what her reasons are or what the consequences would be. Whenever she looks at me with a naughty smile, it takes all my strength not to grab her and slide my hands under her dress.

That last shred of self-control won't hold all night.

Chapter Twenty-Seven

Wild Cards

Madison wanders around the casino floor, hanging on Luke's arm. They haven't dropped each other's hand since we left the hotel room, exchanging dreamy glances every few minutes.

Unlike them, the glances I throw Adrian are more suggestive than sweet. He's as handsome as usual in his dark jeans, the top two buttons of his navy-blue shirt undone, sleeves rolled up to mid-forearm. I want his hands on me, and I want to leave no doubt in his mind about it.

Judging by his hungry eyes every time I brush against him, my choice of dress has the desired effect. Step one of the plan to find our way back to each other is in place — keep his attention on me.

Adrian's deep blue gaze hasn't left my thoughts this past week. His heartbeat under my palm still resonates through my body, just like his pleading voice, asking me to wait for him. How could I refuse? Why would I even want to refuse?

As the days pass, the reasons behind my determination to stay away from him, from his powerful arms, his heady fragrance and soothing warmth all fizzle out. They only made me miserable. Too stubborn, I couldn't admit that the 'right decisions' aren't always the best ones. Or perhaps I was too scared to get hurt.

But I miss Adrian. I have since the first minute I stepped out of his apartment, and the hollowness hasn't died down.

"I want to play Blackjack," Madison says. "Who's in?"

Colin shoots me a warning look. "Now, *you* don't get us thrown out."

All eyes turn to me.

"What's that about?" Madison asks.

Colin answers before I have a chance to. "Eva got us kicked out of the Flamingo, a few years ago."

Daphne smiles wide, no doubt eager for a racy story. "What did you do?"

"I got caught counting cards," I whisper with a tinge of pride.

Adrian's eyes light up with awe. "You can count cards? That's not easy to do. You really have a thing with numbers."

His admiration is empowering and disarming at the same time. I love how much he values my intellectual capabilities, yet I'm helpless, speechless under his intense stare.

I shrug. "Too bad it didn't get me anywhere."

"It could have," Colin says. "We were up thirty thousand dollars when they noticed what she was doing."

"Very impressive." Adrian's eyes never leave me. "I'd love to see you in action."

Before I can find the perfect sexual innuendo to throw back at him after that opening, Madison points a finger at me, shaking her head like a Grinch. "No. Nobody's getting thrown out tonight."

"Right." I chuckle. "Let's stick to craps, then."

We gather around a table, Madison still huddled against Luke, Colin and Daphne slipping in between other players. I slither close to Adrian, my back rubbing against his front for a second, and he blows out a labored breath. *Desired effect achieved again.*

At the table, the current shooter, a skinny man with a dark mustache on his red face, hands them to Daphne as soon as he sees her. "Wow, there's my lucky charm!" He slurs his words.

She indeed looks like an Irish fairy with her wavy red hair, pale skin and dark green dress. Yet his lewd stare on her is disgusting, and his breath reeks of whiskey even from a few feet.

"No, I'm not." Daphne's tone is cold.

The man doesn't take the hint. "Come on, Lucky Charm, blow on the dice."

"Blow yourself!" Daphne says, her tone emphasizing the double entendre of her phrase.

"You're not nice, for such a pretty creature."

The entire table is silent. Adrian stiffens next to me, and Colin fidgets next to Luke.

She opens her mouth, but the dealer speaks first. "Sir, I'm going to ask you to either throw the dice or move away from the table, please."

The man doesn't look at him when he answers. "Yeah, yeah, just a second."

"Just throw the damn dice." Daphne takes a step backward, her stance less confident, and I've had to face unrelenting men often enough to recognize the sudden worry in her expression.

"Come on, be nice with me. You're my lucky charm." The man's hand reaches for her waist.

In a split second, Colin gets around Daphne and slides his imposing body between them, shielding her from the man. "No, she's not." His tone is low, rough, menacing.

But it doesn't deter the drunk. He pushes his fist against Colin's massive chest, but Colin doesn't move even an inch.

"Wow, strong dude." A manic laugh erupts from his stinky mouth.

The dealer warns again. "Sir, please, you ha—"

"All right, I'll throw the goddamn dice!"

The man shifts his attention back to the table, and we all relax. Colin turns to Daphne, who offers him a sweet smile.

"Thank you. Now, put your balls back in your pants and let's play." She winks, making him laugh.

Adrian pushes his body closer behind me. His warm hand slips into mine and squeezes once as he leaves a kiss on the top of my head, lingering there for a moment with his nose in my hair. My body melts against him and my heart falters, overwhelmed by his protective affection. He's here, by my side, if any drunken man ever bothered me. I squeeze back before he releases my hand and steps away, and I miss the contact.

Several players place their bets. The drunk man throws the dice, and he loses. "See that?" he yells at

Daphne. "It's your fault. You should've blown on my dice."

He staggers to the side, lunges forward and grabs Daphne's arm. She seizes a half-full cocktail glass left on the edge of the table and throws it in his face.

"Don't touch me!" She snatches her arm from his grip as his nostrils flare.

We all dash toward her. I'm next to Daphne as Colin steps in as a shield again. The man grips Colin's shirt, unaware that a simple slap from Colin would be enough to knock him out.

The dealer nods as an obvious signal to security, and two men dressed in black suits rush to the table.

A middle-aged woman with an asymmetrical bob cut and cargo shorts runs in our direction. "What did you do to my husband?" she screeches, her wide eyes shooting daggers at Daphne.

She bypasses Colin and charges at us, all claws out. Before any of us can react, she's clutching Daphne's hair, and the two pints of beer she had in hand spill on my breasts, the sticky liquid flowing down my dress. I'm soaked.

Adrian, Luke and Madison encircle Daphne and me. One security guard drags the woman backward as she exchanges a desperate look with her husband blocked by the other guard. She points toward Daphne. "She stole my chips! She stole my chips!"

"What?" Daphne yells.

The woman doesn't stop shrieking. "She stole my chips. All of the chips I had in my purse. She stole them. That's why I was grabbing her."

"Bullshit!" Daphne yells again as the two guards turn to her with questioning looks.

"That's not what happened." Adrian's voice rises, but Colin shakes his head, giving him a pointed look, his lips sealed shut.

Colin knows it's not a good idea to argue with Security on a casino floor.

"Please follow us, now," one guard says.

Daphne doesn't calm down, ignoring Madison's soothing hand on her shoulder or Colin's warning gaze. "This is insane. For what?"

"We're going to review the camera footage. You'll stay with us until the police arrive, if deemed necessary."

"You can't be fucking serious."

Colin steps in front of her. "They are, Daphne. Just..." He gives a head tilt, urging her to follow. "I'm staying with you."

"That's up to us to decide, sir," the guard says, sticking out his chest.

Colin turns around, takes a silent stride, and stretches out his towering frame an inch from the guard. "I'm her lawyer."

The guard seems to deliberate for a beat. "Okay, let's go." He nods to the dealer, who has already resumed the bets at the table, and leads the woman away, her husband following.

"We'll meet up later," Colin says. "We'll keep you posted, but don't worry. Worst case scenario, we find another hotel for tonight."

Daphne gives a quick hug to Madison. "I'm so sorry."

"Not your fault." Madison blows Daphne a kiss as she's guided away by the second guard.

On our way to the lobby for some calm, Luke holds Madison close to him and whispers in her ear. Adrian walks next to me, silent but throwing several glances at me.

When we're isolated in a quiet corner, Luke sighs. "I'm sure Colin can handle this situation easily. They should be back soon."

"Unless Daphne doesn't stop yelling at them." Madison's voice sounds off, distant.

Adrian tilts his head to one side, bending his knees a little to be level with her. "Are you okay, Maddie? You look a little shaken." His tone is warm as an endearing softness emanates from his big-brother voice. He seems so very different from the man with anger issues I saw the first days.

Madison lets out a shaky breath, still hanging on to Luke's arm. "I'm fine. Maybe a little dizzy. I think I need to eat."

"Okay." Adrian nods, and his soft gaze lands on me. "But first, you want to change, I imagine."

His eyes travel down my sticky legs and back to the beer-soaked dress clinging to my body like a second skin. When his gaze reaches my eyes, the lust I expected to see in them isn't there, only thoughtfulness. "Are *you* okay?"

I swallow hard, drowning in the kindness in his eyes, fighting the urge to bury myself against his chest. "I'll be fine after a shower and a change of clothes," I lie. I'll only be fine when I'm in his arms again.

Madison pulls away from Luke. "I'll go with you. You guys find a table in one of the restaurants. Text us, and we'll meet you there." She kisses Luke one more time and walks toward the elevator.

I throw Adrian a smile over my shoulder and follow Madison.

After a few seconds, Adrian calls out. "Eva? Wait a sec." He takes a few strides to meet me, stopping only an inch away. "In this dress," he whispers low enough that neither Luke nor Madison will hear him, "you looked fucking breathtaking tonight." He leans in, his mouth near my ear. "*T'es tellement excitante.*" The soft sounds drip from his tongue like honey.

My breath catches, heart skipping a beat, heat coursing through me and settling between my legs.

Before I can reply or grab his shirt to tear it apart, Adrian steps back, a devilish grin spreading on his face. "Oh, you thought you were the only one who could play this game?" He winks and turns on his heels to join Luke, leaving me out of breath.

I watch him walk away, torn between annoyance and arousal. That smug, handsome, irresistible asshole.

Madison clears her throat. "The elevator's here..."

"Yeah, right. Sorry." I rush to her right before the doors close.

Madison giggles but doesn't say a word.

"What?"

"You're cute. You and Adrian. You're cute together."

The elevator chimes, the doors open and we step into the hallway of the eighteenth floor.

"I'm not sure 'cute' is the best choice of word to describe our relationship," I joke.

"You are, though. In those rare moments when you're not bickering or being stubborn." She chuckles again. "Sometimes there's just the two of you, and you don't even notice us anymore. That's cute."

"Luke and you do that sometimes. Like the rest of the world doesn't exist."

She nods, one eyebrow cocked. "Yes. Exactly. Like Luke and me."

A wave of emotion washes over me at the realization. I've been too scared to let my barriers down. I kept retreating at each complication, convincing myself that it was for the best. But it was only fear of admitting that my feelings for Adrian were already so much more than what I allowed myself to see.

"I'm falling in love with him," I mumble, almost to myself.

Madison lets out a despairing groan. "Oh my God, you're so slow."

She bursts out laughing, and I join her as we make our way down the long corridor.

"I hope you're not too disappointed this weekend wasn't flawless," I say.

Madison shrugs. "It's just a minor hiccup. Daphne and Colin will be back with us in no time."

"There're security cameras everywhere. It can't be that hard to prove she didn't steal anything."

I search inside my clutch purse for the keycard as we approach my room. Madison lags one step behind, and when I turn around, she stands with her eyes unfocused, lips sealed, pale as if all the blood has drained from her face.

"Are you all right, Madison?"

She jolts forward and vomits, the contents of her stomach spilling between us on the beige carpet, and spatters landing on my legs.

I freeze in shock, disgust and fear of throwing up as well, forcing my brain to ignore the acid smell spreading around us.

Madison lifts her teary eyes to me, her chin trembling. "Shit, I'm sorry, Eva." She wipes her mouth with the back of her hand.

"It's okay. It's okay." I try to keep my voice calm but fail. "What the fuck just happened? Are you okay?"

"I don't know." Her voice comes out hoarse. "I was fine, then…I wasn't."

I help her sit and lean against the wall, gritting my teeth hard as tiny pieces of whatever she ate today slide down my legs when I move.

As I send a quick *911* text to Luke, Madison pulls a pack of tissues from her purse and hands me one, using another to wipe her face.

"I can't clean your vomit from my legs," I say, leaning on the wall with her at my feet but not daring to look down. "I swear I'm going to throw up."

"Please don't."

I keep my gaze forward, breathing from my mouth to avoid being submerged by the stench. "There's a potted tree." I laugh softly, pointing to the opposite corner of the hallway. "There's a tree *right there*, and you threw up all over the fucking carpet."

"I'm sorry. I haven't even been drinking that much. Probably ate something bad."

"Are you feeling better?"

"Not really. I'm tired."

The elevator chimes at the end of the hallway. Luke and Adrian dart toward us and pause a few feet away, taking in the scene in front of them.

"What happened?" Luke asks.

"I threw up," Madison says in a weak voice.

Luke rushes to her side, crouching to pull her against his chest.

Adrian remains at a safe distance, hand covering his mouth and nose, and he retrieves his phone from his back pocket.

"I'm calling Reception." He offers me a sympathetic smile and walks further away.

With both hands on her waist, Luke helps Madison to her feet. "You should go lie down, love. At least until we hear from Daphne and Colin."

Madison nods. "I think I need to eat. Can we order room service?"

"Of course." Luke plants a tender kiss on her forehead.

Adrian struts back to us. "They're sending someone up to clean."

"I'm taking Madison to our room," Luke says. "Let me know if you hear from Colin."

Adrian nods, and Madison stretches out her hand to squeeze mine. "I'm sorry, Eva."

"It's okay. Take care of yourself."

Adrian and I watch them leave in silence until they're out of view.

"Which one was your room?" he asks, scanning the succession of doors on the long corridor.

"One-eight-double-zero-four." I motion toward the nearest one.

He lets out a small laugh. "You were *so close*."

I push myself off the wall, the skin of my legs prickling under the drying mixture of beer and bile. Adrian follows as I pull out the keycard from my clutch and open the door. His body is close behind me, and the air between us becomes heavy, electric.

The cards we've been dealt tonight have wiped out the rest of the group. There's only the two of us left. Alone.

Chapter Twenty-Eight

What Happens in Vegas

After a much-needed shower, I exit the bathroom in pajama shorts and a V-neck T-shirt. Adrian is slouched on a chair, focused on his phone. The bedside lamps cast a dim light. The bright signs of the Strip casinos flicker through the window, golden shadows dancing on his square jawline.

He looks up and smiles. "Feeling better?"

"I feel clean," I say, drying my hair with a towel. "Which is a sensation I never thought I'd enjoy so much."

His gaze travels down my body, and he gestures to what I'm wearing. "I take it we're not going back downstairs." Contentment seeps through his voice, mixed with a trace of hopefulness.

"I'll get dressed when we hear from Daphne and Colin." I throw the towel on a chair and sit cross-legged on the bed. "But I don't think Madison's going to be up for partying, tonight. Or the next few months," I joke.

"What do you mean?" He tosses his phone on the small desk.

I hesitate. "I think Madison might be pregnant."

Adrian's eyes open wide, eyebrows shooting up, not blinking. For a long moment.

Madison and Luke's relationship was a secret to him until a few weeks ago. That must be quite a shock.

I snap my fingers in front of his face. "Adrian?"

He inhales sharply as he comes out of his stupor. "Maddie...my little baby sister...pregnant?"

"Could be." I shrug. "She's been tired lately, and she just threw up all over my shoes."

"Fuck." He bends forward to rest his elbows on his knees, fists gripping his hair.

"Wouldn't you be happy to be an uncle?"

Images of Adrian cradling a baby assail my mind, my insides stir, and I shake my head to chase out the thought. *Damn treacherous hormones.*

"An uncle..." He looks at me, a small smile appearing. "Of course, I'd be happy. But..." He pauses. "I also feel stupid."

"Why stupid?"

"Because I would've missed all of that, if I hadn't come back."

"You're here now. That's all that matters."

He nods and watches me, his eyes boring into mine, blazing. "I'm here. In this room, alone with you. Should I leave?"

"No," I answer too quickly, and he laughs.

The air grows thick between us. His gaze never leaves me, and my skin prickles, aching for his touch. I swallow hard and refrain from walking to him to straddle his lap.

He lounges back in his chair, and a teasing glint flashes in his stare. "Why did you wear *that* dress, tonight?" His voice is a low rumble.

Heat creeps up my neck, and I can't help the smug smile lifting the corner of my mouth.

He chuckles. "I think it's safe to assume it was for my benefit." His smile fades a little. "Why, Eva? Why are you doing this?"

My chest constricts. His question stuns me, and uncertainty overcomes me. Did I push too hard, too fast? Perhaps I only set myself up for failure again.

"Because I was…" I ponder my words. "I was worried that, with time, some other woman might catch your attention." I keep my focus on him, but doubt drips from my voice. "I wanted you to see *me*."

In a swift move, Adrian stands from his chair and kneels on the bed next to me. He tucks a loose strand of my hair behind my ear, his thumb caressing my jaw. "You're the only one I see," he whispers, then lets out a small laugh. "Don't get me wrong, that dress was sexy as hell." His fingers trail down my damp hair. He leans in, his fragrance intoxicating me. His lips grazing my cheek set my skin on fire. "All I wanted was to tear it off your body. With my teeth."

He captures my earlobe in his mouth and bites. My head lolls back. I grasp his shirt to pull his body to me.

His phone chiming startles us, bursting the steamy bubble surrounding us.

I sigh, and Adrian grunts. "It's probably Luke."

He stands, grabs his phone and reads the message aloud. "Madison's out. Nothing too bad, but we're staying in. Sorry, party without us. Talk to you tomorrow." He throws his phone back on the desk and smiles. "Well, that settles it."

"No news from Colin?"

"Nothing. I'm not sure if we should wait for them. Let's get something to eat." He picks up the room service menu and hands it to me.

"If you want to." Once again, a slight hesitation veils my words, a sudden worry that he might want to leave, think it through, take more time. I flirted with him all evening, yet I didn't anticipate this remainder of debilitating fear of being unwanted.

As I scan the menu and call Reception with our orders, Adrian watches me, silent, his face unreadable. I lounge on the bed, resting against the headboard, and he kicks off his shoes, scooches up, and sits next to me.

"Eva, I need to say something... I'm tired of pretending that this situation makes sense, or that I'm fine without you." His soft velvet voice warms my entire being.

Adrian lets his barriers down, one after the other, and I still hide behind my wall. Words have been trapped in my brain for weeks, feelings I didn't recognize at first, worries I didn't realize.

I take a deep breath before speaking. "You came back from France, and *I* paid the price of your anger, of your need to be alone." He opens his mouth, but I hold up a hand. "Please, let me finish. We flirted, and *I* got hurt, because your head was a mess." I swallow the emotions washing over me and keep my tone gentle not to sound reproachful. "We spent the most amazing night together, and again, I got hurt. Rushed out of your place before your ex arrived, as if I didn't matter much... Not as much as her." My voice cracks under the remnants of the sadness that crushed me that day.

Adrian's face falls, and he pulls at his hair. "I'm so sorry."

"I'm not asking for an apology. I just need you to understand what that felt like."

"I do." He shifts to sit on his knees. "It's why I thought I should stay away, to avoid hurting you. The more I try to make it better, the worse it gets. Things were so fucked up from the start. It's like I can't get it right with you, no matter how much I want it."

He reaches over to hold my hand. Our fingers intertwine, the warmth of his palm crawling up my arm, and he continues. "We kept fighting, and you annoyed the fuck out of me." He throws me a teasing wink, making me laugh. "All of a sudden, we're almost banging in my parents' bathroom. It happened so fast, I couldn't make sense of it. I didn't trust my own decisions near you." The candor and kindness in his eyes disarm me. "That night with you was perfect, but I still let you walk out of my apartment like a fucking moron. And you seemed more than okay to keep your distance." His gaze follows his thumb tracing circles on my wrist.

The vulnerability in his voice echoes mine. "I've learned not to hold on to people who don't want to be with me. It hurts too much."

His head snaps up. He angles closer, towers over me, cradling my neck and lifting my chin up with his thumb. "None of the fucked-up decisions I made had anything to do with not wanting to be with you. If anything, I thought it was too greedy of me to want you that much." His deep voice wraps around me.

My heart falters, and the last shred of reluctance I had vanishes. My fingers hooking underneath the collar of his shirt, I pull myself straighter, closer to him. "I want to be with you, too."

He blows out a sharp breath, a smile dancing on his lips. "Are we done waiting?"

"Did it do us any good each time we put the brakes on?" I ask in a murmur, unable to focus on anything other than the bright spark of hope in his eyes.

"It didn't."

My lashes flutter close, and a knock on the door startles us.

"No fucking way!" Adrian shoots a death glare at the door as I fall back on the pillows. "Can't we catch a break, for fuck's sake?"

"R...um...Room service," a man stammers from the hallway.

I laugh at the absurdity of the situation. This has happened to us too many times.

Adrian shakes his head. "Can't fucking believe this."

He climbs over me and pauses, his knees on either side of my legs, arms next to my face. He lowers himself, slowly, the feral spark in his eyes igniting every cell in me and stops right before our bodies touch.

His parted lips graze mine. "The next time I start kissing you, the fucking building can burn down, I promise I won't stop." He pushes himself up and stands from the bed with a grunt.

The frustration he leaves me in is unbearable. I barely resist burying my face in a pillow to scream.

Instead, I watch him walk to the door with an enthralling swagger and open it to a babbling young man.

"I'm sorry for the interrup...I mean...the disturbance, sir."

Adrian pulls the food cart inside. "It's fine. I apologize for yelling." He retrieves his room keycard from his back pocket. "Can you charge to this room instead?"

"Of course, sir." The waiter writes down the number, accepts with a smile the folded bill Adrian offers him and leaves.

"You didn't have to do that." I bend over to bring the cart closer to bed to use as a table.

"Twenty dollars isn't much, considering how I yelled at the poor kid."

I arch an eyebrow at him. "I meant paying for the food."

He throws a french fry in his mouth and smiles. "I know."

There is no arrogance in his demeanor, no shade of superiority even though he probably earns around three times my salary. No matter our different career achievements, he never treats me as less than him.

He settles on the bed facing me, and his turkey club sandwich is devoured in two or three bites while I nibble mine.

My phone buzzing on the nightstand breaks the easy silence between us.

I check the screen. "It's Colin."

"He has better timing than the others." He winks at me, licking the mustard from his thumb.

I chuckle before picking up. "Colin, are you guys okay? What happened? Where are you?"

"We got kicked from the hotel."

"What? Seriously?"

"They found nothing on the security footage, obviously, so they let Daphne go. But they wanted to act tough, so they kicked us out for good measure."

"That sucks," I say as Adrian watches me with a worried frown. "What about your bags?"

"They escorted us to our rooms to pick them up. We couldn't even stop by to talk to you." Colin sighs on the other end of the line. "Don't worry, we're trying another hotel, we'll see. There're enough around. I'll keep you posted, but I guess we're calling it a night, anyway?"

"Sure, find somewhere to sleep, and we'll meet in the morning."

"I got Luke's text about Madison. Where are you?"

"We didn't feel like staying downstairs without you. We're in my room," I say without thinking.

There's a pause on the phone, and Adrian's eyes widen in front of me.

Colin lets out a small laugh. "We?"

"Um…yes. Adrian and I… We were waiting to hear from you." I force out the most casual tone I can muster.

Not that I ever keep secrets from Colin, but I also didn't intend to let it slip so carelessly. Adrian's presence in my room feels natural enough that mentioning it seems obvious.

A bright grin spreads on Adrian's face. Laughing silently, he mouths, "Busted."

Colin chuckles again. "Goodnight, then."

"To you and Daphne as well, then," I deadpan and hang up on his guffaw.

I toss my phone on the nightstand. "So much for privacy."

Adrian laughs. "Is there any in our group? Ever?"

I nod. "True."

"I heard bits and pieces of what he said. At least they didn't call the cops. It could've been worse."

He stands and pushes the food cart against the wall. When he turns back, he opens his mouth and closes it, shoves his hands in his pockets, and sighs. "Can I ask you something personal?"

My curiosity is piqued, and I perk up on the bed. "Of course. I reserve the right not to answer, though."

"Fair enough." He smiles. "Have you ever had sex with Colin? I promise I'm not being a jealous asshole again. It's just curiosity." His tone is caring, confident, nothing compared to a week ago when he asked about Diego. As if he doesn't need me to reassure him anymore.

"No, I never have," I say with a smile.

"Not even once, after a drunken frat party in college?"

"Not even then. Although, there were lots of drunken frat parties," I joke. "It just never happened. Neither of us ever wanted to. I imagine our relationship would be much different now if we had gone down that road."

Adrian nods and steps backward to sit on the edge of the desk, but he jolts up with a grimace.

"Shit, the tattoo." He presses a palm to his ass.

The chaotic evening's events had erased it from my mind, but the thought of Adrian pulling his pants down to let me look awakens a wild fever in me.

His dark blue stare burning with a sudden desire, he steps forward. "The one you haven't seen *yet*."

"Show me." My voice comes out raspy.

I stand, inches from his tall frame. My blood boils as he unbuttons his jeans without taking his gaze off me. He turns around, legs spread just enough to block his pants at his thighs.

Before I can lift his shirt, he tugs it over his head and discards it on the chair.

My breathing grows labored. My hands itch to touch him.

He reaches behind his back, fingers hooking in his boxers to pull the fabric away from his skin and down, exposing the cloth pad taped to his firm ass. With the waistband stuck underneath the curve of his ass, his hands slide to the front of his boxers to hold the fabric over his cock.

Adrian peeks at me over his shoulder, waiting, the look in his eyes inviting me to remove the rest.

Nerves prickling, I tear the gauze with care. When the cloth is peeled off, I can't hold back a giggle at the sight of the plump heart gracing his cheek.

"It's cute, isn't it?" he asks with a teasing smile.

"Very cute." My finger grazes the swollen skin around the design. "Does it hurt?"

"It's a little tender." With one hand still on his cock, the other pulls a sample-sized tube from the front pocket of his jeans. "I need to put ointment on it before it gets too dry."

"Do you need a nurse?" I cock an eyebrow.

He twists at the waist to look at me. His tongue darts out of his mouth to lick his lower lip, his stare devouring me. Without saying a word, he passes me the tube.

I slather a thick layer of ointment on the tattoo until it's all smeared evenly. The urge to squeeze his ass, or bite it, is difficult to resist.

Adrian doesn't move, head bent, breathing heavy.

"All done." I wipe my fingers on a napkin and throw it back on the food cart with the tube. "Can you leave it bare?"

"My ass?" He laughs.

"The tattoo." I shake my head and laugh with him.

"Yes. Thank you." One hand reaches behind to pull his boxers up.

Instead of helping him, I give in to the temptation. My hands skim over his hips, arms snaking under his, traveling up his muscular torso. I plant a kiss on his shoulder blade, and he exhales a ragged breath.

His warmth under my palms, the frenzied beating of his heart spur me on. I leave wet kisses on his back, enthralled by the taste of his skin on my tongue. My body presses against his. I caress his chest, greedy, and down his abs.

Our breathing accelerates in rhythm. The heat radiating from him befuddles me. My hands slither under his, grazing the fabric covering his hard cock.

Adrian seizes my wrist to stop me. "Fuck. Slow down," he breathes. "I can't believe the amount of self-control I need to conjure up with you." He lets out a chuckle and turns to face me.

His pants fall on the floor at his feet, and he kicks them off. His boxers barely hold over his bulging cock. I can't help but lick my lips, hungry for him.

His gaze heated, Adrian pulls me against him, his muscular arms encircling my waist as I hold on to his shoulders. He kisses me, soft and unhurried. "Before we go any further, we agree that this is not just one night. Not 'what happens in Vegas stays in Vegas' bullshit. This is us, for real."

I drown in the deep blue of his pleading eyes. "This is for real."

The most breathtaking smile lights his face. Ghosting his mouth over my cheek to my ear, he whispers, "*Ma puce.*"

A shiver courses through my body. "I'm helpless when you do that."

"I know." His smile widens against my neck.

In a few expert moves, he removes my top, shorts, panties and his boxers, almost never breaking our kiss. With the same skillfulness, we're in bed under the covers before I realize.

He lowers his body on top of mine, skin against skin. His lips brush against mine, barely kissing, the soft blow of his breath tickling. "I've missed you, *ma puce.*"

I let out a whimper. My entire being is under his spell, moving as he guides me, surrendering to him.

I drift in a haze of pleasure kindled by his hands caressing every inch of my body. His mouth trails down my neck, my belly. He leaves wet kisses between my thighs, closer and closer to my pussy. The tip of his tongue presses on my clit, licking, playing, relentless, as my back arches off the mattress. And his tongue slides inside me, provoking a burst of pure bliss.

Never letting me come down from my orgasm, with his fingers replacing his mouth, Adrian climbs over me, hovering. He cherishes me with every touch, every kiss, and he pushes his cock inside me.

I gasp, overwhelmed by the ecstasy as he moves in me, heart beating too fast, mind clinging to flashes of sensations…his muscles flexing under my palms, his labored breaths on my neck, the taste of me on his tongue. His hoarse voice when he whispers '*ma puce*' in my ear, over and over.

We never change position, relishing the intimacy. My legs pinned to the sides of his, my nails scratch his ribs, pulling closer his body that is already crushing me. Trapped but protected, safe.

His fist wraps in my hair. Low groans erupt from his throat in tune with the moans springing from mine.

Our feverish passion grows wilder until I fall over the edge of pleasure again, and he falls with me.

Breathless, he shifts to his side, holding me to his chest.

I nestle against him and listen to his heartbeat slow down, letting my own body settle.

"What are you doing next Saturday?" he asks in a casual tone, still a bit out of breath.

Surprised, I pull away to look at his amused expression. "Nothing planned. Why?"

"Would you go out on a date with me?"

The teasing glint in his adoring gaze makes me giggle. "I'd love to."

Chapter Twenty-Nine

Ambush

After a perfect wake up enveloped in Adrian's warmth, my body molded against his, we have even more perfect sex in the shower. My legs locked around his waist as he thrusts into me, his powerful arms hold me up against the wall tiles, water pouring down the contracting muscles of his abs and splashing around us. A most wonderful way to start the day.

However, the rest of Sunday flies by in a daze. Madison and Luke pin her feeble state on indigestion. Adrian and I pretend to believe them. If they've come to the same conclusion I did about a possible pregnancy, they're not ready to share it yet, and the best we can do is allow them to announce it in their own time.

The retelling of Daphne and Colin's misadventures monopolizes lunch, swaying between Daphne's fiery explanations and Colin's insightfulness. Their sarcastic banter sends us into fits of laughter. Their sense of humor is so similar, so easygoing between them that they seem like they've been friends for years.

All day long, Adrian and I can't keep our distance. We hold hands while we stroll down the Strip, he hugs me close when waiting for a cab. We kiss, his hand on my neck, his tongue tasting me, whenever we have a chance. None of our friends comment. It seems natural even to them. We can't help ourselves, anyway. The night in his arms was too blissful, the chemistry between us is too intense, and we're both tired of denying it.

Late in the afternoon, the return trip steers the mood toward gloominess as Adrian and I can't get adjacent seats on the plane, and at the San Francisco airport, the dreaded moment of parting ways is more difficult than either of us expected. It made more sense that I'd go back with Daphne, as Adrian and I both have to work early tomorrow, but now I'm not so sure.

Adrian tightens his grip on my hand before I can approach Colin's car. He gives a light tug, pulling me against him while his other hand still holds his bag. "How about you don't get into this car with Daphne?" His needy tone mirrors the pinch in my chest.

"What do you have in mind?"

"Come to my place instead. Stay with me tonight."

My brain struggles to reason, befuddled by his heady fragrance and pleading gaze. "I don't have any clothes for tomorrow."

"We'll figure it out. I don't want to let you go just yet," he whispers, and my heart skips a beat.

Luke pokes his head out of Adrian's car parked two rows farther. "Are we going or what?"

Daphne snorts. "Looks like they physically can't detach from each other."

"Like teenagers..." Colin mumbles.

Adrian rolls his eyes, making me giggle. "They're ruining the moment."

"We can hear you," Luke laughs. "And we don't care. We want to go home."

Without another word, Adrian takes a step backward, one eyebrow cocked, still holding my hand.

I can't resist the burning need in his eyes, the sexy smile on his parted lips. We'll figure out the logistics later, but I'm sleeping in his arms tonight. If I have to, I'll go to work wearing one of his shirts as a dress, for all I care.

I wave goodbye to an amused Daphne while Colin laughs, and gets in the car with Adrian. After dropping off Madison and Luke on our way to his apartment, he parks by the curb in front of his building.

He pulls his keys from his pocket and hands them to me. "My fridge is empty. I'll go pick up a few things so I can cook for you, and maybe a nice bottle of wine. I'll meet you upstairs in twenty minutes."

"I can come with you if you want."

"You could…" His voice drops to a throaty murmur. "Or you could make yourself comfortable, wait for me naked in bed…" He lays a kiss on my lips. "Or in the shower. Or lying on whatever piece of furniture…"

His tongue grazes my lower lip, and I capture it, sucking it into my mouth before pushing him away with a wink. "Right. Your idea is better."

My heart beats fast, and a tingling sensation settles between legs as I exit the car and enter the building. A little out of breath and with a grin on my face, I make my way up the stairs, down the hallway to his front door, then wiggle the key in the lock.

The door is already unlocked.

A feeling of déjà-vu washes over me, pinning me to the spot. Muffled sounds seep through the door. Someone is here, but this time, it can't be Adrian.

Peeking inside, the living room is steeped in the dim flickering light of a dozen candles scattered around. When I enter on my tiptoes, the smell of freshly baked cookies lingers in the air, and the voice of Edith Piaf singing *La Vie en Rose* echoes from a phone on the coffee table.

My stomach drops. As it's safe to assume Adrian didn't light candles yesterday for me to find them, there's only one person who could have planned this.

Pauline.

I steel my nerves, but before I can muster up the strength to move, she appears from the kitchen door. A tall woman about my age, with slick blond hair and big blue eyes. She stands in high heels, wearing a white slinky dress with a plunging neckline, her mouth agape and her eyes confused.

Too many emotions whirl in my mind. A drop of surprise to find her here, a shade of jealousy at her perfect supermodel-like appearance. But the dash of anger takes over as I ask in a cutting voice, "What the hell are you doing here?"

Her narrowing stare details me from my messy braided hair draped over one shoulder, my loose black T-shirt and worn-out jeans, to my wedge sandals.

"Who are you? Where's Adrian?" Her tone is cold, almost reproachful as she turns off the music. If any doubt remained, her slight French accent confirms her identity.

Fury flares up my throat as I step to my left to switch on the lights. "Why did you come back? And how did you get in?"

"Excuse me?" she shrieks, one hand on her cleavage as if she was clutching pearls. "I'm here to see Adrian."

When I reach for the closest candle, she steps forward to stop me from blowing on it, but the death look I throw her makes her reconsider. Her eyes waver between anger and shock while I battle with myself not to lunge forward and grab a fistful of her bleached hair to drag her ass to the sidewalk. I won't let her win this time.

After putting out a few candles, I stand in front of her. "Adrian's not here. You should leave."

She snorts. "Who do you think you are? You're just some slut Adrian bangs to get back at me, nothing more." She seems to be in a panic, perhaps more lost than angry, and I get the strange feeling she knows who I am. "You met him, what, a month ago? Don't be stupid enough to believe it's more important than almost ten years of our relationship, of love. More important than an engagement. You can go back to your place because—"

"Shut the fuck up, Pauline." My pulse races, teeth clenched. "Before I call the cops, tell me how you got in."

She hesitates. Her hard stare falters. "I... I still have a key. Adrian and I lived here, together, before moving to Paris."

The words hang between us, and the superiority in her eyes hits like a slap in my face. She knows she touched a nerve. My nails cut into my palms, and I swallow hard to stay calm.

She seems desperate, clinging to one last hope of getting Adrian back without realizing she never will, no matter what she attempts.

"Indeed," I say. "You had years with him. Clearly, that didn't end too well. What did you think was going to happen here?" I gesture at the candles. "You already came once, and it didn't work. How did you think Adrian would react to you barging in like this?"

Surprise crosses her features. "He told you?"

I'm not sure whether she's referring to their relationship in general, or her last surprise visit, but either way, it's my turn to smirk. "He tells me everything."

Her eyes are wide, red with tears menacing to spill. "I want to talk to Adrian. Where is he?"

"If you'd called him before trespassing, you'd know."

A sort of cringe fleets over her face, and realization hits me.

"You *tried* calling him," I say in a softer tone, and she looks down. "Adrian was with me the whole day, so I would've noticed. He blocked your number."

My words don't sound like a question, but I get confirmation with the pained glare she throws me.

The anger in me subsides, leaving only pity for her. "Grab your stuff and just go."

"*Non.* I'm waiting for him." She crosses her arms over her chest, feet planted on the floor, her voice rising. "I'm not leaving him. He's my fiancé. You won't steal him away from me, *petite garce*." She almost spits the last word.

Even though my French is limited, I know this isn't nice at all.

My patience wears thin, and my empathy for her pain has limits. My body trembling, I hold on to a last shred of self-control, because at this point, dragging her to the sidewalk by the hair still sounds like a legitimate option. Instead, I grab her purse on the couch, her jacket, and her bag of whatever she brought.

"Don't touch my stuff. *Non!*" she shrieks again and lunges toward me, yet not fast enough. "What are you doing?"

I sidestep her, open the window with one hand, and with the other throw her belongings out.

Her mouth hangs open as she watches the floating descent of her jacket and her bags land on the ground in a thud.

I close the window and make my tone as threatening as I can muster. "You should go downstairs to pick up your shit."

"*Pétasse!* Why did you do that?"

Walking toward her, I force her to retreat until she's in the corridor. "Insulting me won't change the fact that you lost Adrian, so you can go the fuck back to France because he's mine now."

I turn on my heels and slam the door in her face. Maybe it wasn't my place to throw her out, but I don't care. I won't remain passive and risk losing him again.

My heart hammers. With my back against the door, I slide down until I'm sitting on the doormat. After a moment, her footsteps down the hall abate.

Heavier steps approach, and a knock booms on the door, making me jolt.

"Eva? It's River. Are you okay?"

"Um…yes." I stand and open the door to his worried frown.

"That was Adrian's ex I just passed in the stairs, right?"

"Yes, it was her." My voice comes out a little shaken.

"She didn't even recognize me." He snorts. "Well, like she'd give a shit anyway."

"Did she leave?"

"Not sure." With a head tilt, he motions behind me, and we both dart to the living room window.

I push the curtain to peek outside as Pauline appears on the sidewalk.

"I was in the deli across the street with my friends," River says. "I saw you throw shit out the window. That was *epic*, by the way." He glances at me with an amused smile.

My heart not slowing down, I don't reply and watch Pauline kneel to pick up the contents of her purse. Her phone in hand, she dials a number. My throat constricts, but I know that even if she calls Adrian, he won't pick up.

"If she comes back up, I'm calling the cops," River says as we observe. "Where's Adrian?"

"Grocery store. He should be here soon."

Pauline makes a brief call then shoves her phone back in her purse. And waits. My palms are sweaty, my eyes locked on her. *Is she waiting for Adrian?*

Several long minutes pass. Pauline stands there, arms crossed, gaze down. A cab parks by the curb. She gets in, and the car drives away, tires screeching on the road.

"Good riddance." River sighs and turns to me. "You okay?"

"I guess... Thank you for checking up on me."

"Anytime."

I walk him to the corridor but before he enters his apartment, he throws me a playful smile. "Not sure what's happening, but it's great seeing you here again."

I conjure up a weak smile and close the door, locking it behind me. The fury Pauline awakened in me hasn't subsided, and I ache for Adrian's presence to vent and let it all out.

No matter how much I trust him not to make the same mistake twice, not to indulge her delusions, I also can't stand her showing up as if she's still part of his life.

I snatch Adrian's zip-up hoodie off the couch and wrap myself in it before darting to the kitchen to pour myself a well-deserved shot of tequila. My nerves on edge, I swallow it in one gulp. Hopping on the counter, I bury my face in his hoodie, cocooned in his smell, and inhale a deep, soothing breath.

Adrian comes in without a sound, and he chuckles. "You missed me that much?"

As soon as I lift my frowning face to him, he places the groceries on the table and wraps his arms around me. "What's wrong?"

My hands clutch the fabric of his T-shirt. I bring my nose to his neck, tracing a line to his ear, and let his smell settle my nerves before I launch into the painful explanation. "I have to tell you something."

Chapter Thirty

Damage Control

My stomach knots at the obvious irritation hardening Eva's face, her body almost vibrating from nervousness.

She pours a glass of tequila and slides it toward me on the counter. "This one's for you. I think you'll need it."

"*Ma puce*, you're worrying me. Please tell me what's wrong."

"Pauline was here when I arrived."

A wave of fiery wrath washes over me and swallows me whole. Every muscle in me contracts. I fight the rage submerging me as if my life depends on it and grab the glass. I gulp the golden liquid, relishing the burning sensation scorching my throat. *Downing the entire fucking bottle sounds tempting.*

"Fuck." I take a deep breath and settle my voice, as gentle and comforting as I can manage. "Are you okay? What was she doing here?"

I can't believe Eva has to endure this bullshit again. However, this time, I'm putting *her* feelings first.

"She was waiting for you in a pretty white dress, candles lit everywhere. She still has a key, so she just let herself in."

"I'm changing the fucking locks tomorrow," I grumble. "What did she say to you?"

"She called me a slut, among other insults in French, and said that I'm nothing to you but a quick fuck to get back at her." Behind her fury, the hint of hurt that seeps through her words breaks my heart.

With my hands on her waist, I slide her closer to the edge of the counter and stand between her legs. "You know that's not true. I don't need to tell you that, right?"

"It's still nice to hear, though." She buries her face in the crook of my neck, hands on my back clutching my T-shirt.

My brain connects the dots, analyses the hints I didn't pay attention to when I came in. The candles put out in the living room. The persistent smell of cake or...

My eyes scan the kitchen and on the other end of the counter, a plate covered with a towel catches my attention. I release Eva, reach for the towel to unveil what Pauline baked.

"Madeleines..." I whisper, and Eva scoffs.

I grab the plate, tilt it over the trash and let the contents spill inside before striding back to Eva.

My hand under her chin lifts her gaze to mine. "I'm sorry I wasn't clear enough with Pauline, and she thought she could try again. I'm the one who should've kicked her out. I would have, had I been here earlier."

"I know. But clearly, she doesn't."

"How did you get her to leave?"

"I threw her shit out the window." She reaches up to yank my collar. Her mouth devours mine, tongue slipping in, possessive. "I told her that you're mine. Then I slammed the door in her face."

My eyes widen, and I hold back a laugh. "Are you serious? I wish I'd been there to see that." I chuckle against her lips. "I remember you slam doors with a lot of flamboyance."

The underlying strength in her stare, mesmerizing and fierce, takes my breath away. She stood her ground for me, for us.

My heart staggers as I grasp the obvious reality. I'm in love with her.

Not ready to say it aloud yet, and not in these circumstances, I shake my head with a smile. "From what Pauline said, did it sound like she'd come back again?"

"It's possible. I'm surprised she didn't wait for you downstairs." She pauses, hesitating. "I wish I could say that seeing me here will deter her, but I had the strange impression that she already knew about me anyway."

Even though Eva didn't frame it as a question, I know she wants an answer, a confirmation that even in that painful moment, even after I let her walk out, she was already important enough that I couldn't keep from alluding to her. "When Pauline and I talked, I let it slip that there was someone in my life... I mentioned you."

Eyes shining, her body relaxes.

Mine doesn't. "I need to figure out what to do. Pauline asked for an explanation, and I already gave it to her. I won't do it again. I want to live in peace, and not be scared to find her behind the door whenever someone knocks."

"That'd be nice. Although, I'll kick her out as many times as needed to keep you," she jokes.

The irrationality of Pauline's actions has both of us stunned into silence for a moment. Eva slides off the counter as I put away the groceries. Not in the mood for cooking a romantic dinner anymore. We sit at the table, snacking on a bag of Doritos instead.

I rub my hands over my face, rake my fingers through my hair and intertwine them behind my neck as I stare at the ceiling. "I should've known she wasn't going to leave me alone so easily. Luke told me she was a manipulative bitch," I mumble, my head still in a stunned haze.

"This is not manipulative," Eva says. "This is delusional. She was in panic, scared to lose you." She stands and paces the room for a few steps before stopping, hands propped on her hips, head down.

My heart breaks. I rush to her, pull her to me with a hand behind her neck and the other on her lower back. She nestles against my chest, her arms folded between us. I want to apologize a million times, tell her I love her, but words are pointless. She inhales deep, and I squeeze her tighter, my arms wrapped around her, my heart beating under her palm.

Instead of me reassuring her, she's the one giving me strength to deal with this mess.

I plant a quick kiss in her hair and another on her lips, deeper. With a hand on her hip, I pull her with me until I'm sitting, and she straddles my lap. "Maybe Pauline believes that I still care enough about her, love her enough to not kick her out of my life for good."

"Do you still l—?"

"No," I reply before she can finish asking that question.

My thumb skims over Eva's cheek, caressing her soft skin. My gaze drowns in hers. Leaning forward, I nudge the tip of her nose with mine, and tilt my head to press my lips on hers.

Two months ago, I would've broken a few things out of anger, called Pauline to yell and insult her. My resentment for Pauline has morphed into pity. She's lost in delusions, whereas my life now promises serenity and happiness. No matter what she believes, no matter what she wants or attempts, her control over my life, choices and feelings, is over.

My arms clasped around Eva's waist, I keep her against me. "I won't put Pauline's needs before yours. Not again. Not ever. I won't do anything that you're not okay with."

Eva nods, a soft sigh escaping her lips. "What are you going to do, then?"

"I don't want to see her again, especially if it means leaving you behind. But I can call her. This bullshit needs to stop today."

"Do what you have to do." She pauses, her obstinate stare fixed on mine. "I'm staying by your side this time."

The kindness in her voice astounds me. "What the fuck have I ever done to deserve you?" I grin, awestruck by the decisiveness in her eyes, her chin up, and her evident trust in our future together.

A bright smile lights up her face, and she leans in to kiss me. Eva's presence, her support, make this mess bearable. In hindsight, I should've accepted support from my family and friends long ago, when my relationship with Pauline degraded, instead of allowing it to sink to such a low point.

And even if I had made different decisions, changed paths sooner, I'm sure Eva and I would've found our way to each other.

I muster up some courage and swallow what's left of my pride to make the painful call. Eva and I move to the couch, her cold feet tucked under my thigh and her hand in mine when I unblock Pauline's number and dial.

She picks up on the first ring. "Adrian, I was hop — "

"Stop talking." My voice is even, as detached as I am. "We're done."

"Wh — ?"

"I'm not calling to have a conversation or an explanation. I don't care. It's over. For good."

Her loud breathing crackles through the phone, but she doesn't answer. She was probably not expecting this calm on my part.

"This is the last time you ever hear from me," I continue in a firm tone. "And it needs to be the last time I ever hear from you. If you try to contact me, barge into my home or dare insult again the woman I'm building my life with, I'll press charges for harassment. Are we clear, this time?"

Pauline sniffles, silence draws out without her answering, and I hang up.

A weight lifts off my shoulders. After so many months of self-loathing and insecurity, I can finally breathe. I'm where I'm supposed to be.

Eva shifts to snake her arms around me, watching me with a sweet smile. "Are you okay?"

I take a long deep breath and release it in a loud blow. "Yes. But... I said I'd make it up to you, and..." I shake my head, well aware that none of what I've offered her so far has been either easy or dream-worthy.

"You have." She pulls herself up to straddle my lap. "The way you see me, how you listen to me, how you care about what I feel." The intensity of her gaze disarms me, words evading me as her wet lips brush against mine. "You give me more than you realize. I've never felt more wanted, more appreciated, more at home than in your arms."

A thought pops in my head, and I speak without thinking. "You never doubted me."

She smiles. "Is that a question?"

"Not really. You didn't think that maybe I lied to you, that I led her on."

"No, I didn't."

The tip of my nose grazes hers. "Good, because you have nothing to worry about. You know me better than she ever did."

"How is that possible?"

I swallow back the distant unease in my memory. "There were some parts of me that I put aside, locked in the confines of my brain. That's what Luke means when he says I lost myself."

"What parts of you?"

"Small things that I thought didn't matter, but it entirely changed the way I was. I had to bridle how I spoke to her, how we acted in public...how I fucked."

I glance at Eva who listens without interrupting, her caring gaze on me, her fingertips tracing soothing circles on my biceps, so I continue.

"I forced myself to be...someone else. More conventional, more respectable. According to her definition, at least. It all became dull, myself included."

I don't tell Eva how insecure I was, broken, a piece of me obliterated to the point that I couldn't remember who I truly was. Until her. None of it matters anymore.

Instead, I lay a tender kiss on her lips. "Then you stormed into my life, so fucking frustrating." I kiss her again as she pretends to sulk. "I showed you what an asshole I could be, and not only did you push back, as headstrong as me, but you saw past it. Like I couldn't hide from you. You see *me*, and not a version of who you'd like me to be. I didn't know what that felt like, before you."

The spark of love in her eyes reaches my soul. I adore her so much my heart could explode. Although neither of us utters these words yet.

Her plump lips turn into an impish smile. "So I was right?"

I chuckle. "Probably...but about what in particular?"

"You're mine."

Her sultry, possessive voice sends an electric shiver through me, and my cock twitches beneath her.

"I'm yours." I throw her a smug smile. "It seems my hoodie is yours, too, now. Although I'd like to take it off you."

Before I can move, Eva's mouth crashes to mine, her hands gripping me. She tugs at my clothes, and my body ignites under her touch. I let her set a frenzied pace, follow her down a spiral of smoldering need to possess each other. Clothes are off in a heartbeat, piled on the carpet, and I lay her down on top of it. Skin against skin, our fingertips claw, our mouths devour. This feverish connection consuming us both, I push into her, my cock filling her as she squeezes my ass to take me deeper.

In soft whispers in her ear, I repeat, "I'm yours, *ma puce*." Because despite how brave and understanding she was tonight, I know she needs me to say it aloud.

Her nails dig into my back, claiming me. Her teeth biting into my shoulder send a sharp sting through my nerves that spurs me on. The weight of my body pins her down, my thrusts hit inside her, deeper, harder. Until she cries out my name, eyes screwed shut, her pussy tightening around me. An explosion of ecstasy overtakes me as I follow her over the edge.

Without ever letting go of her, I roll us to our sides, pulling the blanket from the couch to cover us. Her body melts in my arms. Her soft lips kiss the red bite mark she just carved on my skin, and the craziest thought crosses my mind that I want it tattooed on me forever.

Chapter Thirty-One

In the Warm Light of Morning

Soft rays of sunlight pour in through the curtains. I stretch under the covers and open my eyes. Adrian stands in front of his closet in dark gray suit pants, slipping into a blue shirt that he leaves unbuttoned.

I let out a wistful moan. "Am I still dreaming? Although if I was, you'd be in bed with me instead."

"I wish." He smiles. "I can't be late for work. Which I will be if I let you lure me back to bed." He picks out a dark-gray tie that he hangs around his neck without knotting it.

I pout. "What time is it?"

He retrieves his watch from his dresser, pauses to look at the time, and fastens it around his wrist. "Six-thirty."

I jolt upright. "Shit, I need to get ready too."

"If you shower fast enough, I can drop you off at work on my way."

"I have no work clothes or shoes, no clean underwear, no hair dryer... Would you mind making a detour to drop me at my place?"

A strange expression crosses his face for a split second, unreadable, and he nods. "Sure."

I kneel on the edge of the bed, and he steps forward to meet me. My hands reach around his neck, the sheet drops, leaving me naked, my body flush against him.

Gaze dark, his tongue darts out to lick his lower lip. The warmth of his skin as my breasts press against him sends my heart racing. The bulge in his pants grows against my pussy. His hands caress down my sides, setting fire on their path. Thumbs grazing my breasts, his palms stroke down to my waist, my hips.

He captures my mouth into a fiery kiss and squeezes my ass as he grinds his cock against me.

The moan that erupts from my throat this time sounds more desperate.

"Fuck," he says in a labored breath.

He peeks at his watch again, brow furrowed, and I burst out laughing.

"Are you trying to decide if you can fit me into your schedule?"

He chuckles. "I'm sorry, *ma puce*. I really can't be late today and I'd like to have time for more than a quick fuck before driving you…back to your place." The last words come out strained, as if it took him some effort to utter them.

In all honesty, they sound off to my ears not only because of his tone. After several weeks, Daphne's apartment still doesn't feel like home, no matter how hard she tries to be welcoming.

With a chaste kiss on my lips, Adrian steps away. I put on yesterday's clothes as he buttons his shirt and tucks it into his pants.

We move around the apartment, to the bathroom where I brush my teeth then to the kitchen for a cup of coffee while he explains with enthusiasm the project he'll present during his eight o'clock meeting. The one he can't be late for, and that deprives me of amazing morning sex.

I tell him about the dull administrative tasks awaiting me at the office without nearly the same level of excitement.

Adrian lifts my gaze to him with a hand under my chin. "It sounds like you don't even enjoy working there." The concern and tenderness in his voice warm my body even more than his hoodie I just slipped into.

Adrian's right, my job is far from fulfilling, between the repetitive tasks I find no interest in and the side-glances I still get from several colleagues since the rumors about Colin and me.

"I love some parts of it. Working with Colin, what I can learn from him. Since Daphne arrived, the bad working atmosphere has been easier to stomach. Now I have an ally."

He peeks at me as he knots his tie. "But?"

I shrug. "It was supposed to be temporary. I'll never build the career I'm aiming for by staying at this job." I straighten his tie and walk past him to the bathroom. "There's only so many new responsibilities I can take on, so I'm not sure it's worth it anymore."

"Working there, you mean?" He looks at me in the mirror as he fixes his hair while I lift mine into a bun.

"Yes. Maybe it's time I find another job. I'm leaning more toward finance than law."

A bright smile graces his features as he turns to me. "I'd love that. I could teach you so much. But the banking world is a shark tank, you know. With piranhas. Swimming in acid."

"Dangerous animals with big...teeth. I'm sure there's a metaphor in there somewhere," I tease, making him laugh. "At least I'd work in a field I'm passionate about."

Hesitating, he opens his mouth but remains silent as he passes by me, planting a quick kiss on my lips before moving to the bedroom. He sits on the bed to put on his shoes and lifts his eyes to watch me for another beat. "There's an opening for a long-term internship at Morland Stanwell. A special program for non-graduates, like a sponsorship with a fast-track through college admissions to eventually get a degree. One of the candidates dropped out last minute." He pauses, his stare on me, studying my reactions with such focus that my skin prickles. "You should apply."

His offer sounds more than tempting. This is a dream position for someone without a college education, like me. If I could accept, I would.

I clear my throat in an attempt to preserve some poise. "It sounds like a great opportunity, but—"

"But you don't want any special treatment, or anything handed out to you, and you're more than capable of finding a job on your own." He raises a defiant eyebrow. "That's what you were going to say, right?"

He knows me well. I smile. "Exactly."

"Good, because that's not what I'm suggesting." He stands in front of me, hands in his pockets, shoulders relaxed, but gaze piercing as a knife. A commanding fierceness rolls off him, proving that when it concerns work, he's one of the sharks. "You apply. You dazzle them on your own. If they're not fucking blind, they'll see what I see in you." Eagerness sparks in his deep blue eyes as he towers over me, igniting me to my core.

"You work your ass off to secure your spot, and *then* I mentor you into a sharp analyst any firm would kill for."

The prospect of going head-to-head with him every day at work is thrilling. Not only because it brings out a dominant side of him which enthralls me, but because he would support me, let me grow and treat me as an equal. "That's an appealing plan. You wouldn't mind having me around your office all day?"

A suggestive smile lifts the corner of his mouth. "Parading in your tight skirts? Never," he teases.

My eyes narrow, although I can't hide my amusement. "I recall you mentioning a fantasy of yours about fucking a secretary on a desk. It's only a trick to fulfill it, then?"

"Let's say it would be part of my year-end bonus. A six-figure check and you, spread out on my desk." A low laugh rumbles in his throat, making my insides flutter.

He shakes his head, his smile still in place, grabs his suit jacket from the hanger and puts it on. "Seriously, though. No, I wouldn't mind working with you. Think about it the other way around." He grabs my hand, making me twirl until my back is against his chest, walking behind me to the entrance. "This would be a great opportunity for you. You deserve it and you have potential. I don't want you to miss it just because it might be uncomfortable to work together some days, when we fight over some random shit."

"You remember what it's like when we fight, right?" I laugh.

With a tug at my hand, he twirls me around again, grabbing my waist to make me face him, pushing me backwards the last few steps until we're at the front door. "Yet, we're together anyway."

The adoration in his eyes makes my heart falter, and words get lost between my brain and my mouth. I watch him speak about a common future, unable to contain the loving smile spreading on my lips.

"This is the rest of your life we're talking about. Grab whatever chance presents itself." He pauses, watches me for a few seconds and throws me an impish smile. "I fucking love the way you're looking at me right now."

My breath hitches at *that* word dripping from his lips, heat creeping up my neck. "You love it?"

Without tearing his fiery gaze from me, Adrian pushes his body against mine. His hand on the nape of my neck tilts my head to him, his fingers tangling in my hair. His lips brush against mine, soft and warm. "Actually, I love *you*."

My heart gallops, I melt against him, hanging on to his broad shoulders. "I love you, too."

He smiles against my lips, his arm around my waist pulling me closer. His tongue strokes mine, tender. A wave of heat enraptures me as his slow rhythm deepens, more passionate. His hands gripping, my body tingles, pressing harder against him, and I let out a needy moan.

A slight groan scratches his throat. He breaks the kiss, out of breath. "We should go."

I can't repress the small huff escaping me, and he chuckles.

Chapter Thirty-Two

Bring Her Back

I fucking hope this day never ends, because I can't stand the thought of going home tonight to an empty apartment, without Eva by my side. Or watching a dull movie to numb my brain, lying in a cold bed, drinking tasteless coffee tomorrow morning...alone.

Why did we even decide we wouldn't see each other again until our first date? *Next Saturday. In five fucking days.*

Diving into work helps, but my phone beeping with a text from her is what eases my despair.

My mind keeps wandering off.

A grin spreads on my face, and I text back.

Where?

A room in Vegas...and the salty taste of your skin as your cock moved inside me.

Fuck. My fingers glide over the screen.

No way I can focus on work, now.

Is that what you were doing? Sounds boring. Here I was, hoping you were thinking about me…

I can picture the teasing smile that must lift her lips as she types. If she wants to play, I'm more than happy to follow her lead.

Ma puce, you're all I think about. Your eyes, your smile. Your dirty moans as I thrust inside you. Just remembering it makes me hard.

I glance around, making sure no one is watching me through the glass walls of my office. I can't wipe the smile from my face and hope no colleague will enter and notice my cock straining against my pants.

I want you to make me moan again. Next weekend is too far away.

Before I can type my reply, she sends me another text.

Shit, gotta go. Admin staff meeting I'd forgotten about. Talk to you soon.

A little disappointed that we can't continue this game, I slouch on my chair and count the white ceiling tiles, hoping it'll help calm me down.

Being reasonable fucking sucks. Another night without her skin against mine is impossible. Five days without her smile when I get home, without her body writhing under me at night, without her sparkling eyes in the morning. Unbearable.

Once again, whether we *should* wait is irrelevant. I want her back, and I'd only be fixing a mistake I should've never made in the first place.

Leaving work early, I drive the few blocks from my office to hers, determined to have her sleep in my arms sooner rather than later. Through the lobby and to the elevator, I find my way without much problem and push the button to the fifteenth floor. Lucky for me, a lot of information is available with a quick internet search.

The elevator chimes open, and I walk to the receptionist's desk as she's preparing to leave.

"We're past office hours, but how can I help you?" She throws me a lewd smile, and I wonder if she's the one Daphne caught fucking in an office.

"I'd like to see Eva Duncan, please."

Her smile morphs into an aggravated frown. "What for?"

A memory of Eva when she was drunk mentioning bitches at her office springs to mind, along with her comment this morning about a bad working environment. I understand now. On top of being highly unprofessional, this woman oozes petty jealousy.

I stand straighter and stare down at her, my tone firm. "Confidential matter that I doubt you're accredited for. Miss Duncan knows my case. Which way is her desk?"

Swallowing back her obvious annoyance, she doesn't bother picking up her phone to announce me, and only points her fake nail to the left. "This corridor, the fourth office after the coffee machine is Mr. Wilder's. You'll find Miss Duncan sitting by that door."

Without replying, I dart to the direction indicated, crossing the almost empty office floor. As I approach, Eva stacks a dozen files on top of her desk perched on five-inch heels, her delicious curves clad in a tight black blouse and wrap skirt. When I clear my throat, her head spins in my direction, her long hair flipping back with the movement.

Her eyes widen. "How come you're here? Is something wrong?" A hint of worry shows in her voice.

I offer my sexiest smile and shake my head without moving closer. Like in my firm, cameras are probably surveilling from every corner.

Except personal offices.

"May I have a word with you in private, Miss Duncan?" I ask in a low voice. "There's a point I'd like to discuss with you."

Dropping the last file she had in hand, gaze heated, she throws me a teasing smile. "Of course, Mr. Hensley." Her voice is dripping honey. "Colin isn't here. We can...*talk* in his office."

My cock twitches, my mind transported into a parallel universe where my favorite fantasy unfolds in front of me. My jaw clenches as I fight to snap out of it. "Perfect."

I follow her through the door and close it behind us. Eva sits on the edge of Colin's desk, and she's even more breathtaking than the view of the San Francisco Bay out of the windows behind her.

"So, teasing aside... What's going on?" She fidgets, growing impatient.

After another moment to admire her, to consider what I'm about to ask, there's not even the shadow of a doubt in my mind. "I've been thinking about our conversation the other night. About how every time we try to make the right decision, it backfires on us."

Her brow furrows. "Okay…"

"I think we should keep making reckless decisions instead."

She bursts out the most beautiful, crystalline laugh. "What are you talking about?"

My tone dips lower, dead serious. "I want you to move back home. To my place. Tonight."

Her laughing stops in a gasp, her eyes boring into mine. "What?"

"I know we haven't even been on a real date yet, and you could just sleep over anytime, and I'm —"

"Asking me to move in with you." She raises an eyebrow, defiant.

"When you put it that way, it sounds even more fucked up." I stride toward her until our bodies are close and keep her gaze on me with a hand under her chin. "It's not like we weren't living together for weeks before you left."

"Before you kicked me out, you mean," she teases, and I chuckle.

"I should've never asked you to leave." I lean closer, hands on her waist, resisting the need to encircle her body with my arms, capture her mouth, or let my hands roam over her ass. Instead, my gentle grip keeps her close. My lips graze hers, soft and wet. I watch her, hoping my eyes convey the sincerity behind my words. "I don't want to spend another night without you. I don't want to come back from work another day without you being there. I don't want you to just sleepover at my place whenever we go out." The tip of my nose nudges hers. "I want to come home to you every night."

"This is crazy," she says in a breath, mellowing against me.

"Not really. Worst case scenario, I kick you out again." I throw her a smug smile.

She pushes me away with a pout on her lips. "You're an asshole." She forces a glare toward me, but she can't hide the amusement dancing in her eyes.

I laugh. "I know. Are you saying yes anyway?"

A moment of hesitation lingers, her eyes unfocused, wheels turning in her head, no doubt pondering the risks. If we fuck this up again, the outcome could be even worse for her. For one, Daphne might have found another roommate by then. Plus, with the possibility of us working together, maybe I'm asking for too much.

Eva reaches for my tie, letting it slide between her fingers before clutching it to pull me to her. "Yes." She plants a small kiss on my mouth, causing my heart to skip a beat. "Although this time, you do all the heavy lifting to get my stuff moved back."

"Deal." I return her kiss, more forceful, passionate, our tongues mingling.

I hang on to my last shred of discipline before my instincts overpower me, before I lay her on that desk, and I step away.

Eva remains immobile, the fire in her green eyes burning deep, hands gripping the edge of the desk at her sides. The slight bend of her knees tugs her skirt open just enough to show a sliver of her thigh.

"It's very exciting to see you in this setting." My voice comes out as a low rumble, and my cock grows hard at the sight of her, at the thought of fucking her on that desk in her sexy secretary outfit. I glance at the door. "Almost everyone's gone."

"This is my workplace," she warns, but her lustful gaze betrays her arousal.

"Maybe not for long. We should take advantage of the situation. My office has glass walls..."

The corner of her mouth twitches. Fuck discipline and restraint. I want her.

I step forward. "You've never had sex at work?"

"No."

Another step, licking my lower lip. "Have you ever fantasized about it?"

"Maybe," she murmurs.

With one last step, I'm in front of her, towering over her, my feet between hers. She peers at me from under her lashes, sliding her hands behind her to shove Colin's cluster of files out of reach. I follow her movement, pressing against her as she leans back, my hands on hers.

Her breasts strain against her blouse with each breath she takes. "You just couldn't wait to have me spread out on a desk, could you?"

The unabashed raw desire in her eyes echoes the primal need in me, tamed for too long. She allows me to unleash the wildest part of me, the most obscene, without shame or fear of being judged.

I grind against her, my cock pulsing. "You're my dirtiest fantasy come to life." I lift my right hand to her breast, tug at her shirt, and three buttons pop open, releasing her lace-covered tits. Her heart hammers under my palm, in sync with mine.

Trailing farther down, I reach between us to open one side of her wrap skirt. My hand grazes the skin of her thigh.

Eva glances at the door behind me, and I pause. "Are you scared to get caught?"

"A little." A hint of worry veils her gaze for a second.

I suck in a breath. "I can't bend you over that desk to fuck you with your panties at your ankles, then." My fingertips dig into the skin of her upper thigh as I struggle to regain some control.

She whimpers, bucking her hips toward my cock. "That sounds so good, though."

"I love how fucking naughty you are, *ma puce*." I leave a soft kiss on her lips. "But if you're not one-hundred percent comfortable, it's not fun."

I push away from her and stride to the door to secure the lock. When I turn back to Eva, she hasn't moved an inch. Leaning back, her breasts bursting out of her tight blouse, her skirt open enough to reveal the black lace of her panties.

I hurry back to her, resuming my position. "Ask me to stop, at any time, and I will."

She nods, and as my fingers graze the lace covering her pussy, her legs spread wider. My mouth brushes against hers, tongue tracing her lower lip. I slide my fingers under the side of the fabric. As she surrenders to me, I drown in her stare, aware of nothing except her flowery fragrance dominating my senses and her wet pussy around my middle finger.

Soft, quiet gasps escape her mouth in rhythm with my thrusts.

With one hand still gripping her wrist on the desk, I rub my cock harder against her hip, aching for more.

"Can't believe you've never done this before." The stubble on my chin scratches her jaw, my voice throaty. "See how much you love it."

She pants, rocking to take my finger in deeper, a thin mist of sweat glazing her breasts. "It's only because it's with you."

A victorious grin spreads on my face, and I add a second finger. "I fucking love the sound of that. Say it again."

She moans. "It's only you, Adrian."

"Fuck yes." I thrust my fingers harder, my palm pressing against her clit, and her pussy tightens, her body trembling from the orgasm I'm giving her.

I bring a kiss to her lips, soft and sweet, as her breathing slows down to normal, then I help her stand straight.

With my fingers sucked into my mouth, I savor the taste of her, fighting hard to keep my dick in my pants and not fuck her good and hard like I once said I would.

Instead, when she's done buttoning her shirt, I hug her close to my chest. This was all for her.

Her arms snake under my jacket, hands flat on my back. She blows out a contented sigh, her body melting against mine. "If you have other fantasies, please don't hesitate to share them."

"Likewise." I search my pocket to retrieve the spare key I'd had made on the way not to lose forty minutes driving back home to fetch the one she'd given back. "Eva, I don't give a shit about what we should do. I just want you with me. All the time." I place the key in her palm and close her fist. "Come home, tonight."

With one hand on her neck, I ghost my lips on hers, almost kissing, before stepping away. I stride to the door, ignoring the throbbing bulge in my pants and slip a hand in my pocket to hide it before I open.

"Goodbye, Miss Duncan. I'm satisfied with how we worked this out."

She bites her lower lip, the lust in her eyes still roaring. "Pleasure's all mine, Mr. Hensley." Her sultry voice and teasing wink don't help my boner.

I shake my head with a smile and walk out, heading straight to the elevator.

The drive home is a whirlwind of mixed emotions. The soothing relief of knowing she'll be in my arms every night collides with the frantic anticipation of putting my hands on her again. This time, I won't stop at foreplay. My heart pounds fast, my body taut, the smell of her on my fingers driving me wild. I push my foot flat on the gas pedal, anxious to be home.

Entering the apartment, I lock the door behind me to give her the opportunity to use her key when she arrives. I scurry to my room, swap my suit for a T-shirt and sweatpants, no underwear. It'll be less uncomfortable, considering I can't get my cock to settle down.

After changing my bed sheets, I walk to the kitchen for a beer. I need to get a grip on myself because at this rate, I'll end up fucking her against the front door as soon as she comes in. *Although that doesn't sound like such a bad idea.*

I pull myself together, set my mind on cooking to quell my excitement and choose a simple mushroom and pea risotto recipe. I focus my agitated mind on dicing the ingredients with care, dosing the spices just right, and I watch the quiet bubbles of the simmering sauce.

The sound of the key unlocking the door makes my heart falter. I lean on the kitchen doorframe as Eva drops a bag on the couch and walks to me with a gorgeous smile etched on her lips.

"It took you three hours to get here," I almost whine like a greedy child, and her smile grows wider.

"I had to pick up some clothes and explain to Daphne that I'm leaving her."

I peel her jacket off her shoulders and discard it on the couch. "How did she take it?"

"Fine. It didn't surprise her much." Her arms reach around my neck as I wrap mine around her waist. "But she said she's not packing or moving a single box again, and that you're probably loaded enough to pay for movers anyway." She gives an apologetic smile.

"She's right." I chuckle. "If you're letting me take charge, I'll hire movers tomorrow. All your stuff will be here by the end of the week."

Her eyes narrow. "Why didn't you do that the first time?"

"Oh, because *that* would've gone well, offering to pay to get you out of here faster," I deadpan.

"Fair point." She giggles.

I'll never get tired of that sound.

She bends sideways to peek inside the kitchen. "It smells good in here."

"I cooked." I tighten my hold on her, not willing to let her go just yet, and pivot so she can see the pan on the stove.

She hums the softest sound. "I'm even happier to be back."

The words hang in the air, tightening my chest.

"You're back," I whisper, as if saying the words aloud will anchor them in reality, unalterable.

Her hands travel down to my waist. "I am." She snuggles against my chest, inhales deep, and a heavy sigh of relief escapes her.

My nose in her soft hair, we don't move, both of us craving this quiet intimacy.

After weeks of fighting with each other and against what we felt, she's here, in my arms — fucking finally — and I won't ever let her go again.

Nothing has ever made more sense. Nothing has ever brought me as much serenity as Eva's body pressed against me at this moment.

I bend down to leave a soft kiss on her lips. "Welcome home, *ma puce*."

E p i l o g u e

Home

With her back against the armrest of the couch and her laptop on her thighs, the focus Eva has been displaying for the past twenty minutes is impressive. Her eyes haven't left the screen, her breath rhythmic, her limbs relaxed. No nail biting, no muscles tensing, only her brain on overdrive as she takes the Pymetrics assessment tests required to validate her application to the Morland Stanwell internship.

Eva seized the opportunity to work in finance with me despite her concerns. Her interest and natural talent for the field tipped the scales on her decision. She's more than eager to start her new professional journey, and I'll be by her side, helping her however I can to build the successful career she deserves.

At this moment, I'm here for moral support, her legs draped over my lap as I'm sitting next to her, my feet on the coffee table. My company seems soothing to her, and a smile lifts my mouth as I remember the beginning of our story, when my presence was anything but.

As her keyboard clicks under her fingertips, I remain as immobile as I can to avoid distracting her. I scroll through my Instagram, pausing on Madison's latest post. The picture of her first sonogram. It took her and Luke weeks to announce their pregnancy to us, and now she plasters it all over the internet. I squint to discern the two tiny peanut-shaped babies, my nieces or nephews, and my heart swells. Maddie and Luke are going to be amazing parents. In between times of us being the most supportive aunt and uncle, Eva and I will spoil them rotten.

"Okay, done!" Eva removes her attention from the laptop and lets out a sigh, stretching her arms over her head. "It was actually not too bad."

"See? Told you it wasn't that hard." I set my phone and her laptop aside to rub my hands over her shins. "I'm sure you aced those tests, even though it's just a formality. It won't change their offer, at this point."

"Are you sure you had nothing to do with it? People don't usually get hired right at the end of the interview."

"I promise. I'd never interfere, and I don't have that kind of influence...yet." I throw her a wink, and she giggles. "I have my sources, and from what I've heard, they'd never seen any non-graduate...fuck, even *graduate*, with that level of knowledge on structured financial products. They said you killed it."

A fiery smile spreads across her face. "This is so exciting. I can't wait to start."

"Me too." My hands slip under her legs, massaging her calves. "Are you sad you won't work with Colin anymore?"

"A little. It'll be weird not seeing him every day. Daphne, too. Plus, I feel bad for leaving her. She's still having a hard time at the office. I think she really misses the work environment she had in Los Angeles. From what she told me, it was much healthier."

"I wouldn't worry too much about her. She'll get where she wants in life. She's headstrong and feisty. No wonder you became friends." I wink, and Eva gives me the most breathtaking smile.

After a second, the expression in her eyes mirrors the sense of peacefulness in me. Our relationship has overcome a difficult period of mayhem and uncertainty. We now relish the comfort of each other's presence.

"You hungry?" I give her legs a squeeze to make her move.

She perks up. "Are you cooking?"

"Sure."

We stand from the couch, and she pulls me into a gentle kiss. "First, I still have some boxes that I should unpack."

"All right. You do that while I prepare dinner. I'll holler when it's ready."

These past weeks, Eva and I have shut ourselves away in a blissful bubble, indulging in our need for intimacy, in our lust, in our love. We haven't seen our friends much, and rather spend all our time either fucking or cuddling on the couch, deep in conversation. Unpacking the boxes stacked in her old room hasn't been a priority.

As I rummage through the fridge for inspiration on what to cook, an unsettling reality dawns on me, and I stop dead in my tracks. I place the zucchinis back inside, slam the door shut and storm to her.

She's in front of the closet, on her tiptoes, reaching up to store sweaters on the top shelf. Even though she never sleeps in this room, she still uses it for the closet space, because mine is too small for all our clothes.

I hadn't realized until now, but the thought upsets me, and I can't shake it. It almost looks as if we both have our own rooms, separate. Like roommates, but not a couple, because she used to live here alone before I moved back. Also, it's still *my* apartment.

None of this is relevant now. I want more for us.

Leaning on the doorframe, I search for the right words.

"What's up?" She snaps me out of my thoughts.

She stands barefoot in the middle of the room, brow furrowed, hands on her hips.

Then, it all makes sense.

"*Ma puce*, do you want to move in with me?" Not budging from my spot, my voice is serene and determined.

Her eyes narrow, amusement sparkling in them. "I was pretty sure I already did."

"Not really. I can't stand what you're doing right now."

"Folding my clothes?"

"Putting away clothes in *your* closet, in *your* old room, in *my* apartment."

"I'm not sure I'm following you..." Her tone has morphed from amusement to hopefulness.

I step forward to meet her and lock my arms around her. "I don't want you to live with me in my apartment. I want *us* to live in *our* apartment."

A small smile graces her lips. "What? How?"

"I'll rent out this place. We'll find something else together. Something bigger, where all our stuff fits into the same bedroom."

Her smile falters. "I can't afford to buy —"

"Not yet, maybe. For now, it's not an issue. Have I asked you to pay rent since you moved back? It wouldn't be any different, except we'd choose *our* home. Together."

The wheels are clearly turning in her head, eyes searching mine, hands holding on to my shoulders. Her heart hammers, resonating inside my chest, and I hug her even tighter. In the depth of her stare, I understand how much this means to her after the wretched youth she endured.

I brush my lips on hers. "Maybe even a house, with a backyard for the cutest puppy we'll probably adopt one day."

She gasps, a teasing smile reappearing. "A puppy?"

"For starters," I whisper against her mouth, and my heart skips a beat with hers. A miniature Eva, someday, who'd have me wrapped around her tiny finger.

"You're serious?"

"Reckless decisions are what we do best, remember?" I tease.

She giggles, her eyes wide, a sparkle of happiness glowing in them. She nods and lays a soft kiss on my lips. "Then let's build our home together."

Want to see more like this?
Here's a taster for you to enjoy!

Crashing the Net
Cheyenne Meadows

Excerpt

"What the hell are you talking about?" Ranger Deacon, the captain of the Denver Wolfpack, voiced the question probably every man in the room had on their mind.

"Piper Darrow is taking Gunderson's place. She'll be the number one goalie for the rest of the year."

"Holy shit," one of the guys in the corner muttered.

"We must be pretty damn awful to have to invite women to play with us," Adam Lancaster, seated behind Ranger, hollered out.

"Who came up with that fucking awful idea?" another asked.

A chorus followed, voices filled with exasperation.

Tommy Smith, the head coach, held up his hands. "It's a done deal. No use in getting all pissed off when we have to fill that crucial position. Besides, she's one hell of a goaltender."

"Let Rayovic play," Des Croft, one of the second line players, tossed out.

Smith pinned the guy with a firm stare. "I am letting Rayovic play. But he can't be expected to play every minute of every game for the next thirty games." His voice rose and turned hard as steel. "You know as well as I do one goalie can't do it all."

Ranger glanced across the room, noting the confusion and frustration painted on the guys' faces. They'd had a tough year thus far. The loss of their goalie had nearly proved to be the final nail in the coffin containing the men's morale. He knew many of them had voiced concerns, even whispering about finding a new home for the next season. As much as he hated to break up a team who'd previously gotten along so well, Ranger understood their sentiment. He couldn't claim to be happy right now either.

But a woman?

He pulled up what he knew about Piper Darrow. Certainly, the last name rang clear as a bell. Her Canadian father had been one of the game's best scorers in the almost twenty years that he'd played. Big, fierce, he had a talent for attacking the goal, combined with stamina, durability and a hell of a backhand shot. The name alone invoked reverence and legendary awe. At least to Ranger.

He'd seen Piper play a couple of times. Quick of hand. Fearless. She defended her goal like a momma grizzly defended her cubs.

Still, she wasn't big or bulky. The nature of the women's game protected her smaller frame from hard collisions commonly found with men. She'd have to be one tough woman to hold up physically for the rest of the season. As a goalie, she had a shot. As a forward, like her father, she'd be likely be out before the week was done from teeth-jarring checks meant to crush her against the boards.

Uncertainly flared. Again.

"She just won the women's league championship and was named MVP," Tommy added.

"Whoopee." Anthony Hillman twirled his finger in the air.

"Big fucking deal," Riley Dickenson snarled.

Ranger swung around to glare at Dickenson for that comment. "I don't care what sport or what gender plays that sport, being the best there is demands respect."

"The decision is final. So if anyone still has an issue, there's the door." Tommy bit out every word and pointed toward the exit. He would have made a drill sergeant proud.

Murmurs answered.

Sometimes being captain sucks.

Ranger stood up and moved to the front of the meeting room. "It boils down to this. We have to have a goalie. As hard as Rayovic tries, he can't do it all." Ranger nodded toward the young rookie, who dipped his head in acknowledgement.

Time to think outside the box and get this motley crew on board. "Think of it this way, you all know who her father is, right?"

A chorus of "yeah" followed.

"Well, who do you think she faced all those years in practice?"

A few laughed. Others began to smile.

"If nothing else, it should prove to be an interesting rest of the season." Tommy grinned encouragingly.

The men agreed. Ranger eyed each one, saw the various reactions, and knew Piper faced a formidable challenge before even meeting their first opponent. She had to earn these men's trust and belief. Hard enough for any new player. Let alone for one who started with predisposed attitudes against them. He had no doubt most men would consider her gender a handicap.

"Get geared up. Practice starts in fifteen." Tommy waved them toward the door. "No cheap shots. The first man who lays a hand on our new goalie will answer to me."

The stern tone told Ranger all he needed to know. The head coach already saw Piper as a daughter figure. To cross him would earn his wrath.

Good. That just might keep Piper standing after today's practice.

Heaven knew she needed all the help she could get.

A few minutes later, Ranger ambled up to the ice, his eyes drawn to the woman with the long blonde hair streaming behind her as she zipped from end to end, chasing a puck with decent skill. She ducked, dodged and finally flipped the puck on edge, pulled back her stick, and let loose. The wobbly shot hit the upper right corner of the net.

"She's the goalie?" Rocky, the left winger on Ranger's line, asked.

"Looks like more of a forward to me," Sven, his linemate and the right winger, pointed out.

Ranger watched the gliding motions, the power contained in a small body. As he stared at her, she stopped on a dime, lifted her chin and turned to face the lot of them. He caught a glimpse of narrowed deep blue eyes, a short sigh and a furrowing of her forehead. Defensive mechanisms if ever he'd seen any. She stood up straight, then rested her hands on the stick before looking back at the guys. Her body language spoke of irritation from having her playtime interrupted along with bracing herself for the impact of dealing with twenty men, all new to the idea of playing with a woman. On the ice. Ranger had no doubt the guys had spent many hours playing with a woman in bed. Including himself.

She checked them all out, sizing them up. As a group or individually, he didn't know. The second her focus landed on him, his breath caught as an electric zing carried through his body. Intelligence showed in her features, along with classic beauty tempered by fitness and strength.

Interest piqued, he skated out on the ice toward her. "You must be Piper."

"Yep." She tilted her head and raked him from top to bottom and back again. Cautious appreciation flared in her eyes. "You must be Ranger." She pointed at the big C on his jersey.

"That's me." He noted the others closing around them.

"She's not dressed for practice," Hillman, another forward pointed out.

Piper cut him a glare. "First of all, I was told practice started at three. It's only two-fifteen now. Plenty of time to put the pads on. Secondly, since I don't have a Wolfpack jersey, the best you're gonna get is my Bobcats one until someone provides me with a uniform." She shifted her gaze to Tommy.

"The order's in already." He offered up a small smile. "Since that's taken care of, do you think you can get into gear so we can get to work?"

Piper grinned at him and saluted. "Yes, sir." She kicked the puck at her feet into motion. In a flash, she flew to the other net, spun and fired.

Another strike.

"Damn." Ranger couldn't take his eyes off her. Beauty. Talent. All with a fiery attitude. Impressed, he found himself staring at his new teammate with avid interest and more than a hint of desire.

"Shit, she's good," Adam remarked.

"Don't start handing out line places yet, Adam." Anthony rubbed his forehead. "Scoring is easy when there's no one in your way."

Ranger had played hockey most of his life, starting on the frozen ponds of Minnesota as a small child. He'd seen a girl occasionally play with the boys during pickup games, but never one in organized play. He didn't doubt Piper had plenty of skills. What he did question was whether she could be the answer they needed and hold up under the pressure of the big leagues.

Time will tell.

* * * *

Piper watched one of the forwards approach, pass the puck off to another guy, then swing his stick as it sailed back to him on the ice. Instinctively, she did the splits, preventing it from sliding under her and across the goal line. Her glove came down fast, covering the puck before anyone could smack at it on a rebound try.

The whistle blew. None too soon, as the two huge men crowded her space just in front of the net.

Tommy skated over. "Nice save."

"Thanks." Piper regained her feet and tossed the puck back out and into play. She'd spent the past hour fending off pucks sailing her direction. None of them had gotten by. A pretty snazzy showing, if she said so herself. Of course, she'd carry a few marks tomorrow morning for her efforts. She'd thought some of the women had powerful line drives. The men had them beat easily. One puck to her chest had stolen her breath and nearly put her down for a good couple of minutes. Sheer pride and determination had forced her back to her feet as if nothing had happened. Good thing she had years of practice with that particular move. Her father had taught her toughness above all else.

Gunther Darrow, her father, could be considered a hockey legend. He'd taken her to the rink with him one day while her mother was away. Piper had been six at the time. He'd strapped hockey skates to her feet as well as those of her brother, Darius, and let them loose. Piper had never once looked back. The ice offered her more than a chance at playtime and exercise. It gave her an outlet.

"Change lines." Tommy waited a beat before tossing the puck toward the middle of the ice.

Piper resumed her butterfly position, her focus completely on the small piece of black rubber zipping across the ice. As the other team brought it over the blue line, a tall, solidly built man took up position three inches from her crease, the blue area directly in front of the net. She craned her neck, shifted back and forth, and struggled to keep her eye on the puck with such a big man right in her way. Tempted to give him a shove, she maintained her composure instead, knowing she'd face this situation over and over again in the near future. Screens weren't limited to the men's game. Women had also developed the practice. Although none were built like the moose presently blocking her view. She'd seen enough of that from peewee games all through college. With no women's leagues at that time except for the professional level, she'd had no choice but to play with the boys. Hadn't bothered her. She had still kicked their butts at every given opportunity.

"Hey, Moose. You might have one fine ass, but I really don't need a bird's-eye view, all the same. So move it."

Ranger turned around and flashed a quirky grin.

She poked him with her stick while keeping a close eye on the puck. A player took it down the middle, then cut across near the face-off circle. He pulled back, then lined up for a shot.

The slash of a hockey stick caught her across the shoulder, the force spinning her around. She maintained her balance, found the puck in her peripheral vision, and grabbed it with her glove at the last second.

After a moment to suck in air, she dropped it in front of her and stared back at the men gaping in her direction.

Aha. There it is. The look of amazement and shock she'd been waiting to see since the rest of the team had stepped on the ice that afternoon.

Hiding a smile, she used her stick to nudge the puck back toward the tall man with black hair and green eyes. Ranger. Ranger Deacon. The team's captain and one of the best power forwards in the league. Built like a true position guy, Ranger towered over her and could easily outweigh her twice. Just now in his prime, he'd played with the team for a couple of years after doing his time in the minors. Skill, talent and plain old hard work had carried him to the pros and landed him a spot on the team. Attitude, people skills and leadership had netted him the captain position as well.

Rumor had it he didn't take crap off anyone. Normally laid-back, he was slow to rile, but once there, he made sure his opponent never trod down the same path again. Big and strong, the guy could generate speed as well as send another player flying when checked.

Piper liked that in a man.

Too bad most of the guys carried a chip on their shoulder and attitudes that belonged in the caveman days. Just another reason she didn't date hockey players. Hell, lately she hadn't dated anyone, athlete or not. She'd lost interest after finding too many toads and none that turned into a prince with a mere kiss.

The couple of men that she had dated hadn't ended up working out, either. Mostly, they'd had sex on their minds. Typical for guys that age, she figured, especially athletes who lacked shyness and had primed bodies to show off. The difference between men and women. Intimacy ranked low on her totem pole behind companionship, friendship and romance. A traumatic childhood had made trust difficult, pushing that level of closeness way down the line. Only time, familiarity and love could motivate her to sleep with a man. Her beaus, on the other hand, had made it known that getting hot and heavy in the sack hovered around the top of their list of goals. At an impasse, they had each gone their separate ways. Since she refused to be a trophy put on display, she'd turned her interests to other, more meaningful activities. Until a man wanted her for her, she wouldn't bother to give them more than a fleeting look.

When and if that happened, she'd reconsider her take on men. In the meantime, she focused on making a place in the world for herself and trying to do a bit of good along the way.

"Penalty shots, then we'll call it a day," Tommy hollered from the nearest blue line. He moved to the edge of the rink and watched them all with a critical eye.

Piper perked up. *Time to shine.*

She banged her stick on the side bars and resumed her stance. The past couple of days she'd spent hours watching video on these guys, in preparation for this very moment. She'd learned their preferences, their tendencies. All that studying would pay off. It always did.

Skater after skater approached her with speed, snaking their way toward her before taking their shot. She rejected each one in turn. Until Rocky flew past her, caught her going low, and shot a nice top-shelf laser that streaked by her before she could do more than blink.

He waved his stick in celebration.

She flipped up her goalie mask and smiled at the team's leading scorer. Since creating masks took time and precision, she'd kept her old one. While the bobcat painted on the side might not match up well with a wolf for a mascot, she didn't really care. As long as it fit well and worked, she would hang onto it. "Good shot. Guess that's why you're the sniper on the team."

"Yeah. You could say that." He grinned at her before tipping his head. "You're not so bad yourself."

She accepted the compliment with a quick grin.

"Nice job." Rayovic skated to a stop in front of her. "You've sure got the fast glove."

"Thanks. You've got some guts standing there with the whole team crashing the net."

Rayovic smiled proudly. "That happened a lot on the ice when I was a kid." His Czech accent came through well, though his words weren't hard to understand, testament to his time and practice speaking English.

"You've got a bright future." She sobered. "I'm sorry it had to happen like this. I feel like you've been given the stick."

Surprisingly, Rayovic offered up a sly grin. "It is okay. I'm not one of those men who have a problem with women playing the game. You play great and the team needs someone like you."

"Thank you." Piper smiled softly. "How do you say thank you in Czech?"

"*Děkuji.*"

"*Děkuji.*" She stumbled over the word the first time, earning a chuckle from the other goalie. "*Děkuji.*" Her second try earned her a nod of approval.

"With your size you have to focus more. If the other team realizes this weakness, they'll take advantage big time."

Piper's grin faded with the heavily accented words. "Stanza. I was wondering when you'd appear." The old Swede had written the record books on goaltending back in his day. He'd turned coach a couple of decades ago and passed his nuggets of advice to his players. *More like beat it into their heads.* Stanza believed in a hardline approach and in-your-face challenges rather than praise and uplifting inspiration.

He snorted and skated closer. "You want to play men's game, you have to think like a man."

Piper rolled her eyes. "That might be a problem. I'm not one to ogle boobs and think with a dick that I don't happen to have. Guess that leaves out scratching the balls as well."

Rayovic laughed openly.

Stanza stared at her for a long moment before his lips twitched. "You're going to be difficult."

"Who? Me? Difficult?" She shrugged. "I'm not the one trying to turn me into a man."

Stanza's lips curled up into a reluctant grin. "Point taken. Now, we still have some work to do."

Piper caught a glimpse of the rest of the team leaving the ice for the day. She had a momentary longing before shaking it off. The ice had become her home away from home years before. With a non-existent social life and the decided lack of hobbies, she had nothing waiting for her at the house anyway.

"When you see the shooter coming..." Stanza rattled on.

She tuned into him completely, needing to get her head on straight before the first game, when she faced opposition in the form of a rival team. Filled with men. Who probably didn't want a woman invading their territory.

The story of my life.

About the Author

I'm French, which is as good a start as any to write Romance, if you ask me. The soft twinkling lights in the winding paved streets of Paris, the warm breeze and spellbinding smell of lavender in Provence…and we invented the french kiss, didn't we?

Although my rebellious teenage self preferred writing crime thrillers, the passion for literature was already there, as well as my interest for languages. I learned Spanish, Italian, and a little bit of German, but English stuck with me.

As I studied english and american literature and linguistics at the University, immersing myself in the language made it impossible for me to write in French, as if my brain couldn't create in French anymore. Luckily, it kept the french romanticism, and I fell into Romance novels.

Fast forward a few years of various choices, different jobs, different lives, my passion for writing romance is still intact, and it's time for me to share it with you!

Mina loves to hear from readers. You can find her contact information, website details and author profile page at https://www.totallybound.com

Home of Erotic Romance

Sign up for our newsletter and find out about all our romance book releases, eBook sales and promotions, sneak peeks and FREE romance books!

www.ingramcontent.com/pod-product-compliance
Lightning Source LLC
Chambersburg PA
CBHW020552260626
47157CB00003B/667